Feather Anne's Song

Elsa Kurt

FEATHER ANNE'S SONG

Dedication

For my husband, always.

Contents

Acknowledgments

I'd like to start with a very special thank you to Dan Tracey. I reached out to Dan—a highly respected guitar player, singer, and songwriter from the Alan Parsons Project, Lipstick Blonde, and Save The World bands—early in the process of writing this book because the character, Nick, is a budding songwriter/musician who writes and sings a song for Feather Anne. My problem? I'm not a songwriter.

So, only knowing Dan through a mutual friend, I gathered my nerve and sent him a message that basically started with, "Hi, random question…" and concluded with these really lame lyrics I wrote. Well, Dan floored me. And made me cry… happy tears, that is. Not only did he offer some helpful suggestions, he then came back with an offer to write a real song for Nick to sing, which he did on the spot (he sang and recorded a couple lines, too, which I will keep forever) all while sitting in a Starbucks.

Dan was also gracious enough to allow me to incorporate a significant symbol of his—the number twenty-seven—in Nick's story. It turned out, the day that I had reached out to Dan, was also the 10th anniversary of his father's passing. Dan's father, Leon Henry, was much beloved by his family and it is a tremendous honor for me to be granted the privilege of sharing a small piece of that homage to him within the pages of this book.

Thank you to my husband, family, and friends for accepting the time it takes to write these books, and thereby takes time away from them. To be afforded not only tolerance, but encouragement in these endeavors, is something I am eternally grateful for. An extra thanks goes to Julie Rubacha for her keen eye and willingness to help a girl out. xo

As you may have noticed in this book and others, I'm not shy about sharing my love of music and old movies. They've both influenced me, inspired me, and entertained me over the years, and I love paying homage when possible. Bringing Up Baby and Cary Grant have found a home in more than one of my books; I guess it's like finding Easter eggs when you spot the reference. The same affection goes out to the bands and musicians that I consider a tapestry of my life. Fleetwood Mac, Rolling Stones, and Nathaniel Rateliff and the Nightsweats were on repeat throughout the writing of this book, and I thank them all for existing and creating music the touches my soul.

FEATHER ANNE'S SONG

1 William

The orange-yellow school bus rounded the corner trailing a plume of gray exhaust. Mae's brow furrowed.

"That's one of the older busses. Do you think it's safe? Maybe we should..."

William turned his wife by her shoulders to face him. "It's a three-and-a-half-minute ride. They'll be fine. Although, I can't say the same for the environment..."

Mae walked into his embrace, rested her head against his chest and sighed. "How are they five already? Time is moving too fast." She tipped her head back and gazed up at William. "Slow time for me, okay?"

William kissed her lips. "You think I have the power to do so, hmm?"

"Of course. You're William Grant. There's nothing you can't do. You're basically Superman."

"That makes you my kryptonite, I believe." They kissed again, a longer, deeper kiss.

"Ew. Get a room, God." Feather Anne trudged past them on her way to the end of the driveway.

"Hey," called Mae. "You coming home for dinner, or going to Moms' house?"

Feather Anne's long dark pony-tailed hair flew out like a whip as she spun back around. "Neither. Softball, music lessons, Brandon's."

"On a school night?"

"Come on, Mae. It's Brianna's birthday."

Mae grumbled, and William cleared his throat; a reminder for Mae to get her annoyance in check, and it worked.

"How *is* Brianna?"

Feather Anne shrugged with one shoulder. "Okay, I guess? The surgery is next week. Right now, she wants to get it done and over with."

The bus for the high school arrived, and the door slid open with a hydraulic hiss before it even came to a complete stop. Unlike the elementary school bus, where the first-time riders sat wide-eyed and obediently, this one transported a raucous group of hormonal teens. The ones not glued to their phone screens shouted and tossed things at one another, ignoring the call of the bus driver to, "knock it off, or you're walking,"

Mae offered a wave to Todd, the world-weary and teen fatigued driver. He rolled his eyes and yelled at Feather Anne. "Move it or lose it, kid."

"Yeah, yeah. I'm coming. See you guys later."

Mae called out, "All right, well, have a great—"

Todd cranked the door close—nearly clipping Feather Anne's backpack—without so much as a glance.

"Charming fellow, that Todd," said William.

Mae chuckled and asked, "Do you think she has any idea about the car?"

They strolled hand in hand back to the house. With Melina Petrova running the café for the day, she and William were free to pick up Feather Anne's new-to-her used car from Ricky Baker's dealership.

William replied, "Well, if her grumbling all morning about being the only seventeen-year-old who has to still take the school bus is an indication, then no."

"Good," said Mae. "I really want this to be a surprise. Will you call Chris and tell him we'll meet him and Gina there? I want to put together a quick basket for Ricky to give to Brianna."

"Of course," said William. "And that's thoughtful of you. I'm sure she'll appreciate it... in her own way."

Mae pursed her lips and made a *hmph* sound. "Yeah, well. I'll never like the woman, but even so… finding out you have breast cancer at thirty-four? It must be so scary. Another reminder of how fragile we are."

William's face clouded, and he nodded solemnly. "It is indeed." He forced a smile. "Go on, now. You make your basket and I'll make my call."

Mae opened her mouth to say something and changed her mind. "Okay. Meet you at the car in ten minutes."

When she'd gone into the kitchen, William pulled out his phone. Before he called Feather Anne's father, he had a voicemail he needed to listen to again.

"William, it's Dr. Nettles. It was a good thing you came in last week. The tests show what I suspected, I'm afraid. Call the office when you get this. I'd like to get you in for surgery as soon as possible."

He deleted the message and looked back at his wife in the kitchen. She hummed as she filled the wicker basket. William's traitorous heart swelled with love.

She looked up. "Hey, you. Stop stalling. We've got a busy day."

William saluted. "Yes, ma'am. I'm on it." He waved the phone at her and made a show of pulling up Chris's number. He hit the call button, gave her a thumbs up, and walked out to the car.

When Chris answered, William said, "Chris, it's William. Mae wanted me to tell you we're on our way to the dealership and we'll see you there."

When Chris asked if Feather Anne suspected anything, William said, "No, I don't think she does. We'll have to park it at your place, though. She has a music lesson with Charles Brightsider and will see it if it's in our driveway." William started the car and said, "Hang on, switching to Bluetooth… and go ahead."

Through the car's speakers, Chris' voice boomed. "Oh, yeah, No problem. Gina's making the bow right now. Thing is huge, man."

William winced, turned down the volume, and smiled. "I'm sure it'll be perfect. See you shortly."

William ended the call and, from the driver's seat, took a moment to look around. Their home, the massive oak in the front yard, their street, the grass—still verdant even in the last days of summer—and the cloudless sky. The window was down and so he filled his lungs with ocean scented air, trying to ignore the ticking timebomb in his chest.

I'd like to get you in for surgery as soon as possible.

The smile that rested on his lips faltered. He would have to tell Mae. Of course, he would. Their lives were about to change drastically, perhaps permanently. Possibly without… no, he wouldn't go there. Not now. Not yet. Right now, and in the upcoming days, they would celebrate the birthday and accomplishments of Feather Anne, the twins first week of kindergarten, *and* their anniversary. His news could wait. It had to.

2 Brianna

Brianna watched the clock on the bedside table, willing it with all her might to move ahead twenty-four hours. She might as well try to stop the tide from going out to the sea.

"Bri? I'm going into work for a couple hours. Need anything while I'm out?"

She forced her head from the pillow and offered Ricky a wan smile. "No, I don't think so. I've got a few errands to run later, anyhow."

Ricky crossed the room and crouched by the bedside, putting them eye to eye. He stroked her hair. "You've got a pass on the whole business-as-usual mindset, babe. Stay in bed if you want. Kids are all in school and Mrs. Teccio is downstairs baking your favorite cake for tonight."

Brianna sighed and lifted a hand to caress his stubble rough cheek. "I want—I *need* to maintain at least some sense of normalcy." She shrugged the shoulder not buried into the pillow. "Otherwise, I'll go crazy."

Ricky nodded. "I get it. Don't overdo it, okay?"

He kissed her temple and stood. When she heard his truck leave the driveway, Brianna hauled herself up, ever mindful of the tenderness of her new breasts. Tomorrow, they would see the surgeon and Dr. Augustin again. The surgeon would check and hopefully remove her drains, and Dr. Augustin would tell her if they got all the cancer.

She glanced down at the clock again. Only four minutes had passed. Beside the clock, her phone vibrated and rattled across the table. She jumped to grab it before it fell and regretted it at once. A hiss of pain escaped her lips.

Brianna did as Lotus Davidson told her to do and breathed in serenity through her nose, exhaled pain through her mouth. After the third exhalation, the pain ceased.

"Fruity granola girl, right again," said Brianna under her breath.

She used the fingerprint sensor to unlock her phone. It was a text, not a call she'd missed. The sender icon showed a band emblem, which she recognized as Feather Anne's latest favorite band, and she grinned. This would no doubt be another of her ridiculous, yet funny memes or GIFS they'd been exchanging daily.

Sure enough, Brianna opened the message to see a screenshot one of the women from Real Housewives of Beverly Hills and a white cat. The camera caught the woman in mid-hysteria, pointing, and the cat's expression looked equal parts bored and mocking. The caption under the woman read, "It's Brianna," and under the snarky cat, it read, "Brawanna."

Brianna laughed out loud. Last week at her appointment, the receptionist had called, "Bra-wanna? Is there a Bra-wanna?"

Finally, Brianna approached the counter and asked, "Are you possibly looking for Brianna?"

The woman patted the top of her head for her glasses, squinted through them, and said, "Huh. That's probably it. Are you her?"

Since telling Feather Anne the story, she'd been calling her Brawanna. It gave Brianna a chuckle every time, too.

She thought for a moment, then did a Google search for Brittany Spears. She saved it, the added her own caption, "It's Brawanna, Bitch!" She pressed send.

Four years ago, no one could have predicted the friendship and mutual admiration the pair had, but there they were. Exchanging memes, going shopping together, and genuinely liking one another.

As it turned out, Feather Anne was a great kid. Smart, funny, definitely a wiseass and a straight shooter, loyal, and compassionate. And she was there the day Brianna got the call from the doctor's office with the results of her biopsy, and therefore, the first to hear the bad news.

Any other seventeen-year-old girl probably would have frozen in the face of something so grown up and awful. Not Feather Anne, though. She took the phone from Brianna's hand, walked her to the kitchen table, and poured her a tall glass of red wine.

She said, in a soothing voice, "I'm calling Ricky right now. You sit, take a couple sips of that. We're going to get you through this, Brianna."

Before Brianna protested—she was in no state of mind to do so, anyhow—Feather Anne had walked outside and made the phone calls. Within the hour, both Ricky and Brandon were home. Feather Anne took Cassidy and Archer to the park, letting the husband and brother take over.

By then, they'd already forged a relationship, but having shared a moment so raw and personal brought the two to a new level. Feather Anne had shown a side that Brianna hadn't known her capable of. Maybe one Feather Anne herself never knew, either.

Years ago, Brianna's therapist told her that people display who they are all the time, but it often goes unnoticed because we're too busy seeing what we want to see. It's only when a crisis or tragedy occurs when we see them clearly—whether they intend for us to or not.

Brianna spent so long caught up in casting Feather Anne in the light *she'd* perceived her in, that she'd been blind to the real girl. It wasn't until Brandon's football injury Sophomore year that Brianna's thaw began. The girl had been at the house daily taking care of Brandon, laid up on the couch with a torn ACL and concussion. Thanks to her, Brianna kept all her commitments and bookings on track.

Months later, Feather Anne came through for the Bakers yet again when they all had the flu at the same time. While they hacked and languished, she and Mrs. Teccio ran around taking care of them, heedless of the likelihood of getting sick themselves.

"Missy Brianna?" Mrs. Teccio hesitated in the bedroom doorway. "You come down the stairs for breakfast, or eat here?"

Brianna lips curved in a slight smile. "Downstairs, thank you."

"You sure, Missy? Maybe you're too tired and need more rest, no?"

"All I do is rest. I'm bored, Mrs. Teccio. I want to get back to my normal life. Starting with eating at the table like a civilized human being."

Mrs. Teccio waved her hands around and shrugged. "Okay, okay, Civilized, it is." She muttered in Italian on her way out and down the stairs though.

Brianna's phone vibrated in her hand again. She half expected another text from Feather Anne—a cry-laughing emoji or thumbs up—but it was Elise calling.

She cleared her throat, smoothed her hair, and sat up straighter as she answered. "Hey, you. What's up?"

"Oh, shut up. I recognize your fake phone voice, so don't use it on me. I'm bringing you dim sum and pho for lunch."

Brianna grinned. "So, you're back in town?"

"Yes, thank fucking God. Florida and my hair do not belong together," said Elise.

"Well, no one told you to open another Oasis Girls' Spa there. In fact, I warned you, you'd—"

"Yeah, yeah. Trevor Lawrence swore the rich grandma population there would go crazy over it, and he was right. Now I'm stuck flying there once a month."

Brianna lowered her voice and teased, "Did you bring your boy-toy along for the trip?"

"He is not a boy-toy," huffed Elise. "He's only four years younger, thank you. And yes, Jeff came with me."

Brianna waited for more and when nothing further came from the other end of the line, she drawled, "And?"

Like a dam being released, Elise burst out with, "Oh, my God. It was amazing. He is amazing. Get this. He wants to *take the next step in our relationship*."

Brianna's brow knitted. "You haven't slept together yet?"

"Of *course*, we have. He means *move in* together."

Now Brianna's eyebrows shot up. "Move *in* together? Wow. But it's only been—"

"I'm well aware it's only been six months. But we've known each other forever."

"Yeah, as Drew van Bergen's kid brother," scoffed Brianna. She thought about how happy her friend had been since she and Jeff started seeing one another and softened her tone. "Anyhow, good for you. Life is short. You never know what's around the bend; Lord knows I'm proof of that. If you're happy, I'm happy for you."

"So, you think I should do it? Move in with him?"

In her most magnanimous voice, she declared, "I think you should do whatever makes you happiest." She paused before adding, "As long as that includes bringing over some pork bao with that dim sum."

"You got it. Can I invite the others, too? Don't worry, I get it; you don't want a fuss for your birthday this year. It'll be low key. Lunch, mindless chatting about whatever, and then we'll be out of your... we'll be gone."

Out of your hair, she almost said. The prospect of losing her hair had made Brianna weep; almost more so than the mastectomy. After they'd biopsied the lump she'd found while showering. The doctor gave Brianna several—all terrifying—options. One of them, the last, being a double mastectomy as a preventative of sorts.

"Do it," she'd said.

The doctor and Ricky advised she takes a few days to consider all the options before deciding. But for her, only one option resonated. Do whatever had to be done to raise her chance of survival. She had a beautiful future ahead, and she planned on seeing it. She made a compromise of sorts to appease the two well-intended men in the room.

"All right. Here's what we do. Schedule the surgery for as soon as possible. I'll go home and think about it some more. If I change my mind, I'll let you know."

Ricky and the doctor exchanged looks that bespoke a clear understanding: do as she said, or else. And so, they scheduled the surgery a week from the day. Brianna never wavered in her decision and only allowed herself what she considered the luxury of tears once.

When—at a follow-up appointment to discuss the next steps—Dr. Augustin recommended chemotherapy as a likely treatment, Brianna asked what many women do when they hear the word *chemotherapy*.

"Will I lose my hair?"

Dr. Augustin gave her a pursed lip, apologetic smile. "I'm afraid it's a strong possibility. There are methods to combat the loss, such as…"

He kept talking but to Brianna's ears, he sounded far away. She raised a shaking hand to her scalp, ran it down the length of her sleek, shoulder-length, straight edged bob. Her hair had always been a source of pride for Brianna and envy from women around her. When she'd had it cut into her now signature bob in college, at least half a dozen girls tried and failed to replicate it. Now, her beautiful, admired hair would be gone.

She held herself together for the rest of the appointment, the car ride home, and until Cassidy and Archer were in their beds asleep. Then she locked herself in the master bathroom and cried for an hour. Ricky, helpless to console her, sat outside the door until she at last let him in, red-eyed and weak. He had a glass of water and a sleeve of thin mints, which he set on the sink counter. Gently, he wrapped his arms around Brianna, stroking her back.

Ricky didn't try to tell her, "It's only hair," or "It'll grow back." He didn't need to say, "I'll love you no matter what." Or, "I'll be by your side through this." He showed her this in his every action.

What Ricky said, was the truth. "I'm scared, too." And, "You can talk to me about how you feel. Yell or cry, when you need to. But don't shut me out. Don't hide yourself from me, okay?"

She'd nodded against his chest and said, "Okay."

When the week of the surgery arrived, Brianna's in-laws took the kids to Cape Cod for ten days and agreed not to say anything to Cassidy or Archer. At their return, they were told that Mommy wasn't feeling well and needed to rest for a few days to get better.

He brought them in to see Brianna in their bedroom and Cassidy asked, "Mommy, do you have the flu?"

"Yes, sweetheart, Mommy has the flu," answered Brianna, ruffling her hair and smiling wanly.

"Okay, Mommy. We'll let you rest. I'm going to make you something special."

Ricky, upon his return to the room after settling the kids downstairs, informed Brianna that Cassidy had gathered her arts and crafts boxes and construction paper and set to work making get-well cards from her and Archer.

It wasn't until he'd told her that his mother had stopped at Whole Foods on the way and picked up all her favorite foods and snacks, that Brianna wept.

Between each weak sniffle she cried, "That's so sweet of her. Tell her I love her. I love your whole family. Even Bethie who drives me crazy."

"Okay, babe," Ricky had chuckled. "I'll tell her. Man, those are some good meds, huh?"

Brianna's head bobbed up and down, "Uh-huh. They really are *so* good."

It was rough going, but she improved daily. The doctors seemed confident they'd gotten all the cancer and didn't believe it had spread. As Dr. Augustin stated it, "The army had gathered to attack, but hadn't decided where they wanted to go."

Brianna visualized a battalion of helmeted cells, lined up in rows with bayonets inside her body when he said this. Part of her wanted to laugh at the image. The other felt violated and angry.

She'd come to her own truce with the cancer, though. Brianna considered the many people who turned toward their faith in times of trial, and just as many who'd raged and railed against and unfair God. As far as she saw it, it was dumb luck... or rather unluckiness.

God wasn't punishing her. Nor would she ask Him to spare her life. She didn't want "Kick Cancer's Ass," or say, "Fuck Cancer," like those well-meaning cancer warriors suggested. All Brianna Baker wanted to do was get on with her life. Have the *chance* to continue it. If that meant cutting off her breasts and losing her hair, or getting sick from chemo, that's what she'd do.

No brave mantras, no martyrdom, no Team Brianna t-shirts or marathons. Life as usual. When she told Ricky and her friends this, they balked.

"Let us be there for you, Brianna," said Elise, Katie, and Charlotte in their respective ways.

Ricky had said much the same, bemoaning his helplessness otherwise. "Babe, I need to feel like I'm doing something besides watching you go through this."

"You *are* doing something. There might be times when you're doing everything. If you want to help me," she told them all, "let me be as normal as possible, for as long as possible."

And they'd agreed. Better yet, they'd stuck to her plan. Brianna maintained a lesser workload, delegating to her staff the tasks that required physical demands and taking over the behind the scenes running of a successful event planning business. Life had continued on as normal. Except underneath the routines and predictabilities something just shy of terror hid in the shadows of her mind.

3 *Miles*

Miles Hannaford cradled his cell phone between his shoulder and ear shouting, "What was that," and "Say that one more time, will you, Nora," as he fed—tried to feed—strained carrots to seven-month-old Fiona. Fiona, however, was too busy delighting in the newly discovered, high-pitched scream she could make. Repeatedly.

At about the same time as Miles tried to conduct a business call involving a million-dollar property and Fiona found her voice, the landscapers fired up the leaf blowers and Rosabelle carried a screaming toddler into the kitchen.

He covered the mouthpiece and hissed, "Poppy, please. Daddy is on an important phone call."

This only made Poppy wail louder.

Rosabelle set the writhing, banshee wailing little monster down and sighed. "She wants her banksie. It's in the wash."

Miles motioned frantically—using the strained carrot laden spoon—between the phone and the baby.

"Careful, you're about to get... too late." Rosabelle stared pointedly at his tailored beige pants, now with a glob of pureed orange carrot on his thigh.

He followed her gaze and swore under his breath. Rosabelle handed him a washcloth and took the spoon from his hand, shooing him away as she did.

"Go on, I've got this," she whispered.

All the while, Nora read off the latest addendum to the contract and the litany of buyer questions and concerns. Miles switched places with Rosabelle who spooned mush into Fiona's mouth with the same amount of ease as he had difficulty. She'd even stopped screaming. Poppy had not.

Her little bow mouth opened wider than he'd imagined possible. "I want banksie. I want banksie..."

She cried this mantra over and over until Miles, in sheer frustration, strode over to the laundry room, yanked open the dryer door, and snagged the warm, damp rag that once was a hospital baby blanket. He pivoted and marched back to where the irate child stood, the wet rag thrust it out in front of him.

"Here, sweetheart," said Miles, pushing banksie in her hands.

The tears and crying stopped instantly and two-year-old Poppy blinked in surprise. In his ear, Nora said, "Well, thanks, honey."

"Very funny," grumbled Miles. "I'll call you back in five." He slipped the phone in his pocket and said to Poppy, "Better now?"

Poppy wrinkled her nose at him. "Uck. It's wet." She dropped it on the kitchen floor and wandered off to the play kitchen set in the corner of the kitchen.

Miles turned a, "Can you believe this kid," look to his wife who merely shrugged, unbuckled Fiona from the highchair and plunked the now sated child on her hip.

"My parents will be here at six to babysit the girls. My gallery showing is at seven. Your blue suit is at the cleaners along with my dress. Pick them both up before they close at five. Will you remember all that, or do I have to send you a text to remind you?"

"Yes, Rosie. I'll remember. And yes, send me a text anyhow. I have three closings today, so I'll be tied up until the last minute. Wait, I thought Feather Anne was babysitting?"

"Change of plans. She has another commitment. Now, don't get distracted. You'll make it, right?"

By her tone, Miles knew she meant it as a command, not a question.

"Of course, babe. Wouldn't miss it for the world." He gave her one of his infamous megawatt smiles. She reciprocated with the death stare.

"This is a big deal to me, Miles."

He missed the days when the megawatt smile worked. Miles bit back a weary sigh. "I know, Rosie. See you tonight."

He leaned in for a kiss, but Rosabelle's phone rang and she turned away to answer. She waved him off distractedly as she spoke to what sounded like the gallery owner.

"Yes, that's fine. No, I can bring the others, too. It's no trouble. Should we..."

Miles' phone buzzed in his pocket. The seller from his next closing. *Shit*. This would be an exceptionally profitable sale for Miles, as long as he kept the buyer and seller from tearing each other's throats out long enough to sign the paperwork.

"Ritchie, buddy. How's it going, my man? Ready to get this ball rolling?"

Miles was pulling into the lot of his office before he realized he hadn't even said goodbye to his children. Not for the first time in recent months, a wave of sadness washed over him. He couldn't understand this melancholy. After all, he was living his dream life. Beautiful wife, healthy children, a huge house on a nice chunk of land. They even had the perfect family dog—a golden retriever they'd named Sunny—and Rosabelle's crotchety old cat Ludo finally seemed to like him... well enough, at least.

He continued his mental list of joys. A career, good friends. Money in the bank. Annual vacations. Good health. Wife. Kids. Dog. House. Repeat. So, why did this oppressive weight keep trying to drag him down? Where had it come from?

A rap on his window startled him. He jumped, looked up and out at the burly frame obstructing the sunlight, and swore. "Fuck."

Miles made a shoo motion not unlike the one his wife had used on him earlier and Bruce Grady stepped back enough to let him out of his BMW.

"Jesus, Grady. You're an hour early."

"Left you a voicemail," said Bruce by way of explanation.

Miles dimly recalled the beep of a call waiting while all hell broke loose in his house less than an hour ago. "Oh, right. Sorry about that. Let's go inside, so we can look over the specs on that property."

Bruce hesitated, squinted, and frowned at Miles. "What's up with you, Hannaford?"

"Huh," said Miles, genuinely baffled.

"I'm more used to your jokes and *yo, brohan* and whatever. You seem... down or something."

Jesus Christ. Miles sucked in air through his teeth. Now he had Bruce Grady—a guy who he'd come to a working truce with and no more—noticed his funk?

He forced a laugh. "Aw, Brucie Moosie, I'm touched. Wanna hug it out, bro? We can have some wine and talk about our feelings?"

Bruce shook his head. "There he is. Never mind, dickhead. Let's get this done. I got shit to do."

Somehow, Miles got through what turned out to be a shit show of a day. Grady harassed him for over an hour on two different properties he thought overpriced. Every buyer thought the property the wanted was overpriced. Each time, Miles explained how market analysis reports assess value and that he had no control over what sellers ask. It always fell on deaf ears.

The first closing ran over but thankfully happened. The second, unsurprisingly, hit a snag and had to be rescheduled. The parties from the third closing got on so famously they wanted to go for drinks together after. Miles tried to back out, but when the seller suggested there were future deals to be made, it compelled him to join them for one cocktail.

At two minutes to five, he skidded into the dry cleaners. The owner already had her shop keys dangling from one hand and the other on the light switches. At the sight of Miles, she heaved an irritated sigh.

"Still two minutes on the clock," said Miles, tapping his watch for emphasis.

She looked up at the wall clock, ready to argue, but the clock read four-fifty-eight with the little red secondhand racing around the display.

She dropped her heavy keyring on the counter, eyed him sternly, and said, "Ticket?"

Miles patted his jacket and pants pockets. He yanked out his wallet and thumbed through the receipts and bills, glancing up at her with nervous chuckles and requests to, "Hang on a sec. I have it here somewhere," as she huffed and sighed and rolled her eyes.

"If you don't have—" she began.

"Ah ha! Here it is." Miles held up the numbered slip of paper in triumph before slapping it on the counter.

He pulled into his driveway at twenty past five, ran inside and nearly collided with Steven Waterman.

"Whoa, son. Where's the fire?" Steven sprang backward, sloshing the coffee from his mug onto the new rug.

"Shit, sorry, Mr. W."

"Language, young man," admonished Ruth Waterman. She bustled past her husband and son-in-law with a dish towel to clean the mess.

"Thanks, Mrs. W. Where's Rosie?"

"Upstairs in her robe, waiting for you. You have her dress, I hope?"

By her tone, Miles suspected she rather hoped *not*. They'd called a truce over the years, but deep down, Miles suspected the Watermans harbored a secret desire for him to screw up and prove them right.

He raised the dry cleaner bag and gave it a shake. "Right here, as promised. I'll go and bring it up to her."

He had one foot on the stair when Ruth clucked, "Aren't you going to say hello to your children?"

Miles face flushed. Ruth made him feel like a bad father for not greeting his children. "Of course," he said. "W-where are they?" He felt even more foolish for not knowing where his children were.

"They're in the kitchen playing with their little play kitchen we got them."

Miles let go the railing and pivoted toward the kitchen. From upstairs, Rosabelle shouted.

"Miles? Is that you? Hurry, please. I need my dress."

Miles froze in place. He turned toward the staircase again, then to the kitchen. The Watermans watched him—Ruth with her arms crossed over her chest, Steven with his coffee cup poised for sipping—in silence.

His phone, locked into his free hand as always, began to ring loudly. On a whim, he'd downloaded an old song from the eighties. It was a fun dance hit by Tone Loc called Wild Thing, and the chorus—*she loves to do the wild thing*—blared from the tinny phone speaker.

Miles hit the silence button, excused himself and sprinted up the stairs. At the top of the landing, he answered.

"Miles," hissed Nora. "What the hell is going on with you? You didn't sign page six of the contract. We might lose this deal."

Rosabelle appeared in front of him, arm extended and hand grabbing the garment bag. "Jesus, Miles. Cutting it close much? We're meeting Mae and William in the bar in twenty minutes. Hurry up and change."

Meanwhile, Nora still yammered in his ear. From downstairs, Poppy's high, squeaky wail of rage pierced the air. Another grievous act by her baby sister, no doubt. The doorbell rang, setting Sunny into a frenzy of barking.

To Rosie, Miles said, "No problemo, Rosie Posie." To Nora, he pacified, "All good in the hood. Scan an email me the page, I'll sign it and get it right back to you."

He tucked the remaining garment bag—his suit—under his arm and stuck two fingers in his mouth to make an ear-splitting whistle, followed by a stern shout of, "Enough, Sunny."

To his father-in-law, he called, "Mind getting that, Mr. W.?" and to his mother-in-law, "Popsicles in the freezer. Usually does the trick."

When all matters were handled, Miles strode to the bedroom and changed into the freshly laundered suit, singing, *wild thing/she loves to do the wild thing* as he buttoned and tied. When Rosabelle exited the bathroom, he told her she looked exquisite and kissed her cheek as he switched places.

Once the bathroom door closed, he locked it. He turned the cold-water faucet on full blast, sat down on the closed toiled lid. Then Miles did something he hadn't done in more years than he could count. He dropped his head in his hands and cried.

4 Feather Anne

Feather Anne sat in the driver's seat of a 2017, royal blue Honda Civic. Her damp palms slipped along the steering wheel, and her heart thudded, but she couldn't wait to get on the road. If only Mae, William, Gina, and Chris would shut up already.

"Now, remember. You have to inch out past that tree at the end of Cardinal before you pull out," said Mae.

"Yeah, but after you make a complete stop at the sign, Feather Anne," said Chris.

"Don't be afraid to go below the speed limit. The cars can always go around you if they're in such a hurry," said William.

"Oh, God, don't encourage her to be a chicken shit. Feather Anne, you gotta drive aggressively out there," said Gina.

"Says the woman without a driver's license," snorted Mae.

The foursome bickered over the roof of the car. Feather Anne pressed the ignition button, turned on the radio, and powered up her driver's side window. She shifted into drive and let her foot off the brake slowly, letting the car roll forward and away from the lunatics. Once certain she was out of sight and hearing, she powered down all four windows and cranked the radio.

She thumped the steering wheel and sang along with Nathaniel Rateliff and the Night Sweats, grinning with the sheer delight that freedom brought. Her first solo drive. No Mae stomping her imaginary passenger side brake. No William lecturing her on motor vehicle safety. No sweating Chris or bitching from Gina. Just her and the open road.

The car behind her honked. Feather Anne startled and stepped on the gas petal. There was a sound–something like a pop and a crunch–and she jerked forward and back against the strain of the seatbelt.

"Shit."

Lotus Davidson climbed out of the car in front of Feather Anne—the car she'd just hit—and Charlotte Asheby jumped out from the car behind her, the car that had honked.

"I'm so sorry," began Feather Anne. Her whole body shook.

"No, no," said Charlotte, wrapping an arm around her shoulders. "It was my fault, honey. I didn't mean to beep at you. Benjamin threw his Batman doll on the floor mat, and I turned to pick it up, but my elbow hit the horn, and… well, here we are."

Lotus, unruffled, said, "I don't see any damage on mine. Yours has a little scuff on it though. Hey is this your first outing by yourself?"

Feather Anne managed a "Yes," before she burst out in tears.

The two women consoled her; each telling her about their first accidents and reminding her it could have been worse.

"Listen, honey, everything is fine. No one's hurt. We can all go on with our day as if it never happened, okay?" Lotus gave Feather Anne a wink and nodded at Charlotte.

"Yep, exactly. All's well that ends well," agreed Charlotte.

"Are you sure?" Feather Anne had gotten ahold of herself, but her chin gave a final quiver.

The two women sent her off after extracting promises to be careful out there and take her time getting to wherever she was going. After Lotus took her turn at the stop sign, Feather Anne creeped up, looked in all directions, and let two opposing cars go before her. There was no beep from Charlotte behind her, even though this time it would have been warranted.

She drove the rest of the trip to Brandon's with the music turned down low and her windows up. When she arrived, she saw him standing on the porch, arms crossed. He sprinted across the lawn to her car before she'd even placed it in park.

"You're seven minutes late. What happened?"

Feather Anne tried to laugh it off and avoid giving an answer. "Wow, dude. Were you *timing* me?"

"Yes. No. Not exactly. I happen to know it takes eight minutes if you hit the stoplights, and six if you don't."

"Okay, Rainman."

"What's a rain man? Wait, never mind that. Why are you late?"

"Oh, my freaking God, Brandon. Why are you being such a spaz?"

Brandon looked down at the ground and mumbled. Feather Anne ordered him to repeat himself, louder and more clearly.

He huffed a sigh. "I called your house and Mae said you left at four-forty-three. I got worried."

"Why didn't you text or call me, dummy?"

"Because Brianna said I shouldn't distract you if you're driving."

Feather Anne threw her head back and yelled at the sky. "You are all trying to drive me crazy." To

Brandon, she said, "So, does that mean you're too chicken to get in the car with me?"

Brandon grinned. "No. Well, a little. Where we going?"

"Beach, duh."

There were only a handful of good beach days left and Feather Anne was determined to get at least one of them before the weather turned cold.

"Okay. Come inside for a minute, though. Bri has an announcement. She's been waiting for you to get here so everyone can hear it at once.

"Shit. Really? Is it bad?"

"No idea. Her and Ricky are being pretty tight-lipped. Ricky's folks are here, too. *And* my mother."

She followed him inside the house. *Brandon's mother, back in Chance*. Feather Anne tried to keep her surprise in check. Martha Bourdreau—who was now Martha Schwartz, remarried to Alvin Schwartz and residing primarily in Naples, Florida—rarely came back to Chance, preferring her children and grandchildren visit her instead.

Inside, the family had gathered in the living room, where Brianna sat in her favorite chair and Ricky stood beside and slightly behind her.

"Feather Anne, we're so glad you're here for our announcement," said Brianna. "Come, sit."

Feather Anne made small waves to everyone and sat on the loveseat beside Brandon. He took her hand and squeezed.

Brianna began right away. "We won't keep you in suspense very long. But first, I want—*we* want—to express our gratitude to all of you. You've made an unbearable experience… bearable."

Ricky echoed her sentiments, and said to Brianna, "Go ahead, babe. Tell them."

Brianna inhaled sharply, exhaled slowly. "The doctor believes they were able to get all the cancer. It has not spread, and they do not believe I need traditional chemotherapy." She interrupted their cheers and congratulations to add, "I'll still have to take a pill every day for the next year or so and I'll likely have side effects, but hair loss is not one of them."

Feather Anne understood how the prospect of losing her hair had affected Brianna, so she easily imagined the relief she experienced. She sprang from her seat and was first to hug Brianna.

"I'm so happy for you," she said.

Brianna squeezed her arm and whispered, "Is it a scuff or is there a dent?"

Feather Anne's eyes widened. Understanding dawned immediately after, though. *Charlotte Asheby*. Sheepishly, she replied, "Just a scuff. I can buff it out before I get home."

Brianna winked. "Can I trust you to drive safely with my baby brother in the car?"

"Brianna, geez," said Brandon, embarrassed.

"Go on with your plans, you two. We're having Chinese food delivered later if you're interested."

Feather Anne and Brandon raced to her car and hopped in. "Ready?" She waggled her eyebrows up and down.

"As I'll ever be, I guess," said Brandon.

"Oh, shut up and buckle up."

Feather Anne drove them to Beach Access Road without incident. They traded the shoes on their feet for the chairs in her trunk and tossed their t-shirts in, too. They had plenty of time for a walk and a game of frisbee or one-on-one volleyball before sunset and Feather Anne commented as such.

"I get the idea you're stalling, Feather Anne. You got news for me, or what?"

Feather Anne popped open her chair and shot him a side-eye look. "Jesus, sport. Slow your roll."

Brandon laughed and grabbed her around the waist, spinning her until she hollered at him to stop or she'd throw up on him.

"All right, all right," she said when she'd caught her breath. "I'll tell you. Sit." Instead of telling him something, she flicked an envelope from her beach bag and handed it to him.

He eyed it suspiciously, squinted up at her, and said, "Is it what I think it is?"

"Oh, my God. Open it," said Feather Anne, shaking her hands frantically.

"Wait. You haven't opened it yet?"

"Does it *look* like I've opened it yet?"

"Okay, damn. Settle down."

Feather Anne punched his arm. "Settle down? Settle *down*? Are you out of your freaking mind? I can't settle down when in your hands might be my entire future. My life-changing moment. My one—"

"Stop, I get it," said Brandon, warding off her flurry of light punches. "You sure you want me to open it?"

She hesitated, then said, "Yes. You're the only one who knows I auditioned for the show. You help me record the audition video, drove me to Hartford. Good or bad news, I want you to be the one who sees it with me. Do it. Quick, before I wimp out."

Brandon took a deep breath, worked his finger into the small gap at the seam, and ripped it open. He turned it away from Feather Anne, pinching the insert between his thumb and forefinger and sliding it out gingerly. Feather Anne caught a glimpse of gold etching and her heart thundered. She thought she might pee her pants if he didn't hurry the hell up and read it.

A slow smile split his face as his eyes tracked the words on the thick, square paper. He read aloud.

Congratulations! Feather Anne Byrd, you have made it through the preliminary audition in your state and you will be moving on to the live taping of The Greatest American Singer competition.

Watch your emails for further information and instructions as well as waivers, disclosures, parental consent forms (for contestants under the age of eighteen), and other guidelines.

Brandon stopped reading and gazed at her; the smile now plastered on his face. "You did it, Feather Anne. I *knew* you could."

It was too good to be true. She couldn't believe her ears. "Holy shit, Brandon. Holy. *Shit*. Wait, read it again."

Had she heard it wrong? But Brandon read it again, and the words were still the same. She was going to be on The Greatest American Singer. She listed the show's credentials to Brandon as if he hadn't watched every single episode with her.

"Number one show for three years running. Discovered five top selling artists in three markets. A guaranteed recording contract. Do you understand what this might mean? The opportunity… the exposure. Oh, shit. The exposure. Brandon, I haven't told anyone about this. Not even Mr. Brightsider."

Brandon grimaced and agreed. "Yeah, that's a problem. So, when are you going to tell them? When the show airs?" He laughed. She didn't. He stopped. "Uh, Feather Anne? You *cannot* wait until the show airs to tell everyone."

Feather Anne made a noncommittal sound. Brandon attempted his, "I'm serious," face. She loved when he made that face at her. He'd been making it at her since elementary school. Hard to imagine that they were approaching their senior year in high school, never mind looking at colleges. That reminded her.

"Have you decided which colleges you want to tour?"

Brandon scooped up a handful of sand, picked out a shell and tossed it at her. "Don't change the subject."

"Don't avoid the question," retorted Feather Anne, picking the shell from her tank top and tossing it back at him.

"Avoid—*I'm* avoiding? No, *you're* avoiding *my* question."

She batted her eyes at him. "Sorry, what was the question? Oh, look! It's the Brightsiders."

Feather Anne used the distraction as an opportunity to jump up and run in the opposite direction.

"Where? I don't—hey," shouted Brandon.

Feather Anne turned, jogged backward, and called, "Last one to the jetty is a rotten egg."

She watched long enough to see him spring up and give chase before she spun back around and quickened her pace. She'd let him catch up, but not win. When he tagged the stone jetty seconds after Feather Anne, she kissed him.

"What was that for," said Brandon, still catching his breath.

"No reason." She shrugged and climbed the rocks using his shoulder to steady herself.

They walked in silence to the end, minding the gaps between the boulders. There, Feather Anne gazed out at the turbulent sea and Brandon—behind her—circled his arms around her waist and dropped his chin on her shoulder.

This was their spot and had been since their very first walk together. That day, and many more since, they'd opened their hearts to each other and spoke of their fears and doubts, hopes, and dreams.

Brandon was also the first to hear Feather Anne sing—*really* sing—and the one who convinced her to try out for the school musical last year, instead of only working on set designs. He was the one who convinced the play director to give her another chance after she froze under the spotlight the first time.

Those were the most recent displays of The Greatness of Brandon Bourdreau. The list, if she ever tried to compile one, would be longer than a CVS receipt. Yet, despite this—or because of it—Brandon still harbored a gnawing worry that he might turn out like his father.

"You're the best person I've ever known," said Feather Anne.

His chest rose and fell against her back; a silent chuckle. He said, "Something tells me you're about to meet all kinds of interesting people pretty soon."

Feather Anne, still within his embrace, spun to look him in his eyes. "Interesting? Yeah, sure. I'll give you that. But better than you? Never."

A smile flickered on his lips, but his eyes seemed sad. She realized how he may have taken her words. *You're the best person I've ever known.* Even to her own ears, it sounded like the beginning of a goodbye.

"Hey," she said. "*Hey.* It's me and you against the world. Always. Okay?"

Brandon rested his forehead against hers. "Okay. Us against the world, no matter what."

They kissed again, longer. This time, when they broke apart, their breath came ragged. Feather Anne laughed and pushed him back with one finger to his chest.

"Settle down, QB." She wagged that same finger back and forth in front of his face.

"Okay, gotcha. Not sayin' it's easy though."

They held hands—Feather Anne leading—and carefully made their way back across the gaping boulders.

She called out behind her. "It's no easier on me, in case you didn't know. But we have a plan and we're sticking to it."

Technically, *she* made a plan and was *making* him stick to it. No sex until graduation. Sure, they got teased for their abstinence pact and most people didn't believe them—including Gina, who kept insisting she go on the pill—but it was something Feather Anne had strong feelings about.

Mae was thrilled, naturally. Feather Anne suspected William, her Dad, and Bruce also all knew, but were too mortified by the topic to commend them. The thought reminded her of where they were supposed to be in less than an hour.

She dead-stopped. "Hey, we gotta pack up and go. We promised Bruce we'd help him at the new place, remember?"

Brandon thumped his forehead. "Shit, that's right. I still can't believe he bought that house."

Feather Anne offered half a shrug. "Eh, doesn't surprise me. He wasn't loving the big commercial properties as much as he thought he would. This is more like him."

They folded up the chairs and shook out the towels.

"I guess. Poor old Mrs. Rudiwitz, huh?" Brandon shook his head.

"Yeah. All alone in that big Victorian for all those years. She couldn't keep up with it anymore."

Brandon slung both chairs onto his shoulder, handed Feather Anne his towel, and they walked to the car. After a moment, he said, "Well, she was, what? Like eighty-something years old, so…"

Feather Anne dead-stopped again and said haughtily, "So? The Brightsiders are in their eighties and they still do everything."

"Yeah, but they're the Brightsiders. No one is like them. They're, like, the only old people I'd ever call badass. They're on their third cruise in two years, and on the last one, they zip-lined. Bad*ass*, man."

They drove in silence for a few minutes. Then, her voice tight, Feather Anne said, "Well, all I know is, I expect them to live until a hundred-and ten or something."

Brandon said nothing but reached over and gave her knee a gentle squeeze and gratitude overwhelmed her. Obviously, the Brightsiders wouldn't live forever. She just wanted them to.

5 Bruce

Bruce shut off the electric floor stripper and wiped the sweat from his brow. From somewhere upstairs the sound of a hammer whacking at… what *was* that kid whacking with a hammer?

"Jesus," muttered Bruce. He yelled, "Nick? What the—what are you doing up there, bud?"

Keep calm. Don't lose your cool. Count to ten before you react.

The heavy clunk of work boots on the stairs preceded the lanky, shaggy haired man-boy that just so happened to be Bruce Grady's son. His *son*. Still took him by surprise every time.

Four years ago, Mia Amendola—Mae's onetime best friend and girl Bruce had lost his virginity with at age fifteen—returned to Chance unexpectedly. However, that wasn't the biggest surprise she had in store. Turned out the derelict teenage boy who'd been lurking around town was her son.

When Mae had told him the story—Mia had gotten pregnant while still in Chance, then moved away with her family—Bruce strongly suspected that this kid might very well be his son. After Mae said Mia wasn't telling who the father was, he found himself conflicted. Should he ask her, or wait for her to come to him? Was the kid even his? And if so, what would that mean? How would the news affect the new relationship he was in with Aileen?

Even though he had more questions than answers, he waited. And watched. Ricky Baker had hired the kid to do odd jobs and errands at the auto shop, so, Bruce found excuses to pop by frequently to observe him.

Like Bruce, the boy was tall and had dark, wavy hair. That was where the resemblances ended though. Where Bruce had always been built broad and muscular, Nick Amendola was lean. Their eyes weren't the same color—although there *was* something in the shape—nor was their coloring. Lastly, their personalities were nothing alike.

Bruce prided himself on his strong work ethics and reliability. Nick strolled into the shop lot and half-assed mostly everything. Bruce had always spoken to his elders with respect. Nick called Ricky and any other adult he encountered, "Dude."

After a couple of months of this—coupled with Mia's bland, indifferent reaction and response to seeing Bruce again—he determined there was no way in hell he was this delinquent's biological father.

Then the little punk rolled his motorcycle and nearly died. Bruce's phone rang in the middle of the night. It was Mia, hysterical.

"Mia?" His voice was gruff with sleep and confusion. Aileen sat up beside him, alarmed. He whispered for her to go back to sleep and took the phone downstairs, repeating Mia's name.

"Mia? How did you get my—what's wrong?"

She was crying so hard her words were nearly indecipherable. He only got the last part.

"Your blood type. I need your blood type right now."

"My—uh, it's AB negative. Jesus, Mia. What's going on?"

She calmed herself enough to say, "You need to get to the hospital now. My son has been in an accident, and he needs a blood transfusion now. He's AB negative like… like his father."

"Mia, are you saying—"

"Just get here, damn it. Please, okay?"

The rest of those pre-dawn hours were a frantic blur. In the same night, Bruce learned he had a son and almost lost him before he properly met him. But the boy pulled through and recovered fully with only a six-inch scar on his right thigh to commemorate the event.

He was pissed at Mia, resentful. He'd had a kid out there in the world for sixteen years and been deprived of being a father to him. It wasn't fair. All the things he'd missed out on. So much time lost. Anger toward Mia boiled inside him and that anger eventually led to Aileen pulling the plug on their relationship.

He couldn't blame her. He'd been more or less consumed by his work, then by the bombshell of finding out he had a kid. *Then* his constant railing against the selfishness of *that woman*, as he referred to Mia.

Never mind all his other commitments. It was a lot to ask of a new relationship. They parted on good terms though and remained friendly ever since. He even did the addition on her house after she remarried last year.

Nick took the news of Bruce being his father with his typical apathetic teen blasé panache. From the hospital bed, he looked from Mia to Bruce, and said, "Cool. So, can you get me some more Jell-O…" he paused, grinned loopily, and added, "Dad?"

From that day forward, Bruce made every attempt to be as much of a father as Nick would allow, even bringing the boy into the business once he'd fully recovered. It was Bruce's hope to inspire some work ethic and passion for something other than weed, girls, and fast cars. Four years later, it was still a work in progress. A sometimes exhausting, sometimes frustrating work in progress.

As for his relationship with Mia, that ended up being a bit more complicated. He'd been furious with her, hurt by her actions, and also by her seeming lack of remorse. It wasn't until Mae gave him some insights that the ice began to thaw.

According to her, Mia feared the growing relationship between Nick and Bruce because she thought it meant she was losing her son. Mia also felt jealous of Bruce, who got to swoop in and be the hero, cool dad while she was stuck playing the role of the evil ogre mother.

With her coaxing, Bruce reluctantly agreed to a dinner with Mia; just the two of them, no interruptions, with calm and honest communication and a chance to set some boundaries and make plans for how to proceed.

It escalated into an angry shouting match... which turned into angry sex. This evolved into an awkward morning goodbye, three days of radio silence, more angry accusations, more sex, followed by regret and repeating twice more.

Eventually they settled into a shaky truce and a mutual agreement that they probably shouldn't keep having angry sex. These days they had occasional, random, semi-friendly sex with no strings and no attachments. They also had monthly breakfast dates at Mae's Cafe to discuss their son on neutral ground.

Their son.

Bruce sighed looking at the goofy kid—who was technically an adult—hammer propped on his shoulder, a bandana tied around his head, and lazy grin on his face. At twenty, Nick seemed no closer to having a plan or any goals to speak of despite Bruce's best efforts to guide him.

Carpentry was, in Nick's words, "okay, I guess." Bookkeeping was, "pretty lame, dude." Roofing, "sucked balls," and operating machinery was, "kinda cool, but boring."

When he wasn't working with Bruce, Nick typically hung out in his room at his mom's house and dicked around. Video games, tv, plucking at a beat-up acoustic guitar, and driving Mia nuts. That made Bruce smile.

"Wazzup, Boss Man?" Nick did a quick foot shuffle intended, Bruce supposed, to look like a dance step.

"What are you doing up there? I thought I told you to gut the bathroom."

"I am," said Nick.

"With a hammer?"

Nick looked at the hammer, then at Bruce. "Uh, yeah. You said knock out the half wall between the tub and the toilet. That's what I'm doing."

Bruce massaged the bridge of his nose, counting in his head to five before he responded. "But why… are you using… the *hammer*?"

Nick looked at Bruce as if Bruce were the idiot, bounced the hammer off his shoulder and mimed hammering as he said in a slow, mocking voice, "Breaking down the wall."

Bruce gritted his teeth. "That's what the sledge is—"

"Hey, we're here!" Feather Anne's husky voice came from the foyer.

"Back here, guys," called Bruce in reply.

Feather Anne and Brandon found them and after a round of hellos, got their instructions. Feather Anne had the task of taking off all the kitchen cabinet doors, while Brandon took on the stripping of wallpaper in the dining room.

"Feather Anne, you good with the power drill?"

"Duh," said Feather Anne with an eye roll to express her annoyance.

"All right, everyone to work. I gotta run to the hardware store. Don't mess anything up while I'm gone."

Bruce looked at his son a beat longer, hoping to emphasis his admonishment with a pointed glare. It was wasted. Nick had already turned away, popping his headphones back into his ears and tromping back upstairs.

All he needed was one hour. Bruce sent a silent prayer to the heavens that the old Victorian would still be standing when he returned. He made a mental list of damages incurred by Nick in the past week.

One antique vanity destroyed. Two Sawzalls broken. A lost level, screwdriver, and nail gun. A gallon of primer spilled. God knew what else. Still, Bruce was determined to find something this kid might excel at. Even if it killed him in the process.

6 Rosabelle

Rosabelle fiddled with her straw wrapper while Mae turned the OPEN sign to CLOSED. As much as she looked forward to talking with her, a surge of anxiousness sped her heart rate. This was something big, and personal. Should she even be discussing it with anyone?

"Two more minutes, and I'm all yours," said Mae as she breezed by.

Rosabelle called out, "Take your time," and meant it.

Both sides of her brain argued. Maybe this was *too* personal. Maybe this could be considered a betrayal of her husband. Unless he was already betraying her. But if he wasn't… and anyhow, it was *Mae*, not some random person. Mae knew how to keep a secret. It was fine. She'd tell Mae what she suspected, and Mae would have a solution.

"Okay. I'm done. Wait. Water? Is that what we're drinking? How about some wine? Better yet, how about homemade white sangria?"

Rosabelle began to say, "No, I shouldn't," but changed her mind. "On second thought, yes, sangria sounds great."

Mae clapped and said, "Yay! Hang on one sec."

She returned with a pitcher of white sangria in one hand and two wine glasses in the other.

After they'd both taken their first sips, declared it heaven, and made small talk about the weather and the kids, Mae sat back and gave Rosabelle a questioning look.

Rosabelle volleyed with a tremulous smile. "I guess you're wondering why I asked for a *just us* get together, huh?"

"What's going on? Everything okay? Do I need to give Miles a slap upside the head for you?" Mae laughed to show she was teasing but when Rosabelle didn't laugh with her, her brow furrowed, and she took Rosabelle's hand. "Hey, you're worrying me now. What's wrong?"

"I-it's Miles. Something is going on with him. I-I think he might be having an affair."

Mae guffawed. "Miles? An *affair*? No way. Rosabelle, he worships the ground you walk on. I mean, the Miles of, like, five or six years ago? Yeah, totally easy to see. But *your* Miles?"

Mae must've seen the despair on her face because the dismissiveness in her tone disappeared with her next words.

"Okay, tell me why you suspect he's having an affair."

Rosabelle took a gulp of sangria and listed her observations. "Well, he's been very... absent lately. Like, he's there, but he's a million miles away. And lately he's been locking himself in the bathroom for long periods of time. He's been coming home late and leaving again at odd times. He says he forgot something at the office, or he has a client meeting. He—"

Mae cut her off. "Honey, these all sound pretty normal. Even the bathroom thing. William says it's the only place he can get a moment's peace."

They chuckled. Mostly because they both knew that *moms* didn't get a break by hiding in the bathroom; the kids merely talked at them through the door.

"You're right, Mae. Separately, it all seems legit. But all together... I can't explain it. He's... different lately. Oh, and he's been taking naps."

"Naps? Miles? Huh. Well, that is strange."

Something in Mae's expression made Rosabelle lean forward. "What? I can tell, you're thinking something."

Mae gave a short head shake. "No, it's nothing. Not really, I mean. It's just…" She trailed off, biting her lower lip.

"Tell me, Mae. What? Did you see him with a so-called *client*?"

"Oh, sweetie, no. Nothing like that. It's silly, really. For years, he usually saunters in, calls me Baby Mae, orders his smoothie, makes me re-blend it, says something snarky, and leaves. Yesterday, all he said was, *hey, Mae*, and he ordered a black coffee. I was surprised, but it got super busy all of a sudden and I kind of forgot about it until right now. Huh."

Rosabelle thought about this. If Miles was anything, he was consistent and predictable. What did it all *mean*? "Well, if he's not having an affair, what is going on with him?"

Mae tilted her head and frowned. "You said he's been taking naps. Are they like little cat naps or…"

"No, actually, I've had to go wake him up. Sometimes he's asleep for hours."

Now Mae looked tentative. "Is it… is there a possibility he's… depressed?"

Rosabelle blinked hard. "Depressed? No, I-I can't imagine it. He's always so upbeat. When he's not napping, I mean. He goes to work every day. Spends time with the girls… no. I think I'd notice if he was depressed. W-wouldn't I?"

Mae offered a helpless shrug. "I'm not sure, to be honest. Do you remember my dad's partner, David?"

Rosabelle did remember him. "Yes, he was so sweet."

"Well, he lived with clinical depression. Most of the time, he did pretty well. Took his medication, saw his therapist and focused on a healthy lifestyle. But sometimes he'd slip and stop taking his meds and seeing his therapist and he'd plummet."

"Oh, but Miles—"

"It doesn't seem as extreme. But the thing is, one of the early tip-offs is the excessive sleeping. When you mentioned the napping… that's what it makes me think of. I'm sorry."

Rosabelle, even as she mentally dismissed the idea as impossible, began to question Miles' behavior under a different light.

"No, don't apologize, silly. Would it make me a terrible person if part of me hopes its depression and not another woman?"

Mae squeezed her hand. "Not at all. It makes you a woman who loves her husband and doesn't want to lose him, is all."

They talked a while longer before going their respective ways. "Well, I can't thank you enough for this," said Rosabelle.

"Aw, any time. If it helps at all, I don't believe for a second Miles would cheat on you. There's something else going on there, mark my words."

"And I plan on getting to the bottom of it, no matter what."

Rosabelle's drive home brought her past the park and she decided to pull in. A walk around the pond seemed like a nice idea. Mind clearing, that's what she needed. Now that her suspicions were offset by a new possibility, she was more conflicted and worried than ever.

She pulled into a parking space, turned off the ignition, and reached over to the passenger side to grab her purse. That's when she noticed the car next to her. More specifically, the man inside the car. His head was bowed, and his hands covered his face.

She saw his shoulders shaking, his torso curved toward the steering wheel. Even through her rolled up windows she made out the sounds of Enya blaming from the other car's speakers.

Her brain struggled to compute what her eyes saw. There was only one man she knew who drove a black BMW and listen to Enya. It was her husband, and he was crying, alone, in his car.

7 Brandon

Brandon used the toe of his boot to slide the garbage barrel closer to the wall. They were on day three of gutting the old Rudiwitz B & B and he was beginning to regret taking on the job, even though Bruce paid well. He saw Feather Anne through the kitchen doorway, but her back was turned. His eyes followed the flow of her long ponytail, to her short shorts, tan legs, and down to her work boots. How did she manage to make even work boots look hot?

From the other kitchen doorway—technically, there were three—he heard a low cat call. Fricking Nick. Brandon couldn't see him from his location, but there was no question of who it was whistling at his girlfriend. Before he said a word, Feather Anne spoke for herself.

"Fuck off, Amendola."

Brandon smirked.

Nick laughed. "Easy, killer. Geez. Can't a guy admire a beautiful girl?"

"What do you want, Nick? Some of us are trying to work here," she said, ignoring his slimy compliment altogether.

"Damn, girl. We used to be cool. Let me guess, your boyfriend won't let you talk to me? Is that—"

"Are you for real? God, you're such a knuckle-dragger," snorted Feather Anne.

Brandon snickered. God, he loved that girl. She could handle herself; he never doubted it. Still, he couldn't stop himself from poking his head around the corner and adding his two cents.

"Dude, why don't you quit bugging her and do your job, huh?"

Nick, who had three years and about two inches on Brandon, smiled lazily at him. He widened his stance and stuck his hands in his back pockets. They locked gazes.

Nick thrust his chin at Brandon. "And what if I don't, tough guy? What are you going to do about it?"

Brandon tossed the putty knife onto the tarp and spread his arms out, palms up. "I'm simply giving you a friendly suggestion, but if you wanna come at me let's go, man."

"Holy fucking testosterone. Both of you, cut the shit. Nick, go do whatever the hell you were on your way to do. Brandon, please get the dining room finished before Bruce gets back," said Feather Anne. When neither moved, she yelled, "Now, idiots."

Brandon twitched his eyebrows at Nick. Nick sniffed and shrugged as if to say, *whatever, man.* Still, he did as Feather Anne told him to do, so Brandon backed off.

"Takin' my break, if that's okay with you Lady Boss," said Nick.

"Good, go," huffed Feather Anne.

Brandon's cell phone buzzed. It was a text from Ricky.

Hey, Bud. Know ur busy,
but need u home for kids 4
like an hr. Sis feelin' meh.
Mrs. T day off.

The timing was shit, but he couldn't say no. "Hey, I have to run home for a while. Bri needs a hand with the kids."

Feather Anne set down the power drill and reached for her purse. "I'll bring you."

"Nah, don't be silly. It's one block over. Gotta get my cardio in, anyhow."

He looked past Feather Anne, out the window over the sink. Asshole Amendola had parked his lazy ass in a wrought-iron chair on the brick patio and had his feet up on the matching table like he owned the place. Brandon scowled and Feather Anne must've known exactly why.

"Relax, I'll be fine."

"He's a loser," said Brandon, jerking his head in the direction of the patio.

"Yeah, well, he's harmless. And don't call him a loser, Brandon. You're being a total Andrew Clark."

Brandon puzzled. "Who's Andrew Clark?"

Feather Anne sighed. "From the Breakfast Club? I literally made you watch it last night. How do you not remember?"

Brandon shrugged. He'd slept through half of it, but she didn't know that. A vague recollection of the characters came to mind. "He was the smart kid, right?"

"No, dummy. He was the jock. Just like *you're* the jock." She raised a hand to block him from her sight. "Go. Just go before I strangle you."

Brandon ducked under her hand and kissed her before sprinting out. Over his shoulder he called, "Love ya. Be back in an hour or so."

As Brandon jogged toward Cardinal Lane, he swore under his breath. He didn't like leaving Feather Anne alone with Nick Amendola, even if she was perfectly capable of taking care of herself. The guy was slimy, had been since the day he came to Chance and probably always would be, no matter how hard Bruce tried to reform him.

How Bruce Grady ever spawned such a low life was beyond Brandon. The mother, Mia, seemed awfully nice, too. Poor lady. Even Brianna sympathized, and Brianna wasn't exactly a wealth of sympathy and compassion. Whatever the case, Nick Amendola—as far as Brandon saw it—was a loser.

The more he thought about it, the more it pissed him off that Feather Anne seemed to not mind Nick's attention. Sure, she told him to fuck off. But she also defended him. Could it be possible that she *liked* him?

The idea made him sick, and he stopped to catch his breath. He shouldn't have left them alone. He considered gathering up his niece and nephew and bringing them back to the house. He'd be gone no more than a half hour if he did.

Decided, he picked up his pace, so he'd get home faster. Once there, he burst through the kitchen door, shouting, "Hey, kids, Uncle Brandon's going to take you—"

Cassidy and Archer were at the kitchen table. Finger paint in a rainbow of colors covered large rectangle pieces of paper, their hands, faces, and hair.

Brianna, looking pale and exhausted, apologized. "Sorry, it was easier to let them go at it. You'll have to get them into the tub after."

"Oh, yeah, sure. No problem," said Brandon. He swallowed his frustration and disappointment and plastered a smile on his face.

There was no way he'd be getting back to the Rudiwitz—he'd really have to start remembering to call it Bruce's—place any time soon.

8 Mae

"All right. Order however many you think will sell. And I really love that new design," said Mae. She looked at the clock. "Nice."

She and Melina Petrova finished their morning meeting with time to spare before the breakfast crowd started rolling in.

"Eh, we're old pros by now," said Melina.

"Hey, how's your sister doing in New York?"

Melina shrugged. "Love/hates it. Her and Ryan keep talking about moving back here, but we'll see."

"You miss your other half, don't you?" Mae squeezed Melina's arm.

"It's hard. We've never been apart this long. I guess I always thought we'd both meet boys from town, have a double wedding, babies at the same time… like in the movies." Melina gave a self-deprecating laugh at her own folly.

"Aw, well, Ryan seems like a great guy, no?"

"Oh, yeah. Definitely. He and Seth get along great when we all hook up. It's good, really."

Mae waggled her eyebrows. "And how *are* things going with Seth?"

Melina blushed. "Very well, thank you. Six months tomorrow. He's sweet. And he understands my attachment to Chance and the café. He's even hinted at moving to town."

Mae was thrilled for both Petrova girls. They'd grown up before her very eyes and now they were embarking on the next chapters of their adult lives. It broke her heart almost as much as it did Melina's when Paulina took an advertising job in the city, but it was the right move for her. And, as her father had been fond of repeating: the only thing constant, is change.

Still, sometimes it shook her to see how much had changed over the years. Sure, most were good, happy changes—life evolving as it should—but some left her feeling sad. They were all getting older. Mae saw it in the mirror, and she saw it most markedly in William.

They'd celebrated his sixtieth birthday that spring. A quiet, family dinner—his insistence— rather than a big party. Mae kept her disappointment to herself; she'd hoped to have something epic to celebrate the man she adored.

Not that William had slowed down. He remained active and fit, worked steadily and toured for his book launches. He helped with the twins and even in the café on occasion. Sometimes, Mae thought he had more energy than her. But lately he'd seemed off. Distant and distracted, and it worried her.

"Hey. Earth to Mae?"

Bruce waved his hand in front of her face.

"Bruce! I wasn't expecting you today," said Mae.

She was as pleased as she was surprised. Ever since Bruce and Pedro bought that very first property four years ago, he'd been almost non-stop busy. Mae heaved a sigh of relief when he'd said it was time to scale back a bit and slow down.

Up until this last year, Bruce had worked at a seemingly manic pace; starting one major remodel on the heels of the last, managing the Brookhaven building, and navigating the new relationship with Nick. Not to mention whatever it was he and Mia had going on.

It had become a complicated life, especially for a man who loved to keep it simple. Mae saw the toll it took on him, but it wasn't her place to tell him what to do. That didn't always stop her though.

"Yeah, well, I had a little free time, so I thought I'd swing by for lunch and catch up with you. You doing okay? You looked like you were pretty far away there." He gazed at her intently, reading her, or at least trying to.

"I'm fine. It's fine. Nothing, really."

Bruce tilted his head. "Mae. You know who you're talking to, right?"

Mae couldn't help but laugh. They'd known each other too long to hide anything from one another.

"Okay, okay. I'm sure it's nothing, but... has William talked to you at all?"

Bruce scratched his head and frowned. "I mean, we've talked. But not, like, *talked* about anything. Why? What's up?"

"I-I don't know. It's nothing, I'm sure. He seems... off."

Bruce gave her a sympathetic look. "Sorry, kid. Although, now that you mention it, yeah. He did seem a bit off last time I saw him."

Mae's eyes widened. "See, I knew it. Where did you see him? What did he say?"

Bruce squinted at her. "Mae, what is it you're worried about? You don't think he's... he's cheating on you?"

"No, of course not." She realized how arrogant that sounded. "I mean, he's not the type of man who'd ever—"

Mae waved her hand dismissively, but suddenly recalled Rosabelle's same concerns over Miles. Was there something in the air affecting only the men in

Chance? She studied Bruce, who seemed perfectly fine and carried on the conversation unaware of her thoughts.

"My thoughts exactly," agreed Bruce, looking relieved. "So, what, then?"

"I guess he's simply tired? Kids are great, but they're exhausting, and... you get it." It seemed traitorous to mention William's age, even if it was merely a fact. "Our finances are fine. He'd tell me if anything was physically wrong. Wouldn't he?"

The question was more for herself, but a look passed over Bruce's face. Like he'd remembered something. She grabbed his arm.

"What? What do you know?"

Bruce took her by the shoulders and gave her one of his famous *everything is under control* looks. "Relax, Mae. I'm sure it's nothing. Last time I saw him was in the hospital lobby. But," Bruce raised a hand to silence Mae, "he said he was there to visit a friend."

"He never mentioned visiting a friend in the hospital to *me*." Instead of easing her worry, this new information stressed her more.

Gina came into the back with an armload of pies. "Want me to fill the case, or leave them back here?"

To Bruce, Mae said, "Maybe he'll talk to you. Will you try?"

"Yeah, sure," said Bruce.

"Thanks, Bruce. Grab a table, I'll get your usual." To Gina, she said, "Here, I'll help you. We'll do half out front and the rest in the cooler for now. They go fast."

It was true; Gina and Chris's bakery next door usually sold out by ten o'clock in the morning. They made everything small batch, and when it was gone, it was gone. Mae had been skeptical in the beginning, but Chris's idea was right on the money. Plus, Mae got the first pick of everything from pies to artisan breads.

Once the day got rolling, Mae had little time to think about anything other than work. But the moment two o'clock came, and the sign flipped, so did her thoughts go right back to William.

Right about then, he was on a plane to Atlanta for a book signing. Tomorrow, he'd be in Virginia. Then home. That's when she'd make him sit down and tell her what was going on. Mae had to trust her instincts on this, and her instincts told her something was wrong. But what?

9 Feather Anne

Feather Anne pulled into the long, circular driveway of the former B&B. Instead of Bruce's midnight blue Ram, there was only Nick's beat-up old Ford truck. The black was so faded, it appeared gray and the rusted-out spots resembled continents.

She bit her lip. Brandon would not be happy to hear she and Nick were in the big house alone. He hated the guy and made a point of saying so every time Feather Anne told him she'd be helping Bruce work on the house. They'd even had a fight over it as she left his place to go to Bruce's that morning.

"It's a *job*, Brandon. I'm getting paid and I'm learning a skill," she'd said.

"Yeah, well, the Big Dipper is hiring. Why not get a job there like every other high school kid?"

She crossed her arms over her chest and stared at him. "The Big Dipper? Seriously? You think I should work in an ice cream shop instead of getting on-the-job training doing something I enjoy?"

"Come on, Feather Anne. Remodeling? *Construction*? Don't you think that's a little... I mean you're a—"

"A what? A *girl*? Is that what you were about to say? Because if so, you better rethink that statement. Jesus. And I thought Nick Amendola was a knuckle-dragger? FYI, jackass: girls can remodel houses. We can be builders. We can—"

"Listen. I'm sorry. I just... it's *him*. I can't stand the guy. I don't trust him around you. I see the way he looks at you. And he obviously doesn't have a problem going for younger girls." Brandon sat down hard on the bottom step of the front porch.

This was an old reference to when Nick first came to town and started seeing Sydney Martin, a girl three years younger. It ended the moment her parents found out and sent her to a private, all-girls school in Farmington.

Feather Anne sat beside Brandon. She uncurled his fist and slipped her hand inside his. "I understand how you feel, okay? But it's not him you have to trust, it's me. We've had this talk before. Guys are going to hit on me. Girls are going to hit on you."

"It's different," he said petulantly.

"It's literally the same. So, shut up. The deal is, we handle it. You handle the skanky bitches trying to move in on my territory, and I'll handle the randos trying to sneak into yours. Problem solved." Feather Anne shoulder nudged him until he laughed.

Brandon smirked and gave her a side-eye glance. "Randos, huh? Is that one of Katrina's words?"

She laughed. "Yep. Last week she told me that, *some rando slipped into her DM and she iced him.* Her exact words."

They both cracked up over this and the tension broke. Brandon said, "Wait. So, did some random guy really send your aunt a DM to hit on her?"

Feather Anne tossed her hands up. "That's what she says. She's actually a pretty big deal on Instagram and Twitter, so she probably gets all kinds of crazy messages."

When Feather Anne stood to leave again, Brandon's expression clouded. "Is *he* working on the house today, too? I know, you can handle it. I'm just asking."

She sighed, kissed his cheek and walked backward to her car. "If he is, I'll ignore him. Fair enough?"

A twinge of guilt had stabbed her chest when she got behind the wheel. Bruce had already texted her to say Nick would be there in his place because, once again, one of the Brookhaven tenants needed him. In fact, they'd been working together alone in the house on and off for two weeks thanks to Brookhaven tenants.

She justified the omission to herself. It would serve no good for Brandon to find out she was alone with Nick Amendola. Especially since Brandon had no chance of getting over there himself thanks to football practice and his own part-time job.

Another twinge followed the first. It relieved her that Brandon couldn't make it to Bruce's. Crisis averted, no tension between the two walking testosterone bags. That's all it meant. It had nothing to do with how much fun she had with Nick doing the remodel. Nothing to do with the way she often caught Nick staring at her. Or the fact that she didn't mind him staring. It didn't matter. Why? Because *it meant nothing*. Nothing at all.

"Yo, legs. You comin' in or what?"

Feather Anne looked up to see Nick leaning into her passenger side window, an unlit cigarette in hand and lazy smile in place.

"Yeah, Jesus. Don't sneak up on me like that, ass."

"Sorry, legs. Bruce says you and me need to do some team work today. Think you can handle being up close and personal with all this?" He stepped back from the car and motioned to himself as if he were a game show model demonstrating to her what she might win.

Feather Anne rolled her eyes. "Uh, yeah. Pretty sure it won't be a problem." She followed him inside.

"So, what is it we're doing today that requires teamwork?"

"Drywall. Upstairs bedroom."

She expected him to make some crude comment about them being in a bedroom together, but he surprised her by saying nothing. She was further surprised to see all the drywall boards already stacked against the wall outside the room.

Nick shot a skeptical look in her direction. "Has Bruce taught you how to drywall yet?"

Feather Anne hooked her thumbs into the loops of her jeans. "Nope. Not a clue."

Another languid smile spread across Nick's face. "Well, then, I guess it's your lucky day, legs."

She gave him the finger and said, "Just show me what to do and shut up. And stop calling me legs. It's derogatory and rude."

"Yes, ma'am. Whatever you say." When she refused to crack a smile, he sighed and changed his tone. "All right. Let's get the first sheet and we'll do it together. There are a few tricky spots—like around the curved door frames—oh, and the ceiling will be a bitch and a half. But otherwise it's pretty easy."

They had six sheets up when Nick said, "Ready to give a ceiling panel a try?"

Feather Anne looked from the four by eight-foot panel, to the two ladders, to the ceiling. "Uh, I guess so?"

Nick laughed. "I'll do the heavy lifting; you spot me and hold the panel while I nail it."

Again, she waited for one of his cracks. None came. She couldn't resist teasing him. "What? No, *that's what she said*?"

Instead of laughing, Nick propped an elbow on the ladder and stared at her intently enough to make her blush. He said, "I'm not always a dick, Feather Anne."

The retort on the tip of her tongue wouldn't come out. Truth was, he was right. He *wasn't* always a dick. The past couple of weeks of working with him had shown a side of Nick Amendola she'd never expected. What she'd learned? The arrogant, doesn't-give-a-fuck attitude was a facade.

Real Nick—the one who wasn't always putting up a front—had a gentler side that came out whenever his grandmother called, which was daily. Plus, he was a total mush when it came to animals, something she learned on day three when he showed her pictures of his three dogs. The way he'd talked about them—"

"Uh, a little help here?"

Feather Anne snapped to attention. Nick's back was to his ladder, and he had one heel mounted on the first rung. The drywall balanced on top of his head. It looked heavy and awkward.

"Shit," swore Feather Anne. "What should I do?"

"Get your ladder as close to mine as you can." She did. "Good. We'll go up facing each other, you keep her steady while I nail her up. Okay?"

They were inches apart, so close she smelled the laundry detergent on his t-shirt and his deodorant. And the gum on his breath. She gulped. "Okay."

He worked fast and efficiently, but even so, Feather Anne's arms began to tremble and a bead of sweat coursed from her temple to her cheek.

"Coming into your space, hang on. Almost…"

Nick stepped one foot onto her ladder, between her ankles. His face was close enough for her to see flecks of gold in his brown eyes. His arms were on either side of her head as he reached up to nail the panel in place. Now she stared at the stubble on his jaw.

"… done." Nick exhaled and set the hammer down on the small platform behind Feather Anne's head, leaving his hand there. He grinned down. "You can let go now."

She lowered her arms. Both of Nick's hands held the platform, momentarily locking her between his arms. It *should* have been momentary. They froze. Held each other's gaze. Feather Anne's breath caught in her throat. Nick's Adam's apple rose and fell.

His head dipped toward hers. Her chin tipped on its own free will. He was going to—she was about to—She blurted, "Lunch break?"

"What?" Nick sprang back, almost falling off the ladder. He hopped down and made a show of checking his watch. "It's only… oh, wow. It's one o'clock? That, uh, went by fast."

Feather Anne mumbled something to the effect of *yes it had*.

"Time flies when you're having fun, right?" Nick's smile wasn't his usual snarky one. It was kind of bashful, hopeful even.

Feather Anne chose to brush off the potentially charged moment. "Uh, yeah. This has been fun. Did you bring your own lunch, or should we order something?"

"I take it *you* didn't bring a lunch," said Nick with a chuckle.

"Nope. Forgot it on the counter at home."

"Okay. Pizza from Lucky Loo's? They deliver the fastest. Plus, my buddy Zeke can get us a discount."

"Is it an *honest* discount? Otherwise, no thanks," said Feather Anne.

"Yeah, totally. Zeke's straight. So am I, by the way."

"Didn't say you weren't," retorted Feather Anne. Good, they were back to their usual banter. Nothing weird going on here. Nothing *wrong* going on here.

But Nick wasn't ready to play along. "You implied it though. I'm aware of what you and your boyfriend—hell, this whole town—thinks of me, Feather Anne."

He'd never called her by her name before. Usually it was by her body parts. *Legs*. *Mighty Mouth*. It disconcerted her.

"I, uh, I'm going grab my water bottle from the car. Meet you in the kitchen."

Halfway down the stairs, Nick called out. "Feather Anne."

She craned her neck to look at him at the top of the landing. "Yeah," she said after a heavy pause.

"You… you mind grabbing my phone from my truck? It's on the center console."

"Sure," said Feather Anne.

An internal argument waged in her head.

He's kind of sweet.

He's playing you.

He's not all that bad.

Nick Amendola is a player, a druggie, and a pig.

He said he's straight now.

You don't like him. You can't like him.

I can be friends with the guy.

No, you can't.

She grabbed her water bottle and slammed her car door. At the steps, she remembered Nick's phone and jogged to his truck. The doors were locked, but the back window was rolled down far enough she could reach in and unlock it.

The first thing she noticed about the interior of the truck was it was much cleaner than she'd have expected. The second thing she noticed was the guitar laying across the backseat. Forgetting the phone for a moment, she pulled out the six-string by its neck.

After a furtive glance back at the house, Feather Anne rested her foot on the step bar and the guitar on her knee and strummed. It was in tune and gave a deep, resonant sound. She'd been trying for weeks to master a Fleetwood Mac song, so she tried the chorus.

A sound behind her made her jump. Nick, standing cross armed and smiling slightly, said, "You can play *and* sing? Damn. I can't seem to coordinate. It's one or the other for me."

Feather Anne's eyebrows flew up. You play? And you sing?"

Nick shrugged and kicked at the grass. "Eh, a little this, little that. Like I said—"

"Can you play Landslide? It's by—"

"Fleetwood Mac, duh."

Shyly, she handed over the guitar. "Wanna play it while I sing? You can jump in on the chorus. Sometimes it's easier when someone else leads."

Nick hesitated, then said, "Uh, sure. Pizza's gonna be awhile anyhow. Zeke is off today so Loo is cooking and delivering." He jerked his head toward the house. "Let's go sit out back."

She trailed behind him, though the house, out the French doors, and onto the brick patio. He yanked the two wrought-iron chairs away from the table and closer together. Feather Anne had to wipe the sweat from her hands onto her jeans.

Nick fiddled around with the tuning keys. She watched him. He looked up suddenly and gazed into her eyes. Softly, he said, "Ready?"

Feather Anne nodded once, and he began. She couldn't look at him as she sang, not at first. But when the chorus came, she caught his eyes and held his gaze, encouraging him to join in.

His voice was smooth and low, offsetting the gravel in her tone, and he harmonized perfectly with her. By the look on his face, Nick was as surprised as Feather Anne. When the last chord faded, they laughed nervously.

"That was—" Nick shook his head, grinning.

"Right?" Feather Anne lightly punched his arm. "What else can you play?"

It turned out Nick's musical tastes were as diverse as her own. They played and sang three more songs together. An old song Mr. B. had taught her, the latest The Lone Bellow song, and one called Picture by Sheryl Crow and Kid Rock. Nick knew it right away.

"Dude, you are full of surprises," said Feather Anne.

Nick half-smiled and strummed. He tipped his head down to look at the strings, letting his long hair hide his face. She almost didn't hear him when he said, "I wrote a song."

"You... what? You wrote a song? Really? Can I hear it?"

He spread his hand flat over the strings and looked into her eyes as if he were trying to make up his mind about her. "You won't laugh?"

Solemnly, she said, "I won't."

Nick nodded and began strumming. The chords evoked a sad, sweet mood and Feather Anne found herself swaying. Then he sang, and the words made her want to cry.

You broke into my soul
You covet what you stole
What was the reason?

I locked out what you seek
Afraid that love would peak
Then be out of season.

One glance into your eyes
And I drop the thin disguise

You don't know my heart
You don't know how I protected it
from the very start.

You don't know my soul
The darkest places that it can sometimes
go
Stay out of my space
It will only keep you safe,
if you don't know my heart.

I could blindly forge ahead
Pay no attention to the dread if I was to
hurt you
It's better just to say, that it was meant
to be this way and take God's cue.

One glance in your eyes
And I dream about another try

But
You don't know my heart
You don't know how I protected it
from the very start
You don't know my soul
The darkest places that it sometimes
goes
Stay out of my space.
It will only keep you safe, if you don't
know my heart…

He stopped and cleared his throat and chuckled
a little. Without looking at Feather Anne, he said,

"Anyhow, you get the idea. It still a work in progress, but—"

"Nick, it's great. I mean it. Let's do it again. This time, sing the whole thing and I'll jump in on the chorus." *If she could just catch her breath.*

He tried and failed to suppress a huge smile as he began playing. This time, they sang it to the end. Feather Anne leaned over the guitar and hugged him. It was impulsive, and she hadn't expected him to hug her back, but he did.

Someone cleared their throat behind them. They turned, expecting to see the pizza delivery guy, dopey smiles still on their faces. It was Brandon, a Subway bag and drink in his hands. Feather Anne gaped at him.

He wore his practice uniform and the white pants were stained with grass and possibly a streak of blood. His jersey had a tear at the waist; it, too, bore grass stains and a red smear. An angry red scrape arced across Brandon's jaw and a small cut rested below his right eye. Feather Anne had seen him like this countless times. What she hadn't ever seen before was the expression on his chalk-white face.

"Brandon, hey. I-I wasn't expecting you—" Feather Anne jumped up, trying to look casual and knowing she failed.

Brandon, with considerable effort, tore his eyes away from her, stared a moment at Nick, and returned his cold gaze back to Feather Anne.

"Clearly," he said. He looked down at the food in his hands as if just realizing it was there. "I, uh, thought I'd surprise you. Practice let out early. Coach wanted us to save the firestorm for the game."

"Why don't we go in—"

"Nah. I'm good. I'll let you and your… friend here get back to whatever it is you're doing."

He spun around and strode toward the house.

"Brandon, wait. Come on," said Feather Anne, running after him and grabbing his arm.

He stopped abruptly, faced her, and shoved the bag and drink into her hands. "Not now, Feather Anne. We'll talk later."

Brandon glanced over her head at Nick, who'd not moved from the chair, but no doubt watched the whole scene. His jaw clenched and unclenched rhythmically.

If she said another word, if—God help her—*Nick* said a word, there would be a fight. That was the last thing she wanted.

"Okay, fine. Are you going to be all right?"

He laughed, a hard, short sound through his nose. "Yeah, fucking great." Shaking his head, he turned and strode away.

Feather Anne took a step to follow. A hand on her elbow stopped her.

"He's fine. He'll go punch a wall or do some donuts in a parking lot. He'll calm down and say he's sorry for being a pus—"

"He's not like that, okay?" Feather Anne yanked her arm away. "You don't know him."

Nick raised his hands—*don't shoot, lady,* the gesture begged—and said, "Sure, whatever you say. Sorry."

He backed away a few steps, stopped as if to say something more, but the pizza guy yelled out from the side of the house, "Yo, you kids order a pizza?"

Feather Anne looked down at the Subway bag and drink, then at the delivery guy. "Oh, for fuck's sake," was all she could mutter.

Nick breezed past her, accepted the pizza, and paid the guy. She watched, mouth open, as he plopped the box on the table, flipped the lid, and grabbed a slice. She continued to watch as he sat back down, his back to her, and shoveled the slice into his face without a care in the world.

Feather Anne fumed. Of course, *he* didn't have a care in the world. *His* girlfriend didn't storm away with the death look on her face, *He* didn't get mortified and made to seem like… like… a *cheater.* Nick Amendola didn't have a care in the world because he didn't have someone who loved him.

And that was the thought that diffused her misplaced anger. None of this was Nick's fault. Or Brandon's. It was hers. *She* lied by omission. *She* let

Nick get almost close enough to kiss her—she stopped it from happening, but still—it was close. *She* was the one singing knee to knee with another guy. And she was the one having not so innocent thoughts about a guy who wasn't her boyfriend.

"Stop overthinking everything and have some pizza, Feather Anne," said Nick without looking back.

"I think I should—"

"You should let him cool off. Sit. Eat. Talk or don't talk." This time he turned to her. "You didn't do anything wrong."

Two forces played tug-o-war with Feather Anne's heart and mind. One pulled her through the house, to her car, and Brandon's driveway. The other, to the chair across from Nick.

Nick fanned the smell of the pizza toward her as a means of enticement. She shouldn't be hungry after such a stress and tension filled moment, but she was ravenous. So, it wasn't Nick who won her over, but the pizza. That's what she told herself, at least.

10 Miles

Miles slowed the car to a crawl as he passed the old Rudiwitz place. He half hoped and half dreaded seeing Bruce Grady's truck in the driveway. There were papers to sign—with a deadline—and if they weren't, he'd lose his deposit and Miles would lose a substantial commission. This wasn't the problem though. The problem was Miles didn't care nearly as much as he should.

In fact, Miles less than cared; he gave zero fucks. Which was a whole other crisis. *He* was in crisis. This was something he had no time for, but now he was being forced to address it finally. He couldn't decide between relief or horror. Both, he supposed.

That morning—after peeling himself off the bed, dragging himself to the bathroom, and hanging his head in the sink and letting the cold water run rivulets down his hair and face—Miles met his bloodshot eyes in the mirror.

"Snap the fuck out of it, Hannaford. You don't have time for this shit," he hissed.

"Miles?" Rosabelle, outside the bathroom door. "Did… did you say something?"

How long had she been there? She'd been hovering a lot lately; she knew something was not right despite his efforts. He'd told her he thought he might have the flu. In fairness, he did think it initially. A deep tiredness, along with body aches, consumed him and his head weighed a ton. No fever came, no cough or accompanying symptoms, yet the fatigue remained.

"Just singing, Rosie Posie. Out in a minute."

He held his breath and waited for the jiggle of the doorknob. He imagined her there, on the other side of the wood, her temple pressed against it, her brow furrowed, and bottom lip trapped between her teeth as she debated whether to come in or not.

Instead, she said in a soft hopeful tone, "I made you a mango and kale smoothie. For after your run? I-I think… maybe a run will do you good. You haven't—"

"Thanks, babe," he said sharply. He winced, softened his tone. "Sorry, still a little blah. I'll, uh, take the smoothie to go, though."

A long pause. "Okay."

He waited for more, but there was none. A relieved sigh escaped his lips and was followed by a scowl of disgust at himself. The only person—besides his daughters—that he'd ever deeply loved in his life, and he was avoiding her. Pushing her away. And he couldn't seem to stop himself.

Back in the bedroom, he passed the bed, its crumpled and tangled bedsheets beckoning him to return to their safety and stood before his dresser. His hand hovered at the drawer with his workout clothes and dropped to the one with his jeans.

He pulled them on, along with a white t-shirt and pullover vest, with leaden arms. It took him a minute to muster the energy to stand and march downstairs to his waiting family.

Rosie would have a travel mug of coffee and the dog's leash waiting for him. Fiona's shouts of, "Beso me, Daddy," would start. Ileana Villeneuve taught her some words in Spanish, and she used them every chance she got. It was cute as hell.

Poppy would begin repeating "De-da," and stretch her chubby arms out to be picked up.

His beautiful, sleep-tousled haired wife would shrug and smile at him as if to say, *what can I say, they love their Daddy,* and kiss him on the lips. The kiss would linger, and Fiona would shout louder, "Beso me, Beso me," and he and Rosie would laugh.

That had been a variation of their morning routine for some time now, one that had evolved from the two, then three, then the four of them. His family. His sweet, achingly beautiful family. At the bottom of the stairs, he braced himself for the scene that normally served as his motivation and inspiration. Had he been concentrating less on his inner turmoil and more on his surroundings, he'd had realized sooner the hushed silence of the house. But he didn't.

So, when he rounded the corner, strolled into the kitchen—easy-going smile pasted on his face—and saw his and Rosie's parents sitting at the table, he froze in confusion.

"Wha—well, hey there, mi familia. What's the occasion I get all four of my favorite parents in my kitchen?"

Was it someone's birthday, and he forgot? Had Rosie told him they were coming, and he hadn't been listening again? Shit. They all looked serious. Jesus. Had something bad happened? Where were the kids? And Sunny? His cold, wet snout should be nudging his hand right about then. He looked to Rosie, his eyes questioning.

"Where are the girls? The dog?"

Steven and Ruth looked down. His mother averted her gaze to the window. His father stared hard at him, like he was trying to figure out who he was.

Rosie tucked and re-tucked her hair behind her ears. She gestured to the empty chair at the table.

"The girls are fine. They're at the Villeneuve's for a playdate. Sunny is outside. Sit down, please."

A knot twisted in Miles' stomach. He took a step backward. Even as part of his brain still puzzled over whether someone had cancer, or died, he knew. They were here for him. *Because* of him.

"Listen, I'd love to join you in this… uh soiree. But I am swamped at the office. Appointments, and—"

"I already told Nora you'd be in later today. Miles, she said you haven't been coming in until noon anyhow."

Now he understood what a cornered rabbit felt like. His gaze darted around the room, at each of them. Ruth, calm and knowing. Steven, uncomfortable. Chet, unreadable. Jeannie, tense.

His mouth went dry. He didn't want to have this conversation. He was fine, damn it. He *would* be fine; no need for… for this. Jesus, was this, like, an intervention? *Fuck.* Their faces. He'd seen this on tv. The next sentence would be something like, "We're worried about you, Miles."

Despite the mounting panic, Miles tried to joke them away. "Ya caught me, I'm having a torrid affair with Starbucks."

Rosie flinched at the word affair. My God, is that what she thought? That he was cheating on her? The notion made him relieved. That was easy to disprove. He really had been at Starbuck every morning.

Alone, in the corner, with his laptop and copious cups of overpriced coffee.

He WebMD'ed his symptoms, pretending he didn't already guess what his problem was. It wasn't the flu, or Lyme disease, or any other physical or neurological disorder. It wasn't a virus, and it wasn't contagious. What Miles had was depression. Somehow the happiest, luckiest man in the world was *depressed*.

In the moments where he could be honest with himself, he understood it embarrassed him, this emotional imbalance. *Chemical* imbalance said WebMD. Whatever the hell the cause, all he knew was Hannafords don't get depressed. Hannafords handle their business and get shit done. Hannafords succeed. Hannafords excelled. They were winners, leaders, and they were happy as fuck.

Rosie's next words deflated the balloon of hope. "I saw you. Yesterday?" When he failed to compute, she said, "At the park, Miles. I saw you at the park."

Tears brimmed in her green eyes. It broke him to see her cry. It always did. Steven spoke next.

"Son, let us help you."

Ruth said, "Miles, we're your family and we love you." She looked pointedly at Jeannie and Chet.

Chet cleared his throat and yanked at the collar of his shirt. "I'm not sure what's going on with you, son, but we, uh, we'll straighten things out. Jeannie."

His mother's normally glacial countenance contorted. She struggled with what to say. Ruth kicked her under the table. Miles didn't see the actual kick, but the thump and sharp glare from Jeannie to Ruth made it clear.

"Miles," she began. "You need—"

He didn't want to hear anymore. He didn't want to acknowledge their sad, scared, worried, awkward faces all aimed at him. Nor could he bear the weight of Rosie's loving, understanding, forgiving gaze. He had to get the fuck out of there.

"Guys, listen. I'm fine. Seriously. All good in the hood. I was a little meh. Touch of the flu, that's all. So, thanks for… this, but I really gotta run—"

"Miles. I love you. You need help. I think you have—"

"Whoa, hey, hey." Mile backed up even though no one was coming toward him. "Rosie, come on."

He forced a laughed, but his Goddamn eyes betrayed him. They stung and his vision blurred. His heartbeat pulsed in his throat and kept trying to laugh but there it was; he was crying. Fucking *crying*.

Once the tears started, he couldn't make them stop. He ground his palms into his eyes, both to stop the flow and block the sight of his stricken family staring at him.

Rosie's arms were around him, her warm body and rose-lemon scent filled his nose, and he never felt so loved and alone at the same time. In between his strangled cries of, "Fuck... fuck... fuck," were her murmurs of, "I'm here... I'm not going anywhere... I'm here, baby."

He dropped his head on her shoulder and buried his head in her soft hair, his hands in tight fists against her back. The more he ordered himself to stop crying, the harder the sobs wracked his body.

More bodies surrounded him. Ruth and Steven, Jeannie, and Chet. All with a hand on him—his hair, shoulders, and back—in silent support.

A bark at the French doors broke up the hugfest. They all turned to see Sunny, snout covered in dirt, and tail wagging. The Waterman's used the moment to busy themselves with pouring coffee, straightening chairs, and general blustering about.

Rosabelle cupped Miles' face between her hands and smiled. "We've got this. Together."

She stepped aside and held his gaze an extra beat. He nodded and released a shaky sigh. Chet stepped in between them and clapped his son on the shoulder. Words of comfort were not Chet Hannaford's strong point, but he tried.

"Let's you and me hit the links this weekend. What d'you say, son?"

"Sure, Pop. Sure," said Miles. He couldn't meet his father's eyes.

Jeannie elbowed Chet out of the way and looked up at her son, studying his face hard. Miles braced himself for a second time that morning. This time for a Jeannie Hannaford buck up and shut up lecture.

"Miles," she began in her smooth steel voice. Rosie stepped forward, ready to defend her husband, but it proved unnecessary. "Rosabelle is right. You can't fight this alone. I'll give you my doctor's number. He's helped me tremendously."

Stunned silence followed. Miles didn't compute, not at first. Neither did Chet.

"*Your*... what are you saying, Jeannie?" Chet's thick eyebrows knitted together.

Jeannie thrust her chin out defiantly and parked her hands on her hips. "That's right. I see a therapist. Once a week, on and off for the past two years."

Now—perhaps for the first time—Miles saw underneath that defiant shield, a different, less confident Jeannie Hannaford. One who, despite her seemingly bottomless well of ageless beauty, refinement, and dignity, still was human.

Chet tried to process. He stammered and sputtered. "You... a-a therapist? For what? Why? You never—I didn't know."

"Yes, well, I wanted to..." she trailed off and looked back to her son. "Truth is, I was embarrassed. All the years of say us Hannafords this, and we Hannafords that." She shook her head and grabbed Miles' wrist. "I'm sorry. That was—it was me telling *myself* to buck up. I never meant for you to feel like—"

"It's okay, Mom." He rested his hand over hers.

And for the first time in a while, it *was* sort of okay. He was okay, or at least he believed there was a chance he would be. With help. The burden wasn't his alone anymore.

Knowing this didn't change the fact that he still had a job to do, bills to pay, and a family to take care of. So, after Rosie extracted a promise from him to make an appointment for the first available time slot with Jeannie's therapist, he climbed in his car to find Bruce Grady and get those papers signed.

As he drove through town, heading next toward Brookhaven, he mused over the morning's events. It wasn't like the shows on television. The problem didn't instantly resolve the moment his family intervened with love and understanding. It helped, yes. But it didn't fix him. He wanted to be fixed.

When they were alone, and after he assured Rosie he wasn't angry with her for calling in the reinforcements, she asked him if he could describe his feelings. At first, he resisted, knowing it might make hurt her. Telling his wife that when they touched lately, it was like he couldn't *feel* her, wouldn't be easy to hear. She'd persisted, though, and Miles did his best to explain the feelings of disconnect and apathy toward things he'd previously enjoyed.

Her genuine understanding and compassion touched his heart deeper than she could ever realize.

She told him, in looking back, she realized she'd suffered a milder form of depression after her car accident.

Her gratitude for being alive—because that's all she heard, *be grateful you're alive*—made her tamp down the feelings of resentment and frustration, and even sadness for losing her independence and physical abilities. Because her injuries were temporary, she thought she had no right to feel the way she did. Complaining would have been selfish. Wallowing, petty. So, yes, she understood the pressure of trying so hard to act right all the time.

"You don't have to be our *everything*, Miles. We're a team, and teammates share the weight." Those were the words Rosie had sent him off with.

Miles collected himself and lifted his briefcase off the passenger seat. Grady stood on his porch, hands on hips and staring at Miles' car. He sighed and climbed out. For now, he'd have to play the role of a man who was all right, but at least it was with a flicker of hope that he might soon be.

11 Brianna

"Pick up your pace, slacker," said Brianna.

"Slow yours down," said Katie. "Jesus, power walking on packed sand isn't easy for some of us, Brianna."

Elise and Charlotte exchanged shrugs and kept their lips zipped. They knew better. Brianna enjoyed this resurgence of power over the group, despite its reason. The *I have cancer card* currently trumped all others, and she planned on using it until it expired. Which, if all went well, would be in another eight months when she stopped having to take her anti-cancer pills and got her clean bill of health.

"Well, Katie, some of us are walking four miles a day *with cancer*, but if you think it's too much for you—"

Katie's lips tightened into a thin line and she hastened her step to keep up with the others. Brianna smirked and continued her previous conversation.

"As I was saying before Katie interrupted our flow, Miles drove by last week and I swear, it looked like he was crying. *Cry*-ing."

"That's so sad," said Charlotte. "I hope he's okay."

"Oh, please. He's fine. He probably saw a gray hair in the mirror and lost his shit," scoffed Elise.

"Not nice, ladies," huffed Katie. "What if something terrible happened and here we are, gossiping and laughing?"

"I, for one, am not laughing, for the record," said Charlotte.

"Oh, be quiet, Charlotte. We get it, you love everyone, blah, blah, blah," mocked Brianna.

"I'd guess Rosabelle finally wised up and kicked him out," offered Elise.

"Nope," said Charlotte, "I saw her yesterday, and she had nothing but sweet things to say about him."

Brianna checked her Fitbit and increased her stride. Katie swore and fell back again. Honestly, she was doing this *for* Katie. She still hadn't taken off the baby weight from Reagan, and that was five years ago.

Wistfully, Brianna asked, "Remember the days when we had a pulse on everything that happened in this town?"

"Yeah, that ended when Brittany moved to Pennsylvania," said Elise.

"Virginia," corrected Brianna, Charlotte, and from way back, Katie.

"Whatever," said Elise. "Anyone hear from her lately? Not that I care."

This time, Charlotte and Brianna exchanged looks. This was one grudge that wasn't fading with time.

Katie, now stopped with hands on knees, called between gasps. I… have… info. But… you'll have to stop… walking if you want… to hear it."

The other three looked at each other, shrugged, and walked back to Katie.

"Oh, for fuck's sake. Catch your breath and tell us what you know."

"Jesus," said Elise, "do not tell me she's moving back to Chance."

Finally, Katie was able to speak in full sentences. "No, but Bart is. She served him with divorce papers and kicked him out of the house."

"Cheating again?" Charlotte crinkled her nose in dread.

"Yep. With—you'll never believe it—the same dental hygienist."

They all gasped, "No," dragging out the 'o' extra-long.

"Oh, yes," confirmed Katie. "She told me herself."

"Wait," said Brianna. "*he's* moving back? Not her? I'm shocked. Her parents are still here. Her brother, too. *He* doesn't have anyone left in Chance to come back for."

Katie dipped her chin to her chest and raised her eyebrows. "The *hygienist* has an apartment in town and he's moving in with her."

"Well," said Brianna. "I'm not inviting them to the party next week. Ricky is forbidden to ask."

Elise threw her hands up in exasperation. "Why are you still her friend, Brianna? You, too, Katie? She's a back-stabbing bitch who dragged us all over Facebook with that anonymous page. And does she ever call *you*? Has she gotten on a plane or driven to see you during any of this?"

"Oh, calm down, Elise," said Brianna, dismissing her rant. "That was four years ago. She apologized—profusely, mind you—and to be honest, I feel bad for her. Oh, and to answer your questions, yes, she calls once a week and offered to come see me when her kids have a school break."

Elise made a sound somewhere between a snort and a laugh. "Well, suit yourself, she's still dead to me."

Brianna's eyes narrowed. "Explain to me how you can forgive your gay, cheating ex-husband, his lover-turned-husband, *and* your ex-fiancé—who you left at the alter because you believed he was still in love with Mae Huxley—but not your lifelong friend who did a shitty thing because she was hurt and left out by us? Hmm?"

Elise's jaw worked like a marionette as she tried to articulate a response. Brianna had her, so she said, "Let's finish our walk, shall we?"

She walked without a backward glance and within seconds, three shadows joined hers. *Bart Sheffield and his floozy, back in town.* She suppressed a shudder of revulsion. Did that mean Ricky would start hanging out with him again? She meant it when she said they weren't welcome in her home.

Thinking of what a slimeball Bart was made her think again of Miles Hannaford. The others had changed topics and were now debating Bikram yoga versus Yolates—a hybrid of yoga and Pilates—and whether they should join a class at Lotus' place.

"Wait, we never figured out the Miles thing," she declared, stopping them all in their tracks.

She realized suddenly that her interest may have been perceived as more than normal interest because of their history. How could she say that she was merely curious and have them believe her? The answer was obvious. She couldn't. This annoyed the shit out of Brianna because she *was* just curious. Nosy, if she really wanted to be honest. But now it was too late to backpedal or justify, so instead, she added, "Eh, it was nothing, I'm sure. Anyhow, who wants to go for fro-yo after this?"

She ignored the exaggerated looks the trio passed around. It served as variation of ones they'd shared since she announced her breast cancer diagnosis. Looks that said, "Let's do whatever she asks," and "Don't argue with her in this fragile state."

Mostly, she didn't mind it; she got her way with almost no effort. One this day, in that moment, it irked her. They were patronizing her. Humoring her. Indulging her, like a spoiled child. Worse, there was nothing she could say to alter the perception.

Brianna turned away and power walked to the parking lot. The others trailed after her. She wished she hadn't suggested a frozen yogurt run. The late September air left her clothes and hair vaguely damp and her chest achy despite the protective wrap that kept the new girls in place while she walked.

Charlotte's phone chimed. "It's the school," she said as she took the call.

Her youngest, Brooklynne, had a fever and would need to be picked up.

"Looks like I'm out for fro-yo. Sorry, guys," said Charlotte.

"It's fine," said Brianna, seeing it as her out, too. "Let's skip it. I'm a little wiped out. Another day."

Neither Elise nor Katie seemed disappointed, confirming her impression they'd been humoring her. She made sure to give them all an icy goodbye. And she didn't give them the leftover party favor bags she'd brought, either. No Godiva for them, hah.

As Brianna turned off Beach Access Road, the sky opened, and rain splattered the windshield. Her headlights and wipers started up on auto. God, she loved her new car, and her husband, of course, for surprising her with it.

She noticed a hunched figure tromping along the sidewalk, no umbrella in hand. "Poor sucker," she *tsked*. Then she recognized the jacket. "Brandon?" She said his name aloud, as if he could hear her, and shook her head in confusion as she pulled alongside him. Brianna powered down the passenger window.

"Brandon! What are you doing, walking in the rain?"

He jerked and crouched to see inside the car. "What does it look like I'm doing? I'm walking home."

Annoyed, she said, "But *why* are you walking home in the rain?"

He didn't answer. She sighed and looked at her pristine heather gray, leather interior. "Get in, Brandon."

He took a few more steps. "I'm fine," he said. The rain fell harder.

"Oh, for Christ's sake, get in the car already," yelled Brianna.

This time, he listened. He climbed in, dripping and shivering. Brianna cranked the heat and turned on his seat warmer. One glance told her he was in a miserable mood.

"Where's your car?"

"Shop."

"Ah, monosyllabic answers. Lovely. Why didn't you have Ricky or one of the guys drive you back?"

Brandon shrugged. "No reason."

Brianna tried to keep from snapping. Obviously, something bothered him. She'd start with the obvious.

"And where's Feather Anne? Why didn't she bring you home?"

Another shrug. He looked out the window and said nothing.

Brianna tried again. "Are you two in a fight or something?"

Still facing the window, he deadpanned, "Or something."

Yes, she saw he didn't want to discuss it. No, she wasn't going to accept this as the end of the conversation. Brianna knew what they were fighting about. Or rather *who* they were fighting about. Nick Amendola. Even thinking the name made her sneer.

He was a punk and a loser, period. Yet, somehow, he'd managed to blind Feather Anne into believing he *wasn't all that bad*. Feather Anne's words, not Brianna's. Little did Brandon realize, but she heard all about this kid and the fight he caused between him and Feather Anne. But she wouldn't let on.

"Does this have anything to do with Nick Amendola, by any chance?"

Well, so much for not letting on what she knew. Brandon threw his head back against the seat. Her imported leather seat. Brianna winced and bit her lip even as she reached around the backseat for a towel or a blanket, or a Goddamn stuffed animal. Anything, something for him to dry off with.

"She told you? What am I saying? Of course, she told you. I liked it better when you two hated each other. Just stay out of it, Bri. Please?"

"Sure, no problem," said Brianna magnanimously. She waited a beat. "All I'm saying—" she ignored the groan from the passenger seat — "is that pushing her away when another dog is sniffing around isn't the smartest move."

Brandon snapped on the radio. The iHeart radio station she had on blasted vintage Madonna, Like A Virgin. Brandon switched it off as quickly.

He slapped his thighs as he spat out, "How? *How* does she not see what his game is? Her, of all people? She's smarter than all those other girls that fall for his... his hair flicking and *I'm a rebel* bullshit."

Brianna smirked. The guy was swoon-worthy... if you liked the bad boy type.

"It's not funny, Brianna. This guy has had Feather Anne on his radar since the day she started working on that house."

"I know it's not funny." After a pause, she added, "I'm sorry," and tried again. "Well, what has Feather Anne said about all this?"

He scoffed, "That I'm supposed to trust her and never mind him."

"And do you?" Brianna took her eyes off the road to look at him.

"Yeah, of course." His tone sounded firm, but his face betrayed the mixed emotions underneath.

"Brandon?"

She only spoke his name, but the question—the repeated question—was implied.

This time, his answer was honest. "I'm not sure. Last week, I surprised her at the Rudiwitz—I mean Grady—house. I thought, hey, I'll bring her some lunch, check in to see how she's doing—"

"And who she's doing it with," added Brianna pointedly.

Brandon ignored her and continued. "And there they were. Singing together."

Brianna waited, but that seemed to be it. "*And*?"

He shifted to look at her in disbelief. "What do you mean, *and*? They were singing a-a love song. *Together*. Their knees were *touching*."

"I see," said Brianna.

And yes, she saw how that scene might have affected Brandon. If that were Ricky, and Brianna was Feather Anne, Nick Amendola would have found himself in a hospital bed with a fractured skull. Thank God, Brandon had more self-control.

"It gets worse. Now, apparently, they are working on songs together every day. She wants him to go with her for the…" he stopped abruptly.

They'd turned into their driveway and the second Brianna put the car in park, Brandon reached for the handle. She hit the lock button and held it.

"Go with her for what, Brandon? You're not getting out of this car until you spill it."

Brandon huffed loudly. "You can't say a word, Brianna."

"Fine. Spill it."

"I mean it. Not a word. To *anyone*." He waited for Brianna to promise. "Okay, Feather Anne auditioned for The Greatest American Singer. She got in, Bri. She'll be on the taped show they're recording in New York. The first one, at least. If she makes it through, then there will be more."

"Oh, my God. Oh, my *God*. Brandon, that's amazing. Wait. Why is this a secret? It's great news."

"You know how she is. She doesn't want all that pressure on her. If she doesn't make it through the first round, at least no one will know until after the show airs."

Brianna covered her mouth and her words were muffled. "I can't believe it. Our little star. I'm so excited." Her eyes widened, and she grabbed Brandon's arm. "Brandon Bourdreau, you cannot stress her out with your petty jealousy right now. I'm serious. This is a very big deal for her, and she can't be distracted by worrying over you."

He pouted and crossed his arm over his chest. "Yeah, I got it, okay?"

"You want my advice? Tell her you love her and you're proud of her. Make sure she knows you have her back no matter what. This Nick kid will show his true colors in no time. If she's at all smitten by him—and I'm not saying she is, so calm down—he'll ruin it all on his own."

He crossed his arms tighter. "I don't like it."

"No shit. I couldn't tell." She eased up. "She loves *you*, Brandon. But big, huge things are happening for her right now and if you love her, you have to let her… spread her wings."

Brandon stared out the windshield, unblinking. After a minute, he nodded his head slowly. "Yeah," he said. "Yeah, you're right, Bri. I gotta let her fly."

Something in his tone struck Brianna wrong. "Brandon, I wasn't saying—"

He flicked the manual door lock and climbed out. Brianna sighed. Then she inspected the leather for water damage. Satisfied there was none, she grabbed her umbrella and followed her brother inside.

12 William

William reached up and unlatched the overhead compartment housing his carry-on bag. He slid the brown leather duffel out and set it on his vacated seat, then noticed the young woman waiting patiently to do the same. He smiled and held up one finger.

"Let me grab that for you," he said, reaching up again.

"Oh, thank you. Careful, it's heavy, I'm afraid," she said apologetically.

The woman's case was a hard shell, with a pretty floral pattern, but the dainty appearance belied its heft. It was, indeed, quite heavy. As it cleared the shelf and William bore the full weight, a piercing pain shot through his shoulder to his jaw. He dropped it down onto the aisle with a grimace.

"Are you all right?" The woman gripped his arm in concern.

William forced a smile. "Perfectly so, my dear. Have a lovely stay in Connecticut."

He recalled she'd come to visit relatives, as per her conversation earlier with her seat mates behind William's row.

"Are you sure? I could—"

"Old tennis injury flaring up. Not to worry. You go on ahead, please. I insist," he added when she seemed unsure.

She thanked him again and sidled past. William massaged his shoulder and worked his jaw. He hoisted his bag on the good arm and strode down the aisle, nodding a thanks and goodbye to the flight attendants by the cockpit.

In the traveler filled terminal, he pulled out his phone and called Mae. She answered on the first ring.

"You're calling to say you've landed safely and you're on your way home to us, right?"

William chuckled. "Exactly right, sweetheart. How's everyone?"

"All good. TK fell at school and has a bruise on his forehead, but that's nothing new. Evvie made a new friend and is already asking for a playdate, so, nothing new there either. Let's see, what else? Café is still standing, as am I. Chris and Gina got another dog. The Brightsiders called from port; they're enjoying their cruise but miss their dogs. Oh, one spot of potential bad news—Feather Anne and Brandon seem to be having trouble. She's not talking, though." She exhaled. "So, what's new with you? How was the last signing?"

He smiled against the phone and maneuvered through the crowds toward the escalators. "Smooth sailing. Or signing, I suppose. Glad to be done and back home."

"I'm glad, too. I've missed my husband."

He heard the smile in her voice. "I've missed you, too. I'll be there within the hour."

"William?"

He'd been about to say goodbye and almost missed it. "Yes, darling?"

"Are you—is everything all right? With you, I mean? Are you all right?"

The tremor—the worry that caused it—pained him to hear. He didn't want Mae to worry, not ever. William stepped off the escalator and moved aside for those harried, hurrying travelers to claim their baggage.

He watched a family of four—husband, wife, two small children—as they waited by the conveyor belt. The little girl kept shouting, "Is that ours, Daddy?" While the boy made repeated efforts to climb aboard the moving belt and the mother repeatedly subverted his attempts.

"Everything is perfectly fine, love. I'll be home soon."

He ended the call but stared at the phone a moment longer. There were two missed calls. One from James. His standard check-in after every signing that William had seen before boarding and let go to voicemail.

Rather than listening to the message, he scrolled the call log. The first missed call showed James' number. The second, his doctor's office. He didn't need to hear the voicemail to know what it said.

Mr. Grant, we really need to schedule your surgery date.

Now that he was home for a long stretch, he'd address the issue. In a day or two, when life had settled back into a routine. It would be cruel to spring such worrisome news on Mae the minute he returned. Wouldn't it? Yes, certainly. He would tell her in a couple days.

13 Feather Anne

Twelve more days. That was all there was until Feather Anne took her turn onstage, under the stage lights, in front of cameras… and ninety-nine other contestants. She felt ready. Then, *not* ready. Okay, she felt ready, but also wanted to throw up.

That was where she mentally was at when her alarm sounded off at six a.m. on Saturday morning. Already awake, heart racing, leg twitching, and sitting up in bed. Sleep. Who could sleep with so much going on?

She went down the list in her head. Feed goats and chickens. Walk the Brightsider's dogs. Pick up Nick. Grab coffees from the café. Go to Bruce's place. Work until 2. Rehearse with Nick. Call Brandon.

Here, she sighed. Brandon. He was trying, she gave him that. But despite his best efforts, she saw the tenseness in his posture and the tightening of his face every time Feather Anne mentioned Nick.

She refused to dance around it or lie about where she was. She did that once, and it was a disaster. From that day on, it was no holds barred, no punches pulled, no—well, no whatever other cliché there was for being brutally honest.

She and Nick had chemistry—*musical* chemistry, nothing more—and Brandon would have to deal with it until after the show. After that, there'd be no more reason to hang out with Nick Amendola. None at all.

"Feather Anne? You up?" Mae called softly through her door.

"Yeah, I'm up," said Feather Anne.

"I'm on my way to the café. William is home with the kids. Can you—"

Feather Anne swung the door open and finished Mae's sentence. "Check in on them today? Yes. In between everything else I have to do today."

Normally, Mae would shoot back an equally sardonic reply. This time, she gave Feather Anne a pleading look with her big, round Little Mermaid eyes.

Feather Anne frowned. "What's wrong?"

"Nothing," said Mae. Her voice rose two octaves.

"Mae," said Feather Anne, punching a hand on her hip. "What's going on?"

Mae shot a furtive glance down the hall, toward hers and William's bedroom, then pushed Feather Anne aside and entered the room. She closed the door behind her and leaned against it.

"William hasn't been acting right. I'm concerned."

"So... did you ask him?"

"Yes," hissed Mae. "Of course, I did. He said everything is fine. But I don't believe him."

Feather Anne gathered her hair into a high, messy bun and took Mae by the shoulders. "Mae, if William says he's fine, he's fine. Stop being such nervous Nelly."

Mae bit her lip. "You think?"

"I *know*," declared Feather Anne. "Now, get out of my room so I can get ready."

When Mae squeezed her into a tight hug, Feather Anne let her, but also let her arms dangle as she groaned in protest. "Stop smothering me."

"Tell me you love me, and I'll let you go," said Mae in a sing-song voice.

"You're so annoying," Feather Anne rolled her eyes but smirked.

"Say it." She squeezed tighter, making Feather Anne *oof* in protest.

"Oh, my God. Fine, you psycho. I love you. Now let go." She shook Mae off, grinning and scowling at the same time.

Mae stepped back with a self-satisfied smile. "There. That wasn't so hard now, was it?" She walked out, but popped her head back in. "Oh, I almost forgot. Mr. B. left a message for you—they were in Barbados at last check-in—something about a message *he* received."

Feather Anne's heart thudded. She'd forgotten she'd put Mr. Brightsider down as her adult contact for the Greatest American Singer show. As a minor, she needed an adult's signature and consent to audition. Since the Brightsiders were on their cruise, he was the perfect one to use.

"Oh?" Feather Anne's voice squeaked.

"Yeah, he was breaking up—bad connection— so all I got was something like, Bob or Beau, from G.A.S. said to call them back about… and the rest cut out. Do you know what that's all about?"

Feather Anne adopted her best *gee, no clue* expression, and said, "Huh. No idea. Strange. Oh, well. So, listen, I really gotta motor, so…" She gave Mae the *beat it* gesture.

The second Mae retreated, Feather Anne closed and fell against her door. "Shit." She hissed.

She'd forgotten all about the whole parental or guardian consent thing. The rules stated that anyone under the age of eighteen needed an adult—someone over the age of twenty-one — with them for taping. Who the hell could she get to go with her that wouldn't make her totally nervous? Or tell her family?

As she showered and dressed, one word echoed in her head. *Who*? The only time it paused was when she stopped in the kitchen to say goodbye to William and the twins. As he set their breakfast before them and moved about the kitchen from sink to stove, to coffee pot, Feather Anne studied him.

"Why are you staring at me, Feather Anne?" One dark eyebrow darted up and his gaze locked on her.

"Staring? I'm not staring." She'd become a shitty liar.

"Let me guess. Your sister coerced you into observing me for *weirdness*. I assure you, as I did her, everything is under control."

"Hmm," said Feather Anne, now genuinely suspicious.

"Hmm, *what*?" William placed his cup on the counter and crossed his arms.

She pointed a finger at him. "You said everything is *under control*. Not *everything is fine*. Under control means something is going on."

William snickered. "Between you and your sister… listen to me. Everything… is… *fine*. Now, off with you. Rufus and Mabel are waiting impatiently at the Brightsider's door, no doubt."

She kissed the twins and left, but not before giving William the *I've got my eye on you* glare. He laughed her off and turned back to his coffee.

Right as Feather Anne hopped back in her car after securing the Brightsider's dogs and house, her phone chirped. It was Nick, asking what was taking her so long.

She looked at the time—six-fifty-four—and laughed. She texted back.

Dude, chill. On my way.

At seven a.m. on the dot, Feather Anne pulled into the Amendola's driveway, then all the way around back to the converted, detached garage Nick called home. Mia waved from her front steps. She was dressed in form fitting blazer and matching slacks, a briefcase in one hand and a travel mug in the other.

Feather Anne liked Mia. She didn't act like a typical mom and didn't treat Feather Anne like she was a kid, either. She supposed it had something to do with her having Nick at such a young age.

She tried to picture herself with a three-year-old at age seventeen and shuddered. *No thanks.* Babysitting the Villeneuve kids, plus TK and Evvie, had been more than enough kid time for her, and they were all good kids. Not like Nick had been, according to him and Mia.

The last time Feather Anne had rehearsed with Nick at his place, Mia invited her to stay for dinner. There, over pepperoni pizza and Caesar salad, Mia regaled her with stories of how bad he behaved.

When she'd looked to Nick for his reaction—expecting him to be mortified—he only laughed and shrugged, neither confirming nor denying his guilt. After dinner, they moved to the living room and Mia showed her pictures of Nick growing up.

"The only one he ever listened to was his Pop—that's what he called my dad—see, that's him right there."

Mia pointed to a picture of a skinny, shirtless Nick at about age six or seven. Nick looked directly into the camera while he hugged the arm of a man who gazed down at him, smiling.

In another picture of the duo, the man—Nick's Pop—had the boy hoisted onto his shoulder and they both mugged for the camera. It was clear by the many pictures that followed, the two had a special bond.

Feather Anne glanced up at Nick from her spot on the floor, a jibe on the tip of her tongue, but she saw the sad, far off look in his glassy eyes and instead reached up to touch his knee. It was on impulse—the gesture—and meant as a nothing more than a friendly show of sympathy. But Nick slid his hand over hers and curled his fingers over hers.

It didn't last long, this hand holding, but it had been enough to send the blood rushing to Feather Anne's ears.

He let go, sat forward, his elbows on his thighs, and pointed to a photograph in the corner of the album.

"My first guitar. A gift from Pop."

Feather Anne looked closer. "Wait, that's the one you played at Bruce's place. When we sang—" Suddenly shy, she stopped and glanced back down at the picture. "The number you have etched into it now… it isn't in the photo."

She knew that same number had a home on all three of his guitars, as well as his inner arm. Despite being curious, she'd never asked before now.

Nick smiled a sad smile. "It came after… after Pop died."

Puzzled, Feather Anne asked, "Twenty-seven… what does it mean?"

"That was the year Leon Henry—my Pop—was born. Nineteen-twenty-seven. I, uh, it's my way of always acknowledging how fucking glad I am he was ever born."

"Oh, Nick. That's beautiful." To Mia, she said, "Nineteen-twenty-seven, huh? That would've made him…"

"Yeah. My dad was a lot older than my mom." She chuckled and shrugged. "Kind of like Mae, I guess. They were as in love as those two are, too."

Mia stood and stretched. "It's ten years this week that he's been gone. Mom never remarried. Said he was her one true love, and no one could ever compare."

She leaned over and ruffled Nick's hair. "We feel that way, too. My Dad truly was the greatest. Loved his family, his country, and his life. I'm glad Nicky got as long with him as he did."

Mia had left them alone after that and once she'd gone, Feather Anne sat down beside Nick and placed the album on their laps. "Tell me more about your Pop, Nick."

And he had. Afterward, their rehearsal had been somber and sweet, their connection somehow deepened. When she left that night, another wild impulse had struck her, and she kissed his cheek. It was quick, and embarrassed, she turned away.

Nick had grabbed her hand and stopped her. "Feather Anne… I—"

She rushed to fill the space where his words tried to go. "I'll see you Saturday. Bye," and slipped her hand out of his without looking back.

In the car, her heart had pounded, and palms sweat. She'd gripped the steering wheel and stared at the dashboard.

What are you doing? Her brain yelled.

"What am I doing?" She whispered.

Now, here she was again, two days later. Would it be weird? Would *he* be weird? Worse, would *she*?

Maybe she was overthinking it. Nick probably hadn't given it—her—a second thought. The guy's phone rang and buzzed constantly from girls calling and texting. Not that she cared.

As she debated whether to honk the horn or get out and knock, Nick opened his door and bound out like a Great Dane puppy, his guitar case slung over his shoulder. He opened the back door, ducked his head in and gave her a lopsided grin.

"You're late, little bird."

Before she responded, he tossed his case on the backseat, slammed the door, and climbed into the passenger side. Because he was so tall, he had to fold himself practically in half. This cracked Feather Anne up and her nervousness dissipated.

"Idiot, push the seat back," she snorted. "And I'm not late. I'm exactly on—oh, okay. Two minutes late. Whatever."

"Late is late, little bird."

"Stop calling me that, freak. And we're still stopping at the café for coffee."

"Your sister make those cinnamon buns for us again?" That lopsided grin appeared again.

She grinned back. "Hells ya, she did."

"Sick," said Nick, and he turned on the radio. After flicking through a few stations, he blurted, "Thanks for hanging the other night."

Feather Anne, caught off-guard, said, "Oh, yeah. Sure. Right. It was—I had—you… good time."

What the fuck was that?

Nick chuckled and looked at her profile. "You having a stroke, little bird?"

Without taking her eyes off the road, she side-swatted his arm. He caught her hand and held it against his chest. Where his heart was. The moment couldn't have lasted more than three seconds, but they were three seconds too long, too wrong.

"Feather Anne, I—" he began.

"I heard Rateliff is touring with the Night Sweats. They're coming to the casino. I thought a bunch of us could get tickets." Feather Anne took a breath and rambled on, giving him no chance to speak. "Mae will probably want to tag along, but she's cool enough. Well, not really, but it's probably the only way she'd let me go. What do you think? About the concert, I mean?"

He was staring at her profile; the weight of it prickled her skin. But all he said was, "Sounds cool, Feather Anne."

And instantly, she hated herself. For being a coward. For letting him hold her hand—even if it was only three seconds. For liking the way he said her name. And the way they sang together. And how the song he wrote replayed in her head all day and night. And how shitty she was being to Brandon. Her boyfriend, best friend, soul mate, future someday husband.

The car was barely in park in front of the café before she jumped out, announcing the obvious. "We're here."

Nick followed her in. She glanced up at him. He'd shoved his hands in his front jean pockets and hunched his shoulders. His chestnut brown hair fell over his face and he shook it back.

"Hey, you… and you," said Mae from behind the counter. She looked form Feather Anne to Nick. "Got your order ready for you. Bruce's is the one with the red stirrer."

"Great, thanks," said Feather Anne, sliding the box toward her and handing it back to Nick. She started to leave.

Mae called out, "I—did you guys come here… together?"

Mae kept her tone light, but Feather Anne knew better. She took a deep breath and turned back. Nick spoke first.

"My truck is in the shop, so Feather Anne is giving me a lift."

"Oh," said Mae. Her eyebrows climbed up her forehead and she stared pointedly at Feather Anne before offering a polite smile to Nick.

"Anyhow, I'll, uh, bring these out," said Nick. He obviously sensed the sisters needed a moment… to discuss him.

The moment the door closed, Mae leaned over the counter and hissed. "What's *that* all about? I thought you couldn't stand him? Does Brandon know?"

"It's… complicated, okay? I'll explain later. And yes." One of Mae's eyebrows twitched higher at Feather Anne. She corrected. "No. I mean kind of. Not that I picked Nick up for work. Yet." Mae said nothing but crossed her arms. "I'm *going* to tell him, God."

She stomped out before Ma further shamed her with her raised eyebrows and knowing smirk. Back in the car, Feather Anne aggressively snapped her seatbelt, cranked the radio, and drove off grim-faced. If Nick had planned on saying anything—and his stare implied he had—he wisely zipped it. Instead, he popped the little tab back on the coffee lid and handed it to Feather Anne wordlessly.

14 *Mae*

Mae pulled up to the Rudiwitz B&B—Bruce's new place—and stopped in front. She observed each car in the curved driveway. Bruce's, Feather Anne's, a plumber's van, and one that surprised her. Brianna Baker's SUV.

"What the heck is she doing here?" She muttered to herself.

Perhaps Brandon had borrowed Brianna's car and was visiting Feather Anne? Mae partly hoped so and partly hoped not. Even though Feather Anne told her very little about the current situation the other day, it was enough for Mae to read between the lines. Her kid sister and her former best friend's son—who happened also to be Bruce Grady's son—liked each other.

It explained Feather Anne's strange behavior as of late, but it opened a can of new questions. The first being, *what about Brandon*? The next being, *isn't he too old for you*? They were questions Mae hadn't hesitated to ask Feather Anne, but the girl adamantly swore she wasn't interested in Nick *that way*.

This led to the third, and most obvious question. *Why are you spending so much time with him, then?* To which Feather Anne confessed they'd been creating music together.

"Nick plays... he's a musician? Mia never mentioned that." Mae had mused over the new-to-her information. "Well, why don't you bring him to the open mic tomorrow?"

Feather Anne had narrowed her eyes at Mae. "Why are you being cool about this?"

Mae smiled innocently at her sister. "Cool about what? He's your friend, who's a musician, and I run an open mic that you often go to and sing at. I'd like to see you two in action. Singing, that is," said Mae.

The younger sister had harrumphed, and said, "Dunno. We'll see. Will Jane and the gang be there?"

Mae smiled. Feather Anne idolized the lead singer of Redhead, Jane Lovett, from the moment the fiery-haired woman walked through the doors of Mae's Café. Jane had taken the girl under her wing over the years and had been the one to get her onstage to sing in front of people finally.

"Of course. Let's see, she'll have John on drums, Freddy K. on bass... oh, and Austin Hills on guitar. Hey, I bet Nick could talk with Austin?" She tried to keep the over-enthusiasm from her voice and failed.

Feather Anne's eyes traveled skyward as she said, "Settle down, spaz. I'll ask him. No promises, though."

And that's what brought Mae to Bruce's place the next day. She couldn't trust Feather Anne to follow through with the invite. Plus, she'd already spoken to Mia, and she was coming, too. So, Nick had to come out, simple as that.

Mae practiced her casual, offhand, *I was passing by* speech and lifting the tray of caramel fudge brownies from the back seat when a voice from behind her made her jump and whap the back of her head.

"It's more believable when you don't walk in bearing a tray of food."

Brianna Baker, arms crossed over chest, a sardonic smirk curling the corner of her mouth, and sculpted eyebrow arched, stared at her.

"Brianna," said Mae warmly. And embarrassedly. "Yeah, no. I was—these were—how are you?"

Brianna's eyes swept over Mae, from her patent leather shoes to cascade waves. "Fine. You're looking... very Mae-esque."

Mae shifted the tray from her hip to in front of her, hating how Brianna made her feel and cursing herself for allowing it. She stood straighter. She would not be baited by this woman.

Ignoring the backhanded compliment—surely, that's what it was—Mae said, "You're looking well, Brianna. I'm glad to hear you're recovering. I'm sure it's been a trying time."

Mae tried not to let her eyes travel to Brianna's hair. She couldn't recall if Feather Anne said she'd needed a wig, or not. If it was a wig, it looked damn good. Shit, she looked. If she was lucky, Brianna hadn't noticed.

"It's my real hair, Mae. I won't be losing it, thank God." The ice queen softened slightly. "It *has* been difficult. Terrifying, if I must admit. Thank you for the food you sent over with Feather Anne. It was very kind of you."

Thank you's were as challenging for Brianna as apologies. Mae let it pass with little attention, as was preferred by both.

"No problem. So, what brings you here?"

A visible debate waged across Brianna's face. She glanced over her shoulder at the house, then back at Mae. Mae waited.

"Actually," said Brianna, stepping off the lawn and closer to Mae, "I'm glad I ran into you. We should discuss this... situation that seems to be developing."

"Oh?" Mae's guard rose. "What... situation is that?"

Sure, she had misgivings—concerns, even— about Feather Anne's budding friendship with Nick

Amendola, but she'd be damned if she'd let Brianna Baker say something disparaging about her sister.

Brianna, clearly a skilled people-reader, said, "Retract your nails, Mae. I adore Feather Anne. I've come to see much of myself in her, in fact."

Mae tried not to grimace at the thought and probably didn't succeed based on the look Brianna gave her.

"Is that—that's... nice," said Mae as neutrally as possible.

"Still," cut in Brianna, "I'm worried this boy is influencing her. Frankly, now that I've seen him up close for myself, I get it. The attraction, I mean. He's like Michael Hutchence reincarnated, for fuck's sake."

Despite herself, Mae laughed. "Michael Hutchence? From INXS? Wow..." She pictured both men, and said, "Okay, yeah, I can see that, actually." When Mae met Brianna's eyes again, she said, "Shit."

"Yeah. Exactly. What girl *didn't* have a thing for Michael Hutchence in the day?" Brianna sighed.

"Still, though. Feather Anne and Brandon are... they're solid. Right? I mean, they're still kids, but—"

"I'm as torn as you are," said Brianna. "That's it, isn't it? They *are* just kids. I don't know whether to encourage them to take a break, or fight for each other."

Mae took a breath. "Well, maybe we should..." she half-shrugged, "let them figure it out for themselves. Like we all did. Look at you and Ricky. All these years later— the ups and downs—and you seem stronger than ever."

Mae hadn't meant to allude to anything, but it hung in the air. *Miles Hannaford.* Thankfully, Brianna ignored it.

"Yes, well..." Brianna threw her hands up in frustration. "shouldn't we lend them the benefit of our experiences? Save them from their own mistakes?"

"That's the thing, though. Who are we to say what the mistakes are? Anyhow, aren't mistakes really lessons learned on our journey? Or, like, choices we make that aren't good or bad, but—"

"Oh, please. I can't even with the philosophizing right now. What do we *do*, Mae?"

Mae shook her head sympathetically. "Nothing, Brianna. We do nothing other than be there for them as they figure it all out."

"Hm." Brianna looked down at the tray in Mae's arms. "Is *that* doing nothing?"

"Touché. I will put my delicious, homemade caramel fudge brownies back in the car and bring them to—"

"Did you say *caramel* fudge?" Brianna's eyes widened slightly.

Mae smirked. "Why don't you take them? For Ricky and the kids, of course." Brianna Baker would never admit to eating such a sinfully calorie filled treat.

"Sure. For Ricky and the kids. I'll have the tray back to you right away."

"No rush. I have tons."

Mae walked around the front of her car and Brianna strode to hers. No goodbyes. No friendly wave. Brianna's SUV rounded the corner before Mae even climbed into her car. She'd stuck one foot in when Bruce called out from the front door.

He bellowed, "Huxley. You leaving without saying hello?"

"Hey, Bruce. Sorry, I was—eh, it's a long story. Looks like it's coming along nicely," she called.

"Come on, I'll give you the tour," he shouted back.

She debated a moment, stepped back out of the car, and walk ran to the house. Why not? She was already there. It would be rude to just leave.

These justifications swirled in her head; an internal, one-sided argument prepared for Feather Anne's accusing glare that was bound to come when she saw Mae. But it proved needless. When Feather Anne saw Mae in the library—where she and Nick were stripping wallpaper—she merely thrust her chin at her and said, "Hey, Mae," and went back to laughing with Nick about something.

When she and Bruce had gone a safe distance, she hissed, "So, what do you make of that?"

Bruce blinked at her. "Make of what?"

Her jaw dropped. "Seriously? Of," she lowered her voice even more, "those two." She jerked her head in the direction of the library.

Bruce followed her gesture and looked back at Mae. "Who? Nick and Feather Anne?" He made a *pshtt* sound. "Aw, come on. They're buds."

Mae scrunched her face at him. "Are you *really* this clueless?"

He scratched his chin, looking down the hall and back to Mae repeatedly. "So, wait. You think... you think Feather Anne and Nick are like... a thing?"

He shook his head against the idea. "Nah. No, her and Brandon are good. Nick's seeing a girl from Old Saybrook. Or at least he was seeing her. Come to think of it, she hasn't come around in a while."

Mae took his arm and pulled him further down the hall. "Did you know they've been spending time together outside of work?"

Bruce's head jerked back, and his palms turned upward. "I—no, first I'm hearing. Shit, I've been so busy with Brookhaven and getting this place up to code. You wouldn't believe—" he caught Mae's expression, "right, yeah. Nick and Feather Anne. So, what do you want me to do about it?"

He didn't say it sarcastically. Mae loved this about Bruce. He genuinely wanted to help and make things right whenever they seemed wrong. Mae gave a subtle shake of her head as she sighed.

"Nothing. Brianna and I promised to stay out of it and let them figure things out for themselves."

"Ah, that explains her visit. She claimed she wanted to bring Feather Anne an iced coffee. But she lurked around so long I offered her a tool belt and safety glasses."

"Oh, I bet she loved that."

Bruce grinned. "She's still holding a grudge about me and Elise. Either that, or she doesn't like me much."

"That was forever ago. Elise has more than moved on. I mean, come on, she's got a franchise business she built from the ground, travels all over the place, and a great boyfriend." Seeing the look on Bruce's face, she quickly added, "And, *you*. Look at you. Mr. Successful developer, property owner person, you."

"Way to make a man feel good, Mae. Don't ever man the Suicide Hotline, huh."

She swatted his arm. Sure, Bruce was still not exactly the luckiest man when it came to lasting love. But it wasn't for lack of interested women. There was even a time when he and Mia seemed like they might make a go of it.

"Stop. You're still the best catch in town. In the *state*."

"Chill, Huxley. I'm busting your chops. It's all good. What's it they say? Good things come to those who wait? I'm in no hurry."

He held her gaze a fraction longer before changing topics. "So, over here, I'm thinking of taking down the wall between rooms and making it a master suite. That wall will be shiplap. Or not. I'm kinda torn because it's a Victorian, so..."

He yapped on this way for the rest of the tour. Mae only half-listened and made the appropriately timed interjections and questions. Her mind fitted between William and Feather Anne. Confronting him, leaving her be. Or, leaving him be and confronting her. What to do, what to do.

"All right, Huxley. Spill it."

Mae rapid-blinked at Bruce. They were back at the front door. "S-spill what?"

He looked down sternly at her. "Sit." Bruce pointed to the pair of rattan chairs in the far corner of the porch.

He trotted inside and came back a minute later with two tall glasses of iced tea. When Mae stared in surprise at the elegant looking glasses.

Bruce chuckled, handing her one. "A leftover from Mrs. Rudiwitz's collection. Seemed a shame to get rid of them."

"Well, they are beautiful. Thanks, by the way for the vintage photographs. They look great in the café.

Oh, and the records! Did you know they were in pristine—"

"Mae? What's bothering you?"

She really wasn't going to say a word. Before the intended words, *I'm fine*, stumbled out her mouth, she blurted, "I think something is wrong with William and he's hiding it from me. Feather Anne thinks I'm being crazy. William swears he's fine. But..."

"But you don't believe him. Okay. So, has your gut ever been wrong?" His blue eyes bore into hers.

"No," she whispered.

"So, what will you do?"

Mae stared out onto the tree-lined street. Jilly and Pastor Pete strolled by with their yappy Pomeranians. They were spared a lengthy conversation with the pair thanks to old Mrs. Treviso and her German Shepherd, Brutus.

Brutus woofed once, loudly, and Jilly and Pastor Pete abruptly dragged their frantic dogs across to the other side of the street as they strained against their harnesses in a murderous, tiny dog rage.

"I'll make him tell me what's going on, even if I'm afraid to hear the answer."

"Atta girl," said Bruce. "Whatever it is—and I'm sure it's nothing, by the way—you two will be fine."

"Yeah. You're right. I guess that's all this is; me looking for a problem where there isn't one. Isn't funny how, when everything is going great, you look for something to go wrong?"

Bruce gave her a lopsided grin and said, "Speak for yourself, lady. I don't go looking for trouble."

Mae snorted, "Yeah, that's because trouble finds you." They clinked glasses. Mae chuckled. "Can I make a confession?"

Bruce eyed her in mock wariness. "Not if it's something you should be telling our new chief of police instead."

"Ha-ha, very funny. No, Joel won't need to take a statement from me anytime soon."

"All right. Fess up. What'd you do, Huxley?"

Mae's nose crinkled. "I kind of, sort of... told Brianna we should butt out of the kids' business, but I came in here planning to—"

"To butt in," finished Bruce. He shook his head and wagged a finger at her. "Well, I'm glad I intervened."

He took a sip of his iced tea, looking thoughtful as he did. When he set the glass down on the small table between them, he turned that thoughtful gaze on Mae.

"Listen," he began, "I'd be lying if I said this... this thing—or potential thing—with Feather Anne and Nick didn't weird me out. I mean, my son and the kid who's been like a daughter to me? Come on, right?"

"Yeah, when you put it like that... really weird," agreed Mae.

Bruce exhaled. "And, hey, maybe they're just friends. I mean, look at us. If we can do it." He blushed. "You know what I'm trying to say. Let's let them handle it and if they come to us for advice, we'll give it. Sound good?"

"Sounds good." Mae stood, smiling. "Well, I'd better get going. I've already been away from the café longer than I said I would."

"Yeah, those clowns in there have probably made a mess. If I don't check in every so often, they go off the rails."

They said their goodbyes and, as usual, Mae became more at ease after talking with Bruce. Feather Anne was a big girl. She'd make her own decisions—good or bad—and she'd learn from them. Either way, Mae would be there for her. As for William, if something was wrong, he'd tell her. She had to have faith.

15 Miles

Relief. That's what suffused Miles' whole body. His secret was out and nothing catastrophic happened as a result. Unless he counted having his parents privy to his mental illness as a catastrophe, which, prior to last week, he would have. But the Hannafords had shocked him with their compassion and understanding.

The one who was no surprise was Rosie. He supposed that was exactly why he tried to hide his depression from her. Rosie always brought her A-game, good days and bad. She seemed unflappable, even when Poppy had pneumonia and Fiona got croup. When life threw shit her way, Rosie handled it. Miles owed her the same level of control and sufficiency.

"I'm failing you, Rosie. I'm failing our family," he'd said to her that night after their little intervention.

Rosie had stroked his hair and smiled at him, looking deeply into his eyes as she did. She sighed. "Oh, Miles. You couldn't be more wrong. I am so incredibly proud of you, and grateful to you for our life. We've done all this as a team, and we'll handle this the same way. Together."

His therapist agreed—with some reluctance—to try a non-medical route. Miles had been adamant, though. However, after a couple weeks, Miles—frustrated that he wasn't instantly cured—relented and accepted a prescription of a low dose anti-depressant.

Despite being warned it wouldn't work immediately, the drug needed time to work into his system, he swore he felt better; more himself than he had in months.

On the third day, he told Rosie, "It's like when Dorothy came out of her house? Like when it landed in Munchkin Land, and everything was in color. Everything's in color again, Rosie."

He'd started running again and quit drinking coffee. He enrolled in the spring 5K marathon. Miles even joined Rosie in her yoga class and signed himself up for Daddy and Me playgroup with the girls.

Dr. Hannah warned him that backslides happened, and he needed to be aware of when that dark tide started to drag him away. She had sessions with Rosie, and also with both of them. He was learning how to ask for and accept help, recognize when he internalized and suppressed his feelings, and to manage his stress.

"I'm guessing you feel like a new man," smiled Rosie when he came whistling into the kitchen.

"Better," he grinned back. "I feel like the old me." He brought his orange juice glass to his lips, but let it hover. "The new and improved old me, that is."

"Well, new old Miles needs to remember to drop off my package at the post office, please and thank you."

"Can do, Rosie Poo." Miles kissed all his girls goodbye, grabbed his keys and Rosie's package, and strutted out the front door.

First stop, post office. Next, Mae's Café. Then, Dr. Hannah. It surprised him to find himself looking forward to these appointments, but he did. Today, they would discuss his progress, whether the medication had begun to help, and if he noticed any side effects.

At ten of nine, Miles took a seat in the waiting room. The walls, chairs, and carpeting were all in shades of beige. A huge rectangular canvas bearing a splash of scarlet and a dash of burnt orange—an abstract that probably cost a ridiculous amount of money—provided the only color in the otherwise drab room. Each visit, Miles mused over why a place for helping depressed people would be so, well, *depressing* to be in.

Dr. Hannah's office was thankfully better appointed. Bright and airy, yet cozy. A difficult balance to achieve. Unlike the waiting room, her office looked as if it had an interior designer's touch. He glanced around the boring room again, trying to find something of interest.

One chair — which he sat upon — a coffee table, and a small, hard cushioned loveseat. Brown, of course. With beige pillows. Only, something ivory poked out. It had a zipper. Miles stood and took the four steps necessary to cross the room. He lifted the cushion to reveal a small purse.

Miles looked at the door. It must belong to the patient—*client*, as Dr. Hannah preferred—in with her now. Normally, outgoing clients leave through another door on the opposite side of the office. It was a privacy thing, according to Dr. H.

He stood still—purse in hands—and tried to listen for voices through the wall. No sound escaped or rose over the white noise machine sitting on a small table in the corner and emitting the natural music of the rainforest. Caws from parrots, birdsong, gentle rain pattering fat leaves. Miles liked it so much that he'd ordered three of the same machines on Amazon for the bedrooms.

The door opened a crack. The back of a platinum blonde head turned away in conversation. "I'll take a peek to see if it's in here."

Dr. H.'s voice. "Oh, why don't you let me—"

"One sec," said the platinum blonde. She turned and looked directly at Miles. "Oh," said Brianna Baker.

Miles looked from Brianna to the purse in his hands. So did she. "I, uh, it... here." He stepped forward and thrust the purse toward her.

She took it, eying him in that damn Brianna way. Cool, smirking, silently but blatantly judging. Her mouth opened, but before any words came out, Dr. H. appeared beside her in the doorframe.

"I—this—my apologies," said Dr. H. to Miles. Her eyes, magnified by her round glasses, blinked owl-like at him. "Mrs... you should," she extended her arm, theater usher-like, back to the interior of the office.

"Yes, of course," replied Brianna. She nodded ever so slightly at Miles, the smirk never leaving her lips.

The door closed between them, leaving Brianna's perfume in her wake. Miles sat down on the couch and raked his hands through his hair.

Shit.

Until then, his problem had been that: *his.* A private matter only his immediate family had been privy to, and no one else. Now, with Brianna Baker having seen him in the office of a therapist? Well, it was as good as front-page news for all of Chance.

She didn't care if the world knew she was in therapy; she had cancer as her excuse, and before that, Gordon Bourdreau. What could *Miles* use as his reason? Nothing, that's what. Within the hour, all of Chance would hear Miles Hannaford was having a problem big enough to require a therapist's help.

"Miles, do come in." Dr. H. startled him from his inner panic.

He followed her into the office and sat in his usual chair, a plush, navy-blue wingback. Dr. Hannah took her spot across but slightly diagonal from him and offered him a glass of water.

"Thanks, no. I'm good." His smile was tight. He tried to loosen up.

"Miles, let me start by apologizing again. My previous client should never have been allowed to re-enter the waiting room. *I* should not have allowed it," she corrected.

"Ah, it's cool. Totally cool. No problemo, Doc."

The doctor pushed her glasses up further onto the bridge of her nose and owl-blinked at him. He spread his arms out and awarded her with his megawatt smile to prove he was as cool as he claimed.

"Your body language says otherwise, Miles. My previous client indicated that you two are acquainted."

Miles waited for her to say more, but she only stared at him, waiting.

"Uh, yeah. You could say that." He laughed, Dr. H. did not. He shrugged and looked away. "Yeah, it was awkward, okay? I mean, her of all people, seeing me *here*." He sniggered.

"Therapy, for many, is a very personal, private thing. Whereas, for others, is less so. I have some clients who hand out my business card like they're party favors. Others who cross to the other side of the street to avoid me in public."

Miles gave a perfunctory laugh at this. She continued, making it the longest he'd ever heard her speak in session.

"What I'm saying, Miles, is that the client/therapist relationship is sacred to me. I never, ever discuss my clients with anyone. If you choose to tell people you came here to, oh, I don't know, sell me a house, or a new office building, I'd certainly never contradict you."

She was offering him an out; a way to excuse or justify his being there. Miles sat back and thought about it. It was his dime, after all. He could talk or not talk as much as he wanted.

After a few minutes, Miles sat forward, rested his elbows on his knees and steepled his fingers under his chin.

"No. You know what, Doc? Fuck it. I'm not ashamed of needed help. I mean, yeah, I was kind of embarrassed at first. And, sure, it *did* freak me out to see Brianna here, and now she is on her way to tell everyone she knows that she saw me at a therapist's office."

"I specifically reminded her of the ethical—" interjected the alarmed Dr. Hannah.

Miles stopped her with a look that said, *oh, please*, and continued. "I've been doing my reading. About mental illness and the stigma of needing help? And how so many people suffer in silence because they're too embarrassed? Shit, Doc. That was *me*, to a T. Like, I almost blew up my family—not literally, obviously. I'm not—anyhow, what I'm saying is, I'm not ashamed to be here. Not anymore."

"I'm glad for you, Miles. By not allowing the unfortunate stigma to impede your emotional growth, you open yourself to so much."

They continued in this vein and he quickly realized he may have overstated how fine he was with people knowing he was in therapy. So, Dr. Hannah strategized with Miles as to how he'd address the possible reactions of others.

"I'll tell them before they even ask. Right? I'll be, like, *hey I'm in therapy and it's great. You should try it.* Easy peasy, problem solved." Miles shrugged.

Dr. H. clasped her hands together on her lap. "Well, will you be sharing that information because you want to help them, or because you want to head them off, so to speak?"

"Uh, both?" Miles offered a sheepish smile.

Dr. H. blinked and waited.

"Okay, you got me. I guess I'd be trying to head them off. I don't want them thinking shit."

"Let's explore that for a moment, Miles. You've mentioned before this concern with other people's thoughts as they pertain to you."

"Well, yeah. I mean, don't you care what people think about you?" Getting no reply, he scoffed. "Come on. Really? You don't care?"

The therapist smiled briefly. "What would happen if someone thought negatively of you?"

Miles said, "What would happen? Ah, well, nothing, but listen, they can think I'm an asshole or whatever. That I don't care. I just don't want anyone to think I don't have my shit together, okay? Hannafords always keep their shit in order."

"I see," said Dr. Hannah. "So, would you say that it's the *appearance* that matters most to you?"

"My mother has a saying. It's not how you feel that matters, but how you look. Her own twist on a cliché. I've heard that since...well, since forever."

Even after Jeannie Hannaford's confession of seeing a therapist herself, she still pulled Miles aside later and said that their business was their own and no one needed to know. She reminded him that he represented the family, so handling his little problem was imperative to keeping up the integrity of the Hannaford name.

"I've handled mine, Miles, and I expect you to do the same," she'd concluded, handing him the business card with Dr. Harold Kellerman's name and number. He went with the therapist Rosabelle found instead.

"Well, Miles, " said Dr. H., "I think this is something worth exploring more, don't you? Let me rephrase my question. What do you think would happen if someone thought you didn't have your... shit together?"

Miles smirked, but bit back the teasing comment on his tongue. Doc didn't seem to get his humor. Instead, he considered the question. After a moment, he said, "I-I don't know. Nothing, I guess?"

Well, shit. It was true. Abso-fucking-lutely nothing would happen. What *did* he care? Why? He had no good answer.

The therapist interrupted his revelation. "I'm afraid we've about concluded our time today. I'd like for us to explore this more next week though."

She stood, as did Miles. At the exit door, Miles stopped. "Thanks, Doc. I mean it."

"No thanks needed, Miles. You're doing the hard work and you're making great strides. See you next week."

As he had after every appointment, Miles left with mixed emotions. Equal parts positive and negative thoughts—*I've made great progress today* versus *I am sick to my stomach*—volleyed like a ping pong ball.

This time, added to the internal monologue, he reminded himself that Brianna Baker now had the knowledge he was in therapy. He reminded himself to care less about this fact. As he told himself this, he barked a voice command to his car's Bluetooth.

"Call Rosie."

The smooth but impersonal voice replied, "Sorry, could you repeat that?"

Miles swore under his breath and annunciated, "Call Rosie," emphasizing the *Ro* in Rosie because sometimes the system called Josie, his office manager. This time was no different

"Calling… Josie."

"Disconnect. Disconnect," he shouted

Josie answered, and he had to spent ten minutes pretending he'd meant to call and check in on the office. This led to him being nominated to pick up coffees for everyone. After she'd talked his ear off for another ten minutes, he was able to make the call he'd intended.

"Hey, Rosie. How are my girls?"

"Hey, you. I was beginning to wonder when you'd call. We're good. How about you? Your appointment go well?"

"Yes, indeedie, it did," said Miles. He cringed.

"Miles?" Her tone spoke the warning. *Don't try to fool me, Miles.*

"It was fine," he sighed. "Except one little, tiny, massive fucking glitch. I ran into Brianna in the waiting room."

"Brianna… Baker? But how? Why? I thought Dr. Hannah's office had one door in and one door out?"

"It does. She'd forgotten her purse on the couch. I guess she got to the door before Dr. H. could stop her. You know how Brianna is."

"Yep, I sure do. Oh, Miles. I'm sorry."

She knew as well as he did what that meant. A new serving of gossip, with Miles Hannaford as the main dish.

"I'm okay. I'm *trying* to be okay, I mean. Dr. H. says I need to start caring less about what other people think. She's right."

"She said that, huh?"

"More or less," said Miles. He may have paraphrased, sure, but that was the gist.

"Well, I agree. Screw Brianna and anyone else like her. Therapy is nothing to be ashamed or embarrassed about."

"Thanks, babe. I—"

Rosie cut him off. "And, guess what? That's not even the point here. If that... that bitch thinks she's going to get away with trying to make you look bad, she'll have me to deal with, Miles. I will—"

Miles chuckled. "Easy, there, killer. I appreciate your mama bear mentality, but really, it's okay. *I'm okay.*"

Rosie made a sound that indicated *she* wasn't okay with it, even if he was. He loved his wife's sweet, gentle nature—it's what he fell in love with—but he got one hell of a kick out of her ferocious side, too. Especially when it was in defense of him or their girls.

After a pause, she said, "All right. But I will kick her ass, Miles. Just saying. Anyhow, are you stopping back home before the office?"

"I wish. I got roped into picking up coffees, so I'll be going straight there after. Why, you need something?"

"No, no. All good. But if you're going to Mae's for the coffee, will you tell her I got the limo for Friday?"

Miles wracked his brain. *Friday, Friday. What the hell was Friday?*

Reading his thoughts—as she so often did—Rosie said, "Tickets to see Hamilton. We're going with Mae and William, the Villeneueves, the Davidsons, and the Ashebys. We're taking a limo, so no one has to drive. I'm sure you didn't forget, *right*, Miles?"

"Me, forget? No way, Ro-zay."

She let him off the hook easily; a perk to having an issue with depression. Not that he'd say that to her. Or anyone. Apparently, people were pretty damn touchy about depression jokes.

At the café, Mae herself stood at the front counter. "Hey, baby Mae. How's it going?"

Mae smiled warmly at him—an indicator that his wife had given her at least some intel about his situation—and returned the greeting.

"Pretty good, thanks. You grabbing something for home or work?"

"My work wife has ordered me to get coffees for the troops in the trenches," said Miles, eyeballing the pastry case. "Ah, hell, might as well throw in some incentive to work. I'll take that whole tray on the top shelf."

"You got it."

Mae set about filling his order and chatting with him as she did. Mere weeks ago, Miles couldn't bear the task of idle chit-chat. Now, and once again, he enjoyed it. They bantered about the kids, the new ice cream shop opening down the street, and their spouses. He marveled at how normal it all felt.

On the way out, he remembered what Rosie had told him. "Oh, hey, baby Mae. Rosie says we're all set with the limo on Friday."

She grinned at him. "Okay, fess up. Did you remember about Friday on your own, or did Rosabelle have to remind you?"

"Of course, I remembered," said Miles feigning surprise that she'd even suggest it.

"Because *my* husband clean forgot."

Miles relaxed. "Oh, well, in that case, yeah, I totally spaced."

Mae waved a fist at him. "You men. I swear."

If she, or anyone, knew how good it was to be lumped in with the rest of the male population… well, she'd never understand. Then again, maybe she would. This was one of the things his therapist had helped him see: the connectedness of people.

Miles had never really experienced that before Rosie. Even then, it remained only her—and their daughters—that Miles saw in sharper focus and as real people until he'd started seeing Dr. Hannah. It was like seeing and feeling for the first time in his life.

16 William

"William, you need this operation. There are no two ways about it. I thought I'd made myself clear weeks ago. By rights, you should be admitted as of last week."

William rolled down his shirtsleeve with slow, painstaking care. He was stalling his response. Biding his time. Procrastinating.

At last he said, "What about that experimental drug you mentioned?"

"That was on the table before your results came in. William, you have five blocked arteries. I've told you the percentages, none of them good. I'm scheduling the surgery for Monday morning, and even that is pushing it."

"I need to get through the weekend. I'll prepare my wife. Monday it is."

He left the office with a surgery date scheduled, waivers signed, and a heavy weight on his mind. William wasn't a superstitious man, but he had a bad vibe about this upcoming procedure. Or, it was merely fear.

Not fear for himself—surely, it existed—but more fear for Mae and the twins. The worry and burden she'd be facing. All because he couldn't leave her be like he should have six years ago. Had he stayed away, she could have met and married a man her own age and had a normal life. Instead, she was saddled with an old man in need of... of *heart surgery.*

He wondered once again if she and Bruce would have ended up together. William knew as well as anyone else that Bruce Grady loved Mae. And Mae, in her own way—one that took nothing away from him or their life together—loved Bruce.

If something were to happen to William—*if he should die*—would they find their way to each other? Or would Mae, out of obligation and love for him, deny herself to a second chance at love? She was too young and had too much life ahead of her to shut herself off. But he could see her doing it.

God damn it though. He didn't want to give up his wife or his life. Why was he thinking so pessimistically? Thousands of men and women lived through open heart surgery and even moved on to live richer, fuller lives because of it. Why wouldn't he be one of those success stories?

William ticked off the reasons why he'd be fine. He was physically active and fit—aside from the heart issue—and he ate well. Studies showed that people who did those things had the best chance of survival and smoother, faster recovery times. Even the ones like William, with genetics against them.

Now, with the surgery scheduled, William's sense of foreboded shifted into one of anticipation. He wanted to get it over and done with and resume his life. His mercurial mood shifted yet again, back to the darker realities of a major surgery. As a practical-minded man, William had instructions prepared, letters—already written, naturally—sealed in their envelopes and labeled. One for Mae, Feather Anne, TK, and Evvie.

He'd updated his will on the day of the twin's birth and notarized days later. Neither his wife nor his children would want for anything, even if Mae were to give up the café. This, above all else gave him comfort.

The lump in his throat belied his contentment. William had to tell Mae, prepare her for what was to come. The series of well-deserved emotions—anger at not being told sooner, fear, and worry, and finally a facade of calm confidence—all would take their turn on her face and words.

He understood his wife perhaps better than she did herself, and vice versa. Their love and relationship defied expectations, survived gossip, and grew stronger daily. They were, if not an anomaly, an exception to the rule. As with everything else in their life, William credited Mae.

His beautiful inside and out, old soul of a wife. She loved fiercely and wholly, but not blindly. William, thinking of his wife's penchant for calling him and the children out for even the smallest transgressions, chuckled as he pulled into their driveway. He'd said to her once, "Mae, if you were a royal, you'd be a cross between the Queen and Princess Diana."

"I'm not sure how to take that, William," she'd responded. One eyebrow quirked up.

"It's a compliment, I assure you. You see, you have this sweet, fawn-like beauty—not unlike Diana—yet you have a backbone of steel and an unwavering commitment. It's what they call the *iron fist within the velvet glove*."

"Hmm," she'd mused. "I'll take that. Now come with me to get the twins in the tub."

"See? Point proven." He'd laughed.

William sat back in the car, collecting himself before going inside. He wanted to give Mae a lovely, worry free evening. After the play, once they were home and alone again, he'd tell her. Surely, it could wait that long.

17 Brandon

"I'm losing her, and I can't stop it from happening." Brandon threw another shell into the sea.

Leia, his now six-year-old chocolate lab, gazed woefully up at him as if she understood. She woofed once, low in her throat.

"That's the best advice you got, huh? It's okay, girl. My ideas aren't any better."

The dog sneezed and laid down on the flat boulder. Brandon sat beside her, letting his legs dangle above the choppy water ten feet below. It didn't escape him that normally, Feather Anne would be sitting on the other side of Leia and Rutger would be trotting back and forth the length of the jetty and barking into crevices at the crabs. At least, that's what they guessed he barked at.

"Well, old girl, I guess she's not coming. Again."

He checked his phone for the fifth time. No call, no text. Not from Feather Anne, that is. Brianna had texted twice. Ricky once. His buddy, Kade, also texted, as did his boss at the vet clinic. Brandon didn't bother reading any of them.

Feather Anne hadn't called or messaged him since Friday morning. Nor had she responded to his calls and texts. Their last exchange had been innocuous.

Him: Jetty tomorrow before work?
Her: It's a date. Miss your face! Xo

But it had given him hope that all was well again between them. But twenty-four hours of radio silence followed. Part of which she'd spent with Nick the dick. Something he knew because he'd driven by Bruce's new place and seen their cars in the driveway.

It'd taken all he had not to pull in and surprise them. But the last time he did that, he and Feather Anne got into a big fight. Eventually, he backed down and accepted her promise that nothing more than music went on between her and Nick.

"You don't want to hear this, Brandon, but Nick and I are really, like, musically compatible," she'd said.

The thought of Feather Anne being compatible in any way with someone other than Brandon made him crazy. He said as much. Feather Anne rolled her eyes and tossed a hamburger bun at him.

"Listen, let me get through this whole competition thing, then life will go back to normal, okay? You hate him, but Nick has been a huge help. Mr. B. won't be back in time to coach me, and besides you, Nick's the only one who knows."

Brandon didn't dare mention he'd told Brianna. They'd stopped yelling at one another, and he didn't want to start up again.

"All right, all right. It's fine, I guess. For the record, I still don't trust him. But I do trust you, Feather Anne."

That's when she'd made him promise to not stop by Bruce's place unless she invited him. It was done grudgingly, but the promise was made. And regretted.

Brandon looked at the time again. Nine-twenty-three. He stood up, brushed the sand off his pants, and gave a short whistle.

"Come on, girl. Let's go home."

He had a scrimmage at eleven and work right after. If they were going to get together at all, it wouldn't be until Sunday night. Feather Anne might not even want to hang out, since the next day she'd be driving to New York for the show.

That was another thing that yanked his chain. She didn't want Brandon to go with her. Said she'd be too nervous if he was there watching her and she was best off going alone. He'd argued against her going into the city by herself, but she'd tuned him right out.

A figure sprinted toward him from the beach. His heart lurched even as his brain computed it wasn't Feather Anne. It was Kade, in his scrimmage uniform. When he reached the sand, Kade was there panting and waiting for him.

"Dude, what the hell? I've been texting you for, like, an hour. Scrimmage is at ten. Someone screwed up the schedule and coach is rip-shit. Said if we aren't all on the field by ten sharp, the whole team's gotta do extra laps."

Brandon looked at his watch again. Nine-forty-three. No way he'd get home to change and at the field in time.

"Shit, man. I can't—"

"Yeah, you can. I stopped by your place and got your gear. Let's go, bro."

"Wow, thanks, man." Brandon's brow rose in surprise.

"Please. This ain't for your sake, it's for *mine*. I got a date with Jenna Walthran tonight and I am not missing it because of you."

Kade sped through town—making Brandon cringe internally—and made small talk. Brandon spaced out; his head turned to the window.

"Dude, yo!"

Brandon's head snapped. "What? Yeah. Wait, what did you say?"

"The fuck, bro. I said your name three times. What's your deal? You and Feather Anne fighting again?"

One shoulder lifted and dropped as he shook his head. "Nah. Not really. It's just… ah, never mind. It's cool. So, where are you taking Jenna?"

It was Kade's turn to shrug. "Movies. Beach. The usual, I guess. So, uh, you and Feather Anne *aren't* fighting?"

Brandon narrowed his eyes at Kade's profile. His tone sounded off. "No, why?" Before Kade answered, he scoffed, "And the beach, man? Really?"

"Yeah, the beach. The ladies love the romantic stroll. What can I say?"

Brandon waited for Kade to elaborate on the Feather Anne question. Or rather the rephrased and repeated question. Finally, as he pulled into a parking space by the football field, he spoke.

"Listen, it's none of my business, man. And I'm not trying to start shit, so you—"

"Spit it out already," said Brandon.

He ears burned and a sudden rush of sweat stung his armpits. What the hell was Kade going to tell him? Did he see Feather Anne and Nick somewhere? Doing some*thing*?

"It's nothing, man. Not really. Just something Jenna said yesterday. She claims Maddie mentioned her and Nick Amendola working together a lot."

Kade looked to Brandon with a *sorry, man* expression.

Feather Anne must have confided in Maddie. It surprised him a little; she'd always kept to herself for the most part. Still, if this was all it was, no big deal. His shoulders relaxed.

"Yeah, it's cool. I know all about it." It wasn't cool. Especially not if people were talking.

Kade yanked at the tight curls at the back of his head. His expression told Brandon there was more.

"Uh, yeah. She also said Nick Amendola was in Feather Anne's car the other day. She saw them go into Mae's Café together." Kade must have seen Brandon's body tense. "Sorry, man. I was hoping you knew…"

"It's cool. Come on, let's get to the field." Brandon reached for the door handle.

"Bro… you still gotta change," said Kade.

Brandon looked down. "Shit. You go ahead. I'll change here."

Kade hesitated before clapping his shoulder and leaving him to change… and fume. He did both simultaneously. At the same time, he tried to reason with himself. Maybe Maddie saw wrong. It was possible.

Sure, two people identical to Feather Anne and Nick in an identical car at her sister's café.

Still, it could happen.

Yeah, I call bullshit.

That's why Feather Anne was avoiding him. She knew he'd be pissed. Well, she'd be right about that. He was beyond pissed. Part of him wanted to call her and put her on blast. He went so far as to unlock his phone, but he saw the time. Nine-fifty-nine. Not enough for what he wanted to say.

Brandon climbed out of Kade's car and tossed the phone on the seat. "Fuck it." He shook his head and sprinted to the field. If she wanted to talk to him, she'd have to work for it.

18 Feather Anne

What she would remember about that night for years to come—her whole life, probably—were three things. The antiseptic smell of hand sanitizer thanks to the countless times someone pumped the lever on the wall beside her. The sweet, melancholy sound of Clair de Lune coming from the piano in the hospital foyer. And Mae's soft, gut-wrenching cry when the doctor broke the news.

The rest she recalled—Mae's knees buckling, the young emergency room doctor grasping her elbows and guiding her to a chair as Feather Anne wrapped an arm about her waist—but not with the same sharpness.

In those moments, she'd temporarily forgotten about Nick, who'd driven her to the hospital the second she got Mae's phone call and sat beside them all night and offered to get them coffees, or food, or make phone calls. They'd wanted no calls made, not until William was out of the woods—those were the doctor's words, *we're trying to get your husband out of the woods*—and the ones they'd clung to.

William would be all right. Of course, he would. He was *William*, God damn it. This is what Feather Anne assured Mae as she held her sister's ice-cold hand. To herself, Feather Anne reasoned, *he'd had a massive heart attack, yes. But people survive those. He would survive.* They'd brought him back, and now they'd make him better.

That's what was supposed to happen. So, when the doctor whose name she never learned said the impossible, she refused to believe him. Not even Mae's acceptance convinced Feather Anne.

She sprang up. "Bullshit. He is not. Fuck you. He's *not.*" She couldn't control the waver in her voice, and it made her furious.

The doctor turned his stupid kind eyes on her and she wanted to punch him. "I'm very sorry for your loss," he said. He reached out a hand to touch Feather Anne's arm, and she jerked away.

"No," said Feather Anne.

Mae came up behind her and turned Feather Anne around. "Sweetie, oh sweetie. He's gone. He is."

She wrapped her arms around her kid sister in a tight embrace. Comforting *her*, even though she'd just lost her husband. Shame at her selfishness filled Feather Anne.

"I'm sorry," she whispered. And they cried together.

The doctor spoke. "Mrs. Grant? Would you like to…"

Mae stepped back from Feather Anne, wiped her eyes, and sniffed once. She nodded sharply. "Yes."

"Do you want me to come with you," asked Feather Anne. She hoped and feared the answer would be yes.

Mae somehow managed to smile. She touched Feather Anne's cheek and stroked back her hair. "No, I need…" her voice shook, "I need to say goodbye to my husband alone. If you'd like to come in after, you can. But it's okay if you can't."

Feather Anne bobbed her head and choked back a sob. "Okay."

She watched her sister—still as elegant and regal as ever, yet somehow smaller, frailer looking—as the doctor led her to the room where William lay. Feather Anne's chest hitched, but she couldn't breathe. Nor see. Scalding tears blinded her, and when a pair of arms enveloped her, she didn't care who they belonged to. All Feather Anne wanted was to be carried away from this moment.

"I've got you, Feather Anne," said Nick against her hair.

She stiffened and stepped back. She couldn't fall apart; not when Mae needed her to be strong. *The twins*. Jesus. Her little niece and nephew, home with Chris and Gina.

"What time is it?" Feather Anne scrubbed the tears from her eyes and took a deep, shuddering breath. *Pull your shit together, Feather Anne.*

Nick slipped his phone from his pocket and illuminated the screen. "Four a.m." He studied her, waiting.

"Okay," she said. "Okay. I have to call Katrina. And, uh, fuck. Who else? Think, damn it." She knocked her fist against her forehead.

"Hey, hey. Listen, it's four in the morning. You call people now you'll give them a fucking… I mean, how about we wait a couple hours? It's not going to change anything. Sorry," he added.

She blinked unseeingly at the tiled floor; like she was in a trance. Shock. Was she in shock? Poor Mae *had* to be.

"Gina," said Feather Anne. "I, at least, have to call our mother. She's probably already at the bakery." She checked for her phone. "Shit. I left it in your truck."

Nick handed her his phone, and she tapped the number to her mother's cell phone. Gina answered on the first ring.

"Hello." She sounded wide awake and anxious.

"Mom?" It was all Feather Anne managed before her throat closed.

"Feather Anne," said Gina sharply. "He's not… oh, shit, no."

"Mom," she said again, this time warbled by tears. Nick gently took the phone from her.

In a low voice, he said, "Mrs., uh, Byrd? This is Feather Anne's friend, Nick. She's okay." He paused—listening to Gina—and said, "Yes, ma'am. That'd be a good idea." Another pause. "Yes, ma'am."

He looked at Feather Anne and stepped further away, speaking in a lowered voice for a minute longer. He came back as Mae returned from the hospital room, composed but red-eyed. She walked slowly to Feather Anne. They didn't speak. Mae pinched Feather Anne's sleeve between her fingers for a moment or two before the sisters bent their foreheads together.

A nurse appeared beside them. "Mrs. Grant? Would you like more time before we…" she trailed off, hoping the obvious was understood without elaboration.

"Just a little longer? Please?"

"No problem," said the nurse with a compassionate smile.

"Gina's on her way," said Feather Anne.

Mae sighed. "Okay. Good. Wait. I'll need someone to stay with the twins while—"

"Uh, your dad—Feather Anne's dad, I mean—said he's going stay there for as long as you need," supplied Nick. "I hope you don't mind, but I called my folks, too. I thought you'd want the company." He blushed slightly.

Feather Anne mouthed, "Thank you," to him. "Mae, I haven't called Auntie Tree yet. Do you want me to, or…"

"Oh, Feather Anne, would you? I'm not—I can't. Not yet. I'm not ready." Her huge gray eyes pleaded.

"Of course," said Feather Anne. Her gaze drifted down the hall at the darkened room.

Mae followed her gaze and took both her hands. "There's no right or wrong here, Feather Anne. If it's too hard to see—to go in there, that's okay. But if you think, even for a second, you might regret not going…"

"I-I want to say goodbye to him. He was…" the words, *like a father to me*, came between tears.

Mae squeezed her hands. "He loved you so much. *So* much. And he was incredibly proud of you."

She nodded, unable to speak. That was the thing about William. They always knew how he felt about them. Never once did Feather Anne question whether he loved her or wanted her around, because he told her so. That was just William.

Feather Anne slipped her hands free and moved down the corridor. She stood in the doorway as a nurse unhooked some machines and stepped aside when she rolled them out with an apologetic nod. The privacy curtain around the bed was drawn back halfway, exposing the outline of his covered legs.

I can't do this.

Yet one step followed the other, bringing her bedside of the first man—the first person—she ever fully trusted. At first, she looked no higher than his hand lying still on the bed. Instinctively, she reached out her own hand to hold his, but hovered above.

Maybe she wasn't supposed to touch him? But that was stupid. People on television do it all the time. At Gloria van Bergen's wake, Mrs. B. held her hand, and she was in a coffin.

She let the hovering hand settle gently over William's. It was cool to the touch. Not icy, as she'd expected. It seemed morbid to think such thoughts, but there they were.

Feather Anne forced her gaze up his arm, to his shoulder, and finally, his face. She had to keep swallowing back the knot in her throat. She fought back the urge to shake him and tell him to wake up. She had to… she had to not fucking cry.

"I auditioned for that show, William. The one I made you watch with me every week? And guess what? I made it. I made it on the show. Out of all those auditions, they picked *me*."

She swiped away a tear before it fell onto his sheet. "It's enough knowing I got on. I'd probably have gotten voted off on Monday, anyhow. So, don't worry, okay? I'm not going to leave Mae's side. She needs me now, more than ever and I won't let you down."

The tears spilled freely now. She couldn't stop them if she tried. This was her last chance to tell him how much she loved and respected him. But all she managed say was, "I love you, William. *You* were the good stuff."

She kissed his temple and inhaled the scent of his manly shampoo, knowing but not believing it would be the last time she'd ever get to do so. When she reached the door frame, she was surprised to see Nick waiting for her. He gazed at her intensely.

"You're not going Monday?"

She gaped at him. "No, of course, I'm not going. And lower your voice. I told you, no one in my family knows about the show."

"Yeah," he looked around, then repeated quietly, "Yeah, I *know*. And I think you're crazy to not tell them, Feather Anne. I've met these people; they're like the freaking Walton's."

"How do *you* know who the Walton's are?"

"Shut up. You get what I'm trying to say. They'll support you no matter what. You should tell them."

She grabbed his arm and yanked him further down the corridor. "And what? Miss William's funeral? The show is in two days. I'm nowhere near emotionally prepared for this, anyhow."

"I heard what you said in *there*, Feather Anne. I'll bet you anything, William would want you to do it. And so would your sister."

"Yeah, well, it doesn't matter because I'm not telling her. And neither are you. Got it?"

Nick raised his hands in surrender. They walked back to Mae, who was joined by Gina, Bruce, and Mia. The trio, despite their own shock and sadness, poured all their attention into bolstering Mae.

Mia stood, giving Feather Anne a quick hug before offering up the space beside her sister. She went to Nick, ruffled his hair, then hugged him. Feather Anne watched this dispassionately. A numbness was taking over her body and mind. It was like a defense mechanism or something. Emotion overload equaled shut down.

Bruce reached across Mae's lap to take Feather Anne's hand. She let him. At Katrina and James' arrival, the barely scabbed over wounds of their loss were ripped open anew. Fresh tears fell down the tracks of the dried ones and the story of what happened had to be repeated for their benefit.

The toll it took on Mae was obvious, yet she insisted on re-telling it to them. Feather Anne suspected she needed to hear it again herself in order to make it sink in. Each sentence was chopped short, sounding almost like a recitation of a recipe's instructions.

"We had tickets to see Hamilton. At the Bushnell. We took a limo. With the Ashebys, and Davidsons. And Miles and Rosabelle. Everything seemed. Fine. We had dinner. William had salmon. But he didn't finish it. H-he had heartburn, he said."

She stopped and frowned.

Katrina said, "Sweetie, you don't have to—"

Mae ignored her. "The show… it was wonderful. After, we were all supposed to go for drinks. William said he felt under the weather, so we called an Uber. We'd just gotten in. The others had already gone. That's when… he…" She inhaled sharply and brushed away any attempt at comfort. "The hospital was only five minutes away. *Five minutes*. They should have been able to…" she rocked and buried her face in her hands.

The sobs. They were like nothing Feather Anne had ever heard before. She didn't scream or wail. She didn't tear at her hair or fall to the ground. It was worse. It was a cry of grief so deep it sounded like physical pain. Something bottomless and unmendable.

Feather Anne wanted to run. She wanted to run to the end of the earth to get away from that crushing sound coming from her sister. Even as guilt suffused her for wanting to run, she still wanted to run.

It was Katrina who rescued her, wittingly or not. "Hey, kid. Why don't you get some air, huh? You could probably use the break."

Feather Anne looked at her sister, unsure.

"It's okay, honey," said Katrina. "You did amazing. William would be so proud of you, how you took care of your sister."

The ache in her throat returned. Had it ever left in the first place? She looked around for Nick. She needed her phone from his truck. She spotted him by the hospital phone talking with Bruce. They were looking back at her with unreadable expressions. Not that she cared.

All Feather Anne cared about in that moment was getting her phone and calling Brandon. Shame suffused her as she realized she hadn't thought of him throughout this whole ordeal. What did it mean? Shouldn't he have been the first person she'd want beside her in a crisis?

For a few seconds, Feather Anne stood inside her own island, observing everyone and everything as if from afar. Mae, flanked by Gina and Katrina, sat on the edge of a family waiting room chair. Across from them at the other side of the room, Bruce and Nick had been joined by Mia where they huddled by the phone. She was alone.

She been there before, in her aloneness, unmoored and adrift. And it had been William who tethered her with an arm around her shoulders and his rich, warm voice telling her they were her home from now on. Who would tether her now?

Until then, she hadn't realized how much she'd depended on William. How much she needed him. How much she loved him. The realizations crashed against her. He would not be in his chair, reading a book, when she came home at night. He would not be in his seat at the dining room table at dinner. Nor would he be playing with the twins in the yard, or dancing in the living room with Mae when they thought everyone was asleep. So many things were now *would nots*.

Panic rose from deep in her stomach. How could she help Mae through this? She was only a kid still. Not equipped to handle someone else's grief. It was too much. There was no way. She'd say the wrong things. *Do* the wrong things. She'd—a pair of hands gripped her shoulders. Feather Anne looked up from her silent hysteria to see Bruce's worried face.

"Hey, sport. Come here."

He pulled her into a hug and Feather Anne let him, even though she hated hugs and he knew it. After a moment, he stepped back and held her shoulders again. His gaze was steady and firm, like he was about to give her a lecture or something.

"Everything is going to be all right, Feather Anne. Katrina, Gina, and Chris, Mia… we're all here for you and Mae, TK, and Evvie. *I'm* here for you guys, okay?"

A flash of anger surged through Feather Anne and she stepped out of his grasp. He looked confused, but she didn't care. She blurted, "He's not even in the grave yet and you're making a move?"

Bruce recoiled as if she'd slapped him. She wanted to take it back immediately. He saw this, and the instant forgiveness in Bruce's eyes somehow made everything worse. Feather Anne did the one thing she'd wanted to do since the doctor gave them the worst news of her life. She ran.

Nick called her name, and she heard Bruce call out to him. "Let her be, son." She didn't stop or turn around. Somehow, through the maze of the hospital, Feather Anne made her way outside. She found herself in a courtyard, one likely for mobile patients and families to escape the sterile hospital air.

The bright daylight disjointed her. It had been the middle of the night when Nick drove her—at breakneck speed—to the hospital in Hartford. All she knew of the area was the theater where she'd seen a few plays and shows with Mae and William, one or two restaurants, and the new baseball stadium. As for how to get to any of those places; she hadn't a clue.

"Fuck."

She hissed the word. Her choices were to sit out there on one of the benches and wait for someone to come look for her or go back and face Bruce. A man walked by with a bag of delicious smelling food and coffee. Her stomach grumbled.

The audacity of hunger at a time like this shamed her, but it was there, nonetheless. So, Feather Anne gave herself a third option after checking her pockets for money. The crumpled ten-dollar bill she found would get her something decent enough. She walked back inside and followed the signs to the hospital restaurant.

It wasn't until she extended her hand to pay for her selections that she remembered where the money had come from. *William.* Could it only have been yesterday morning? She'd been about to leave and called out her goodbye. Mae had already gone with the twins. It was only William at home, long in front of his laptop by the time she'd woken and readied herself for school.

"Hold up," he'd called.

Feather Anne groaned, dragged her feet to his office and whined, "Come on, William. I'm going to be late."

He had on his reading glasses and tipped them down to the end of his nose to see her better. "First," he'd said officiously, "You look lovely, my dear."

Feather Anne rolled her eyes, but smirked. He always made a point of saying something complimentary before she left the house. It was sweet... not that she'd ever admit to loving it.

It wasn't always something superficial, either. Instead, it varied with the day ahead. Like if she had a big test that day, he'd have probably told her something like, "You look ready to take on the day, Feather Anne." And even if she hadn't walked in the room feeling that way, he somehow managed to make her believe it on her way out.

That morning's good words were perfectly timed, too. It was picture day, and she'd changed ten times before settling on an outfit that she deemed tolerable. Her hair hadn't cooperated with her efforts, and a pimple threatened below the surface of her chin. It would be in full bloom by the time she sat for the photographer, no doubt.

"Thank you, William," she said in a monotone. "May I go now?"

"Do you have any cash on you? You should always carry some cash. You kids and your pay apps and debit cards… here, take this." He reached into his wallet and pulled out a crisp ten-dollar bill.

She laughed and took it, and as she shoved it into her pocket, she said, "Thanks, William. Love you," then dashed out the door. The last thing she heard William say to her was, "Love you, too."

"Eight-fifty-nine," said the woman wearing a hair net behind the register.

By the tone of her voice, Feather Anne understood it wasn't the first time she said it, either. She looked down at the bill in her hand—blurred by tears—and realized she hadn't let it go. The cashier had her fingertips on the other end and was gently tugging it. The man behind her cleared his throat forcefully.

No, she couldn't give away this last gift from William. She'd rather starve. A shadow fell over her and a male voice said, "Here." A hand with a twenty-dollar bill reached over hers to the cashier.

Feather Anne's head jerked up. Nick stood beside her, a plastic boxed sandwich in his hand and a bottled water under his arm.

"These, too," he said to the cashier who merely grunted and took his money. To Feather Anne, he said, "Grab your stuff. Come on."

He led her to a corner booth and wasted no time in popping open his food and digging in. Feather Anne still held the ten-dollar bill tightly.

"Put your money away, Feather Anne. Eat."

He didn't look up at her, and for that, she was grateful. Tears were once again coursing down her cheeks onto her lap and she couldn't muster the energy to stop them. Nick reached his free hand to the napkin dispenser, yanked out a clump of them, and pushed them across the table to her side. She took a few and wiped her eyes and dabbed under her nose. She needed to blow it but, God, she hated when people did that in restaurants.

At last, the tears dried up, and she hoarsely said, "Thanks, Nick. I'll—"

"Eat," he said before she finished.

Feather Anne nodded and dug in. The food, despite smelling good, tasted like nothing. She let the sandwich fall back into the tray and pushed it away. Nick pushed it back at her.

"I don't want it." She heard the surliness in her tone and didn't much care. "Tastes like crap. No, not even crap. It tastes like—"

"Nothing. Eat it anyway. You'll need it."

He made a sound somewhere between a snort and a sniff and Feather Anne glanced up at him.

"What?" She asked.

He looked thoughtful as he chewed, then—not looking at her still—said, "After my Pop died, I thought my taste buds were, like, broken or something. Couldn't taste a damn thing for days. Hot sauce didn't even help. My mom even took me to the doctor. He checked me out, said I was fine."

He finished his sandwich, balled up the napkin, and shrugged. "My mom told him about my grandfather and they kinda figured it was something to do with, like, the grief."

"When did it get back to normal?"

He shrugged again. "Dunno. It was, like, all of a sudden I could taste stuff again."

She nodded and picked apart her sandwich for the bacon. She'd at least eat that. Unable to control the falter in her voice, she asked, "When does it stop hurting so fucking much, Nick?"

He took a big breath and exhaled it slowly before answering. "A long time… and none at all."

"W-what do you mean?"

"It's, like, you start off feeling like nothing is ever going to be okay, right? But then—it's crazy— but everything keeps going. Life, I mean. Like, you still get up the next morning and brush your teeth." He waved his hand between their trays. "You still eat. You laugh at jokes and watch tv. But there's always a spot in you that hurts. You live with it, Feather Anne. That's the way of it. Can I give you some advice?"

Feather Anne wasn't sure she wanted any, but she said, "Sure."

"Try not to be a dick to everyone, okay? I was. For a long time, too. Everyone around you is gonna be hurting. Just try to remember that. I wish I had."

She thought of what she'd said to Bruce. It was such a shitty thing to say, to even *think*. Yeah, everyone knew how much Bruce loved her sister. But he also loved and respected William. And he was— right after William—the most decent man on the planet. She'd lashed out like a child, but now it was time to grow the fuck up and do the right things by the people who loved her the most.

"Yeah," she said. "Okay."

They drank their coffees in silence, watching people come and go with no real interest. In wordless agreement, they stood, tossed their garbage, and made their way to the elevators and back to the family waiting room to bring Mae home.

"Oh, here," said Nick, handing her phone to her. "I, uh, hope you don't mind, but your boyfriend left a shit ton of messages, so I called him and gave him the head's up."

"You talked to him?" A wave of nausea swept through Feather Anne. Nick called her boyfriend from her phone.

"No, it went to voicemail. I left a message. Don't worry, I wasn't an asshole."

Despite herself, she laughed and said, "For once."

He elbowed her and grinned. She realized how right he was earlier. Life goes on and so does the hurt. Like roommates who never speak to one another. This was to be the new normal, and even as she accepted it, she decided it really, truly, and completely sucked.

19 Bruce

For the first time in Bruce's memory, the café's doors were locked, and the sign turned to closed on a Saturday morning. The bakery as well.

"Someone needs to be there when the seafood delivery comes," Mae had said an hour earlier.

Her voice, scraped raw from crying, came out as barely a whisper, but Bruce heard her. He, along with Gina and Chris, Katrina, and James, and Mia had all stayed with her and Feather Anne overnight—what was left of it—and into the morning. They were there to do whatever she asked; whatever she needed.

Katrina and Mia made the necessary phone calls. Chris and Gina took care of the twins. James slipped into William's office and did… Bruce wasn't sure what he did, really. When Bruce had gone to knock on the door, he paused at the sound of the man's sobs, and gave him his privacy.

As for Bruce, he stood ready to jump at any command, great of small, from either the two grieving women. If they'd asked him to lasso the moon, Gad damnit, he'd do it. Anything to chase away their soul-crushing sorrow.

He didn't want this. He'd never hoped for it, not ever. Feather Anne's words in the hospital had cut him deeper than any knife. He forgave her for them, but they'd hurt. For as much as he loved Mae—no, *because* he loved Mae—he loved William, as well.

That's what love is. To Bruce, at least. Loving someone fully, whole-heartedly, means you only want for their happiness. And Mae was so happy. So in love with her husband and her life.

Sure, it sucked for Bruce that it wasn't *him* that made her that happy, but he'd accepted that a long time ago. There was no bitterness; it was enough being a part of her life. If he were to tell anyone that, they'd probably call bullshit, yet it really was the truth.

William Grant had become a genuine friend to Bruce. One who, despite knowing of the other, younger man's love for his wife, welcomed Bruce into their home and their life every day. He treated Bruce as an honorable man and seemed to respect him. It was mutual, too.

Most importantly, William had loved Mae the way she deserved to be loved. Had it been otherwise Bruce didn't think he could've born it. A woman like Mae… well, you have to love her right or not at all.

"Hey, man. Where's Mae? Is the café closed?" A husky man in a baseball cap rolled a dolly toward the back door. Six boxes of refrigerated seafood.

"Yeah, it is. Death in the family," said Bruce. *Just unload the damn stuff.* He wasn't in the mood to talk to this guy.

"Aw, damn. Sorry to hear that. Who was it?"

Jesus. Fucking nosy much?

Bruce took the clipboard, signed it so hard it tore the paper, and thrust it back to the man. "Her husband," he said.

The delivery guy tugged his cap off his head, revealing a shiny, bald pate. "Oh, man. I'm so sorry. What was it? An accident? The cancer?"

He hadn't started unloading the boxes yet, so Bruce took the liberty. He needed to get this guy the hell out of there and get back to Mae. The driver prattled on.

"I had a cousin with that prostate cancer. Bad news, that was. Wait, maybe it was the pancreas? Anyhow, one he was fine, the next—"

"Thanks, man. We're all set here," said Bruce. He rolled the dolly back to the truck, tossed it in the back, and gave him a sharp nod.

"Ah, sure, sure. Say, give my condolences to Mae, will ya? She's a good girl, that one. Sad business."

"Will do," said Bruce.

Jesus. Was this what she'd be dealing with when she came back? People asking all kinds of personal questions and trying to mask their nosiness with concern? It made him sick. He had to protect her from it all. How, he didn't know. But it wouldn't be from lack of trying.

Once he'd deposited the boxes in the walk-in refrigerator, he brought the invoice to Mae's office and set in on her desk. He cringed at the sight of the mementos that faced her every time she sat down. A candid, eight by ten photograph of her and William was flanked by smaller ones of varying sizes and subjects. The twins and Feather Anne. Mae, Feather Anne, and Gina. Bruce, Mae, and the Petrovas. One of William gazing into the lens.

He lifted it and held it in his hands. His brain still refused to compute that the man staring back at him from the frame would not be clapping him on the back and offering him a drink ever again.

"What the fuck, William? Jesus, man. We are all going to miss you. But Mae…" His throat tightened around a lump that wouldn't go away.

"We'll all be here to help her through."

Bruce spun around at the familiar voice. "Georgie. Charles," said Bruce.

The sight of the Brightsiders released the tears he'd be fighting so hard to hold back. He was like a damn kid trying to keep it all together in front of everyone, but relieved to the point of tears that his parents had shown up to make everything all better.

Georgie opened her arms to him, and Bruce went to her. He had to bend low and even though he felt a bit silly and awkward, it was so damn good to be comforted.

Charles patted his shoulder and said, "There, there, son."

It lasted only a minute and when Bruce straightened, he apologized. "Sorry, Mr. and Mrs. B. I—it's the—"

"We understand, sweetheart. If I know you—and I do—you've been keeping everything together and under control. It's all right to have your own feelings, too, dear."

"Man, it is good to have you guys back. But how did you—"

"We had a message from Feather Anne when we got off the plane."

"Weren't you staying in Florida for a bit after your cruise?"

"Not when we heard the news. All we thought about was getting home and being here for those poor girls."

Charles added, "We've been to the house already. That's how we knew you'd be here."

"I'm sure you were a welcome comfort," said Bruce.

"It'll be a long road. Our poor Mae. My heart breaks for her." Georgie dabbed at the tear rolling down her tan, lined cheek.

"Grief is the price we pay for profound love," recited Charles, a sad, knowing expression on his face.

Together, the threesome gazed down at the photograph of William. Georgie took it from Bruce's hand, patted Bruce's cheek, and set it back on the desk.

"Should we put some of these away for when Mae comes back?" Bruce gestured to the photos.

"Leave everything as it is. I get it, you want to fix this for her and make everything all better." Georgie took both his hands in hers and forced him to hold her gaze. "But you can't fix this, Bruce. You can't fix *her*. All you can do is be a good friend to her."

"But I—"

"I understand." It was in her eyes that she did. "You want to protect her and shelter her from all the pain and sadness. But you can't, nor should you."

Georgie Brightsider was right, of course. His brain told him so. But his heart was another matter all together.

"Come on," said Charles. "Let's get back to the house and see what we can do next."

Bruce locked the door again and followed the Brightsiders back to Mae and William's house. His phone rang, and he jumped, thinking it might be Mae.

"Hello?"

"Pop?"

"Hey, son." Despite everything, he smiled a little at Nick's use of the name Pop. It didn't happen often, so he secretly cherished it when it did. "What's up?"

"Nothing, really. Working on the house, keeping busy. How's Mae? And, uh, Feather Anne?"

Bruce's mouth twitched again. The whole Nick, Brandon, Feather Anne situation gave him mixed emotions, but he still had pride at how his son had stepped up when everything happened. *Yesterday.* Not even twenty-four hours had passed.

"As well as can be expected," said Bruce.

"Yeah, I figured. Listen, there's something I gotta tell you. I mean, I gotta tell *someone*, and you're like the only one I can think of who might know what to do."

Bruce's gut clenched. What had the boy done? Another speeding ticket? He'd warned him the last time, Joel Asheby's hands were tied when it came to stuff like that. Age of electronic ticketing and shit.

"All right," he sighed. "Lay it on me."

Nick snorted. "Chill, Pop. I didn't do anything wrong... this time. It's about Feather Anne. Well, and me, I guess. I mean, not like—"

"Spit it out, kid. I'm almost back at Mae's," said Bruce.

"Yeah, okay. Right. So, you've heard of that show, Greatest American Singer?"

Was this kid really talking to him about a stupid television show? Now? Barely keeping his calm, Bruce said, "Yeah," stretching the word out.

"Well, Feather Anne got on it."

"What," said Bruce not computing, "you mean she got tickets to see it?"

"No, Pop. To be *on* it. A contestant. She auditioned, and they invited her to be on the show. She's got an actual chance to compete for a record label."

"A record label." Bruce's brain was filled with molasses. "Wait, she auditioned for the show? The actual television show? And she won? When? I mean… shit. I'm so confused."

Nick repeated everything again, and it sunk in—sort of—the second time. He spoke Nick's words back to him, then said, "But why wouldn't she tell us? When is the show?"

"It's Monday. That's the problem. She's not going because of William. Don't get me wrong, I understand it. But this is a once in a lifetime chance, Pop. It's the only thing she's ever wanted, and she's been practicing so hard."

It hit him. "You love her," said Bruce.

Nick was silent so long Bruce thought he'd hung up. But he answered, his voice gruff. "Yeah. Don't make a thing of it, okay?"

"Sure. Whatever you say, son," said Bruce, aching for the boy.

He wasn't sure if Feather Anne had feelings for Nick. She and Brandon had been an item for a long time. Whatever happened, it wasn't going to go easy.

"Anyhow, I'm supposed to take her there—the city—Monday morning. If she's not there for check-in at nine a.m., she forfeits her spot."

"Jesus, Nick. The timing—"

"Yeah, exactly," said Nick. "Believe me, I'm aware it sucks, big time. But from everything she's said about William, he'd want her to do this, I think."

It was Bruce's turn to be silent. He sat at a red light long after it changed to green. The blat of a car horn behind him startled him back into action.

At last, he said, "I think you're right, son. I'll see what I can do. No promises."

Nick's voice was full of relief when he said, "Thanks, Pop. I knew I could count on you."

Well, that was better than being handed all the money in the world right there. Bruce's chest swelled. There was a time when the weight of other people's expectations and their dependence on Bruce burdened him. Now, it filled him with pride and gratitude.

Nick's words were a reminder to him that Bruce was *that guy*. The one people trusted and relied on because he'd earned that level of confidence. He could do all the things thrust in his lap. Help Mae through this. Help Feather Anne realize her dream. Help Nick keep his life on track. All of it.

"Damn right you can, son. I'll call you later. And Nick?"

"Yeah?"

"Thank you," said Bruce, his voice thick.

"For what?" Nick gave a small laugh.

"For letting me be in your life."

"Yeah, yeah. We're cool, old man."

And even though it was awkward and new to say, Bruce added as casually as possible, "Okay, bye. Love you."

There was no pause on the other end of the line. "Love you, too, Pop."

When he slowed the stopped alongside Mae's house, he spied Feather Anne on the front porch swing. She was alone. What the hell had that girl been thinking, keeping such a secret from them? Didn't she think they'd be proud of her and happy?

He clomped heavily up the stairs and sank down beside her on the swing. Without a word, she plunked her head on his shoulder. They swung for a bit, saying nothing.

"We need to talk, Feather Anne."

20 Rosabelle

A light rain fell outside the window. Rosabelle's hand shook as she poured hers and Miles' coffees. He touched her hip and offered a sympathetic smile. *I know*, said the smile. Ruth and Steven came in through the kitchen entrance—Rosabelle had left the garage open for them to walk in—without their usual boisterous chatter and fawning hellos to the children.

Even Poppy and Fiona seemed cognizant that something was amiss, and they sat quietly in their respective highchair and booster seat.

"I'll take the girls to the mall. Steven's going to stay behind in case you need anything; he hates the mall, anyhow," said Ruth.

She kissed her daughter's cheek and bent down to give a one-arm hugged to Miles, still sitting.

Rosabelle nodded and smiled gratefully at her mother.

"Dad, coffee?" Rosabelle waggled the coffee pot.

"If you have enough, sweetheart." Steven scratched a line up and down his scalp, shaking his head as he did. "Terrible news. I can't believe he's—"

"Not in front of the children, Steven," said Ruth, cutting her eyes to the round-eyed girls watching the adults with avid attention.

"Oh… I don't think we want to hide these types of things from them," said Rosabelle, looking to Miles for assurance.

"Yeah, uh, Rosie and I talked about it, and we think they should—"

"Age appropriately," interjected Rosabelle.

"Right, yeah. They should age appropriately learn about… about death." He gulped after the word *death*.

Ruth and Steven shot raised eyebrows at each other and Ruth said, "All right, well, you're the parents. Just, in our day—"

"I understand, Mom. You told me Grandma Lulu took a trip and she wouldn't be coming back." Rosabelle scowled at her mother.

Ruth shrugged. "What, we thought it would be too sad for you. You were only six."

Steven asked Miles, "What about you? What'd your folks say when someone died?"

Miles rubbed his chin and looked up to the ceiling. "Let's see. When our dog died, my father said he ran away. When my grandfather died, they said he'd gone to another country." A look of surprise came across his face. "Wow. Guess what? Those are the only two I can think of from, like, childhood."

"Well, you two were lucky. When I was a girl, I lost my father, my uncle, one of my classmates, and my oldest brother—your Uncle Jacob you never met," said Ruth. "Went to every funeral, and the classmate? Open casket. I had nightmares for years."

"Didn't your parents explain, or prepare you?" Miles asked.

Ruth snorted. "Prepare me? Sure. They said get your best dress on and comb your hair. We're going to pay our respects."

Rosabelle poured her father's coffee and said, "Well, even though they are too young to understand anything now, I want the girls to grow up with a-a better... a healthier... oh, what am I trying to say? It's all so—"

"Unexpected? Sudden?" Steven nodded his understanding. "For what it's worth, sweetheart, I understand, and I agree. Don't hide your feelings from the girls; let them see you're sad when you're sad. It'll help them name their own emotions as they get older."

They all stared at Steven in open surprise. "What," he said with a shrug, "I've been reading those parenting articles on the internet."

"All right," blinked Ruth. "Well. Are the girls ready for their Bubbe?"

"Yes, they are packed, fed, and changed. Thank you so much for doing this, Mom."

"Nonsense. You give my love to Mae and her sister and I'll see you later."

Ruth gathered up Poppy onto her hip and shuttled Fiona out the door, calling out in a sing-song, "Say bye-bye, Mommy, bye-bye, Daddy. We love you. See you later." And like that, they were gone.

Steven bore the expression of a man who'd survived a war and could finally relax. He sipped his coffee, sighed, and asked, "You going straight to Mae's?"

"I am, yes. Miles is going to stay here with you, Dad. I'll bet you two can put together that toddler bed while I'm gone?"

She made sure to imply she expected it to be done, even though she posed it as a question. It struck Rosabelle how crazy life was. There she was, living her normal life, while two blocks away, her dearest friend was suffering the devastating loss of her husband—her life altered permanently.

She looked at Miles and he at her. He understood. "Come on, Rosie. I'll walk you out."

Outside the drizzle had stopped, but the sky was gray and the air damp. She slipped her arms around his waist and rested her head on his chest. Miles folded her tightly against him and he kissed her hair.

Rosabelle pulled back to gaze up at his face and thought, *I love him more than ever*. And because they'd gotten the shocking reminder of short and cruel life could be, she told him as much.

"Same, Rosie. You and our girls are my universe. Now and always."

Her eyes stung. They kissed and Miles opened the car door for her. She keyed the ignition and rolled down the window to kiss him again.

"Give baby Mae my love, will you?"

"Of course. Call you later."

The drive to Mae's house, quick as it was, gave her a moment to collect and prepare herself. At thirty-three, they weren't meant to be consoling and grieving the death of a spouse. And how could they have just been all together the night before? Now William was... she couldn't bring herself to accept the word.

If this is how I'm feeling, poor Mae must be in even deeper shock.

Cars filled the driveway, so she parked behind Bruce's truck on the street. On the top porch step, she startled at Bruce's voice. He and Feather Anne sat on the chair swing, the toe of his boot moving them back and forth.

"She's out back. With the goats. Everyone else is inside."

"Oh, okay. Feather Anne, I'm so sorry."

"It's okay," said Feather Anne.

The girl tried to smile, but it faltered and fell. Rosabelle hesitated. "Should I not—"

"She'll want to see you. We've all been driving her nuts, I think. You'll be a relief." Bruce smiled and jerked his head toward the backyard.

Rosabelle nodded and backtracked down the stairs and around the house. She unlatched the gate and walked across the patio toward the goat pen. There were only two now; Ginger and Gracie. Fred and George has passed away some years back. Rosabelle found this poignant and oddly fitting.

She found Mae sitting on an upturned feed bucket in the pen, scratching behind Gracie's ear and staring blankly at the ground. Rosabelle stood uncertain and afraid to surprise or intrude. Her concern was unwarranted; Mae sensed her there.

"I knew. I *knew* something was wrong, and I did nothing." She turned ever so slowly to look at Rosabelle. "I did nothing, Rosabelle, and now he's gone."

Rosabelle pursed her lips and opened the gate. She grabbed another empty feed bucket, flipped it, and sat beside Mae. She took Mae's hand and forced her to look into her eyes.

"You listen to me, Mae. This is *not* your fault. Even if you suspected something wasn't all right, it is not your fault. Things—sometimes terrible, unfair things—happen and they are out of our control. This was one of those things."

Even though Mae nodded and seemed to accept this, Rosabelle wasn't sure she believed it in her heart. "I'm going—we're *all*—going to help you through this, Mae. We're here for you, and the kids, and Feather Anne, too."

Mae's lips formed a wan smile, and she briefly rested her head on Rosabelle's shoulder. When she picked her head up again, her gaze became far away, and her words came out thickly.

"They let me go in after… after. He looked—it wasn't right seeing him there. Like that. We were supposed to be home, in our bed, reading our books before one of us fell asleep and the other had to turn off both reading lamps."

A dry, humorless laugh heaved her chest. Rosabelle waited; there was more.

"Instead," said Mae, "I was in a hospital room staring down at my hus—" her voice broke. She breathed in through her nose and out through her mouth several times. "Staring down at my husband and trying to comprehend that he was not coming home with me."

Rosabelle touched Mae's back but said nothing. Her friend needed to purge, and she would let her.

Mae gave Gracie a gentle shove, and the goat snorted and walked off. She sighed and tipped her head to the gloomy sky.

"I got mad at him, Rosabelle. Furious at him for leaving us. Leaving *me*. I-I said it out loud. I said, *damn you for leaving us, William*."

Mae covered her mouth, pinching her nose. When she dropped her hands back in her lap, she said, "I wanted to take it back the second the words came out. I don't *want* to be angry at him. In six years, I can count about twice when I was legitimately angry at him for something. Crazy, right?"

"No. It's sweet, Mae. You two had a very special relationship and love."

Mae nodded. "William is… he was one of a kind. Not another like him in the world. I'd rather be angry at myself than at him."

"So, you want to take on all the burden of blame, do you? You think that will make this any easier?" Rosabelle said this gently, but with a firmness, too.

Mae's small chuckle was genuine. "It's my way, after all."

Rosabelle stroked her friend's hair. "Oh, sweetie. This one is too big to take on alone. You're going to have to let us all in to help. *And* let us grieve with you. We all loved William so very much."

This time it was Mae who reached out for Rosabelle's hand. They sat like this for a while, occasionally tossing bits of scrap for the goats and stroking their coarse backs. When the patter of raindrops began, they stood and brushed themselves off.

"You ready?" Rosabelle looked hard into Mae's eyes.

"Not much choice, I suppose. But yeah, I'm ready."

Inside the house was a busyness, a hum of activity. It had the look and feel of take action people in a crisis. Like a room full of military personnel giving and awaiting attack commands. It was both comforting and jarring.

On one hand, the relief of having grownups handle the difficult business of death and its aftermath was palpable to Rosabelle. Even having her own home and family to care for, it was in times like these when she reverted to being a child again. She looked to Mae and suspected she felt much the same.

On the other, the buzz and crackle of tension altered the normally warm, cozy, and joyful house to an almost assaultive degree. No Rosemary Clooney crooning from the record player in the living room. No Mae at the stove stirring a homemade sauce or William uncorking a bottle of Merlot or Cabernet. The twins, rather than being center stage of the kitchen, were shunted off to the playroom, the door closed. Again, a look toward Mae told Rosabelle she felt this, too.

Knowing Mae as she did, Rosabelle realized her friend need to regain control, and quickly. She whispered to her. "Without thinking, tell me the first thing you need right in this second."

She blinked and stared wide-eyed at the houseful of people, she blurted, "For everyone to get out of my kitchen."

Rosabelle patted her shoulder and announced, "All right. Everyone…" she waited for their attention. "Out of the kitchen."

With little grumbling—especially after seeing Mae's slightly frantic expression—they left the kitchen.

"There. That's done. Give me my next marching order," said Rosabelle.

Mae's purposeful manner and take-charge attitude crept back into her posture. The dazed, haunted expression cleared and was replaced by resolve.

"Right," she said. "Shit. Jesus, I don't know what's going on with any of this. I need everyone to report to me. My husband is getting the—" her voice wobbled and steadied, "the send-off he deserves and I'm the one who needs to do it."

"Okay. I'll get your aunt first. I think she's made calls and such."

Mae bobbed her head once and braced her hands on the island. "Good. Will you check on Feather Anne?"

"She was with Bruce when I came in. Seems as okay as can be."

Another nod. "Okay. I'm going to make fresh coffee and roll out some dough for quiches. Would you tell *them* they don't need to tell *me* I should relax or—"

"Totally understood. Consider it handled."

Rosabelle left in search of Katrina, who was quickly found hovering outside the kitchen entrance.

"You're a great friend, Rosabelle," said Katrina.

Rosabelle thanked her and stepped aside. She made the rounds to the others, sending home those who Mae wouldn't need anything from in the immediate. When they'd all been sent off—leaving Bruce with Feather Anne and Gina with the twins—Rosabelle slid a record from one of the dozens of sleeves lined up in Mae's record cabinet.

She suspended the needle over the spinning record and bit her nail. Perhaps she'd be overstepping? What if she chose an album that made her friend cry? At last, she resolved to trusting her gut and placed the needle carefully on the vinyl.

With the volume gradually raised to five and the sweet, sultry low sounds of Helen Merrill filling the room, Rosabelle swore she heard the house itself saying thank you. Back in the kitchen, she watched as Mae's tense shoulders lowered and her face smoothed. She glanced up at Rosabelle and mouthed, "Thank you."

"I'm leaving for now, Mae, but I'll check back with you a little later."

"Thank you, again. We're going to Sullivan's to make the funeral arrangements in a couple hours. We're going to have a wake and then a memorial service. William wanted—" Mae's breath caught. "He wanted to be cremated. Would you, Lotus, Charlotte, and Marisol come by tonight? I'm not ready to—"

"Of course," said Rosabelle. "You'll be here, too, Katrina, yes?"

"I will. For as long as this one needs me," said Mae's aunt. "I'll send James home tonight. Fuck. Has he come out of that office yet?"

Mae and Rosabelle shrugged at her. She swore under her breath again and excused herself to find him.

Mae called after her, "Go easy, Tree." To Rosabelle, she said, "Poor James. They've been friends for more than thirty years."

How typical of Mae; worrying about how someone else was coping when she'd suffered the greater loss. Rosabelle, speechless, hugged her friend and promised to return later.

"Bruce, Feather Anne, I'm leaving now, but I'll be back again later. Text or call if you need anything," said Rosabelle once again back on the front porch. The pair hadn't moved from the swing and looked as though they might never. But Bruce surprised her.

"I'll walk you to your car, Rosabelle." He stood and followed her down. Feather Anne gave a weak wave and resumed swinging.

"Listen. I need your opinion on something."

Bruce told her how Feather Anne had won a chance at competing on Greatest American Singer. Her eyes nearly popped out of her head.

"Bruce, that is amazing. The odds of getting on that show… can you imagine? But what's the problem?" Rosabelle couldn't fathom why her opinion was needed.

"It's on Monday. She has to be in New York by nine A.M. or she loses her spot."

"Oh," said Rosabelle. Now she understood. "And she wants to go, of course." "No, that's just it. She's giving up on it because of… well, the obvious."

"Okay," said Rosabelle. She was back to not understanding the problem. But then she did. "Ah. I see. You think she should go, but you're not sure how to handle it?"

"Exactly."

"Mae needs to know. She'd want to, I'm positive."

Bruce exhaled. "Okay. Yeah. That's what I thought. Shit. Feather Anne's gonna flip out on me. Again."

Rosabelle shrugged and nudged him. "Oh, the joys of parenting, right?" He was, after all, like a second or even third father to the girl. More seriously, she said, "She'll be needing you more than ever now, Bruce."

He half-shrugged and dug his fists in to his pockets. "Ah, well. She's got Chris and—"

"Yes, yes. No disrespect to them. But you two have a special bond."

"As did she and William."

"Which is why you'll be needing to fill that void. Not that you need me to tell you any of that."

She blushed at her pushiness. Of course, Bruce knew what to do and how. He kissed her cheek; a gesture to say he hadn't minded and opened her door for her.

On the way home, she called Miles, hungry for his voice.

He answered on the first ring. "Hey, babe. You okay?"

She sighed and slumped against the seat. "Yes and no. I'm glad I went over, obviously. I think *she* was glad for it, as much as she can be about anything right now. But it was so sad, Miles. So, so *sad*."

"Aw, Rosie Posie. Sorry you had to do it alone. Your dad and I got the toddler bed together, though."

She smiled. "How does it look? Are we *really* ready for a toddler bed?"

It seemed impossible, but they'd caught Fiona climbing out of her crib twice now and Rosabelle feared she'd hurt herself.

"Tell me about it. I'm freaking out over here." He laughed but quickly sobered. "So, how is baby Mae holding up? They have the arrangements made for the funeral yet?"

"Not yet. They're going this afternoon. She asked if I'd go back over after it was done. I said yes. Hope you don't mind."

"Nah, do what you gotta do, babe. I'll hold down the fort."

"And how are you, Miles? I feel like I haven't asked in ages."

"Babe, you check on me every day. I'm good. Seriously. Feeling almost back to normal, actually."

"Good. You'll tell me if—"

"Detective Rosie will probably know before I do if I'm not good." He chuckled to show he was teasing.

"Yeah, yeah," she said. "Home in ten." She almost hit the end button but stopped. "Miles?"

"Yeah, babe?"

"I love you."

In the pause, she sensed him smiling. "Love you, too. Now get your ass home, will ya?"

She tried to not let a day go by without telling or showing her family that she loved them. But was it enough? She knew how these things went. Something terrible happens, and everyone tries to—what was that Tim McGraw song—Live Like You Were Dying. *That.* She knew this all too well.

After her car accident, Rosabelle had made a promise to herself to love and live big, without reservation or letting fear dictate her choices. For the most part, she'd stuck to it. But life… is life. People, no matter their best intentions, fall into routines and habits and take each other for granted. Maintaining that level of intensity and passion was impossible. It wasn't realistic.

She tried to imagine it; living so intensely, *loving* so intensely and constantly and wondered at how or who could possibly do that. The answer—her husband—bound down the steps of their house at the sight of her car and met her in the curved driveway.

He wore a ripped t-shirt and a huge grin. The same grin that greeted her from the day they'd begun dating. And that's when it sank in: *her husband.* He was the Tony Robbins of love. Huge, epic, and all encompassing. With every fiber of his being.

She was out of the car and in his arms. Crying and laughing at once and not caring one bit about it.

21 Brandon

Downstairs the doorbell rang. Brandon's practice jersey was halfway over his head and steam billowed from the shower. He waited, listened for who it was. Probably one of Brianna's friends. But maybe, just *maybe*, it was Feather Anne.

When no call of, "Brandon, it's for you," came, he whipped his mud and grass-stained shirt at the hamper and forced back the shower curtain with equal vehemence. The water scalded his back, and he jerked away, swearing and reaching around to turn it cooler.

As he lathered, washed and rinsed, he seethed. No call. No text. No nothing from Feather Anne since the morning before. *What the fuck.* He slammed the shampoo bottle on the ledge. How could she be so insensitive? So thoughtless?

Yes, the show loomed, and she was excited and nervous. But she should be talking to *him* about it, not that dickhead, Amendola. Why hadn't *he* ever learned to play the guitar? Then this wouldn't be an issue.

He wondered if she was avoiding him because she didn't want Brandon to find out Nick was bringing her to New York on Monday. That *had* to be it. Feather Anne was probably going to try to avoid him until afterward. That'd be like her; run away and hide from anything too difficult.

This was the kind of bullshit she did anytime they had a fight. She'd ghost him knowing full well it would drive him insane, and he'd track her down, apologize—even if she was the one who was wrong—and beg her not to be mad at him.

"Not this time," said Brandon.

He towel dried his hair and wrapped the damp cloth around his waist. With the side of his palm, he wiped a clear streak across the fogged mirror. Brandon clenched his jaw and stared down his reflection before he repeated, "Not. This. Time."

In his room, Brandon cranked his music up and dressed. Saturday afternoon, and he couldn't think of a damn thing he wanted to do. Besides seeing Feather Anne. There was a Biology test on Monday. He'd study for it.

This lasted for about two minutes. He slapped the book shut and opened his laptop, intending on checking Feather Anne's Instagram and Snapchat.

"No. Don't do it." Hearing the command aloud somehow made him more apt to listen to himself. He closed it and turned his music up louder to drown out his thoughts.

A knock on his door made him sigh and sit up. Brianna, there to tell him to turn down the racket.

"Sorry," he called out and lowered the volume.

She knocked once more and cracked the door. "That, too, yeah. But here," she held out Brandon's cell phone. "Kade stopped by. Said you forgot it in his car this morning."

"Toss it," said Brandon, cupping his hands like a baseball mitt.

She threw it and winced.

"Shit, sorry, Bri. I forgot," said Brandon.

"I'm fine. Certain motions still hurt a little."

"Can I do anything?"

Brianna shrugged. "Pick up your wet towel from the carpet?"

"Yeah, yeah," said Brandon.

Brianna closed the door again, and he pressed the power button to illuminate the screen. It flashed and turned off. His battery had drained. *Probably no calls anyhow*. Still, he reached around the floor beside the bed for his charger and plugged it in. He wasn't going to check it though.

Two minutes later, the phone balanced in his palm, he powered it back on. It had only two percent battery, but it was enough to show he had a missed called and a voicemail from Feather Anne. He pressed play, anticipating her husky voice offering a vague apology-like explanation. Instead, Nick Amendola's voice assaulted his ears in a long, halting message.

"Yo. Hey, uh, this is Nick? Sorry, but, uh, something has happened. Not to Feather Anne. Not, like, directly. It's her… shit, what is he to her? Her brother-in-law? Yeah, I think that's right. Uh, anyhow. William? He, like, died last night. Or, like, early this morning. We're at the hospital in Hartford. Thought you should know. I mean, I thought Feather Anne would want you to know. She's, uh, pretty torn up about it. Sorry to be telling you like this, in a message, Okay, well, bye."

A beep followed, then a request whether to save or delete the message. Brandon did neither. He merely stared at the phone in his hand. Blinking. His heart pumped blood so quickly into his veins that his temple throbbed. William Grant… dead? No. It couldn't be, could it?

A quick, double knock on his door again. He looked up mutely as Brianna burst in again, this time breathless, pale, and with her own phone clutched in her hand.

"Brandon, William Grant—"

"He's dead. I-I heard," said Brandon. His lips felt full of Novocain. He sat rooted to the bed.

Brianna furrowed her brow at him, bringing her phone back to her ear and staring hard at him. "I told him, yes. He says he knows. Okay, yes. Please do. Bye." She ended the call and stuck her hands on her hips.

"*Brandon*." It came out as a hiss. "What do you mean you heard? How long have you known? Why didn't—"

"No, I mean, I just found out. Same time as you. M-my phone was dead and I—holy shit, Bri. I gotta go."

Time—which had seemed to have stopped for those brief moments—caught up. He leaped from the bed and yanked on his sneakers. At the same time, he reached around his dresser for his car keys.

"Fuck," he slapped his forehead, "my car's in the shop. Can I—"

"Hell, no, you're not driving my car. I'll bring you."

He wanted to argue, but not as much as he needed to get to Feather Anne. So, he raced down the stairs to the garage with Brianna close behind and calling instructions to Mrs. T.

"Just let them watch Frozen again, Mrs. T. Ricky will be home in an hour. Cassidy, help Mrs. T. with Archer, please."

Brandon heard all this as if from far away. His own swirling ruminations sang louder in his mind. He considered his thoughts from less than an hour ago. Spiteful, petty, selfish. It hadn't even crossed his mind that something could've been wrong. He wanted to puke.

He also wanted to climb over the passenger seat and mash his foot to the gas petal. "Can't you go any faster," he asked.

Brianna opened her mouth—likely to offer a snarky retort—took a glance at him and thought better of it. She sped up, but not by much. They drove in silence; Brandon running his hands down the length of his jeans over and over, and Brianna biting her lower lip.

There was only two cars in the driveway, Mae's and William's. Easy to believe it was merely another day and nothing amiss.

"I don't see Feather Anne's car," said Brianna.

"She's here," said Brandon.

He spotted her straight away, on the porch swing with her legs folded up to her chin. She looked so small and forlorn. Brandon's heart lurched.

Brianna followed his gaze. "Listen, as much as I want to hug her and give my condolences, I think I'll drop you here and come back later."

Brandon shook his head. "It'll be weird if you don't come up, Bri."

She sighed and scraped her bottom lip with her teeth. "Okay. Just for a minute though."

They climbed out and walked slowly up the walkway. Feather Anne didn't look at them or unclasp her arms from around her shins, but she scootched to the center of the swing to make room for them. Brandon and Brianna exchanged a look and sat on either side.

Brianna wrapped an arm around Feather Anne's stooped shoulders and she in turn rested her head against Brianna. Brandon sat with his hands on his lap and his head bowed.

Brianna spoke. "Is Mae inside, sweetie?"

Feather Anne shook her head slowly. "They went to the funeral home to make… arrangements."

"Okay," said Brianna. "Is there anything I can do for you?"

"No," said Feather Anne in a small voice.

"All right, honey. If there is anything—anything at all—you say the word, okay? I'm going to let you two have some time alone. Brandon, call me when you want me to come back."

He nodded and mumbled his thanks. Even after Brianna's SUV had rounded the corner, Brandon couldn't figure out how to say he was sorry in a way that showed the depth of his sincerity. *I'm sorry* wasn't enough. So, he sat there, saying nothing with his heart thudding and his hands sweating.

Minutes stretched on like this—Feather Anne curled up into herself, Brandon with his hands in his lap. His arms should be around her. Her head should be against his chest. Why hadn't he just done it? Did she even want him there? Feather Anne sniffled once and rubbed her nose against her jeans. Back and forth, back and forth.

Brandon turned his head in her direction—not quite looking at her, but close—and finally said the only thing that ran through his brain on repeat.

"I'm sorry."

Feather Anne spoke into the denim at her knees. "Yeah, me, too."

Suddenly, Brandon wasn't sure what they were referring to. William... or their relationship? He reeled internally; his mind in frantic chaos, searching for what to say next. He needed clarity, and he hated himself for being so selfish in his concerns.

"He was... he was the best."

Guiltily, Brandon relaxed. "Yeah. Is Mae—how's Mae holding up?"

She let her knees drop into a crossed leg pose and exhaled hard. She looked up at the porch ceiling and shook her head slowly.

"Not good. She's putting on a decent show of it, but she's not okay. Right now, she's kept busy. All the planning and the non-stop company. When everyone's gone, though..." She trailed off.

"Reality sets in."

"Yeah," said Feather Anne. She looked at him. "I'm sorry I didn't call you myself. I just—"

"Hey, no. No explanation needed; I get it. Really." He didn't, but it was the only thing to say.

He wanted to say, "Why didn't you call *me* to bring you to the hospital?" And, "Didn't you wish I was there to hold you?" Or, "I bet Nick was more than happy to comfort you."

Brandon knew not to ask those questions or make snide comments. But he thought them, and that was bad enough.

"I—everything happened so fast. One minute we were rehearsing. Then, that call. Mae's voice." Feather Anne shuddered. "All I thought about was getting to her."

Now, at last, Brandon did reach out. He closed his hand around hers and squeezed. She didn't pull away, but she also didn't turn it palm up to squeeze back. Brandon refused to let himself wonder if it meant something more than weariness on her part.

"You must be exhausted," said Brandon.

She blinked and her brow drew together as if it was a curious question. "Oh," she said, "I guess I am. I'm… kind of, like, numb. Like, you've seen that stuff the twins play with—Floof? It's like moldable foam. Well, I'm, like, inside the Floof and I can't move, and I don't want to, either."

Brandon made a soft chortling sound through his nose. "Floof, huh?"

"It's stupid—"

"No, no," said Brandon. He squeezed her hand again. "Not at all. I get it. It's not the same, but I remember feeling like that when everything went down with Gordon and my mother." He'd never refer to that man as his father again. "Although back then there wasn't Floof to compare it to."

Feather Anne's mouth curved into a smile. It was small, miniscule really, but it counted as a smile. It was a smile he'd put on her face, and it gratified him more than he could express.

Still, it killed him not to ask her if they were okay—he and Feather Anne—and he had to physically bite his tongue to keep the words from sputtering out. While he groped for something to say, Feather Anne slipped her hand out of his and stood.

"Come inside, if you want. I'm going to get some food out. Mae will be back soon, and she hasn't eaten anything."

"Yeah, sure. If it's okay, I mean. Like, if you'd rather I—"

"Stop being a freak and come inside," said Feather Anne with a snort.

And somehow, this was the best thing she could have possibly said to him. Underneath the sadness and shock, and their weirdness of late, Feather Anne—real Feather Anne, *his* Feather Anne—was still there.

They walked inside and he helped her line the kitchen island with platters of food. Deli meats and salads, rolls, and condiments. Because he'd be such a long-time visitor to the Huxley-Grant house, Brandon moved with comfort and familiarity around the kitchen; pulling plates form cabinets and silverware from drawers. He liked this, despite the reason, and his confidence grew.

The doorbell rang. Feather Anne, slicing a tomato, called over her shoulder, "Get that, will you? It's probably Rosabelle or one of Mae's other friends."

Brandon wiped his hands with a dishtowel as he strode to the front door. He swung it open with a warm smile ready. Only, it wasn't Rosabelle or Lotus, or Marisol, or any of her other girlfriends. It was Nick Amendola with his floppy hair and hands in pockets. Oh, and his fucking guitar slung across his back. Can't forget that.

"Hey, man," said Nick. As if it were the most normal thing for him to be at Feather Anne's door, with Brandon answering it.

"Hey," said Brandon. He drew the door toward his side, blocking the view.

Nick rose onto the balls of his feet and tried to glance around Brandon. "Feather Anne here?"

Where the fuck else would she be right now, dickhead?

Brandon dipped his head out the small opening and spoke in a conspiratorial tone. "Yeah, she is. But now's, uh, not really the best time. Maybe you should—"

"Who is it, Bran?" Feather Anne stepped up behind him and peeked over his shoulder. "Oh, shit. Hey, Nick. Get in here. Sorry, I lost track of time."

Mind reeling, embarrassment and frustration bringing color to his cheeks, Brandon stepped back and let Nick in. *What in the actual fuck*? She was *expecting* him? *Him*?

Feather Anne looked between the two boys and quirked an eyebrow. "This isn't going to be weird, right? You're both cool? Because it's not like I lost someone special to me like a hot minute ago, or anything."

Brandon and Nick made a big show of expressing how totally not an issue was to be had. Well, Nick made a show, Brandon was being honest and sincere. He was mature and, naturally, the situation called for a higher level of respect. As for how Nick would behave? He doubted the guy had the ability to class it up, but whatever.

"All cool," said Brandon.

"No worries, babe," said Nick.

Brandon's hand curled into a fist, but he kept his composure. "Feather Anne and I are getting some food ready for when Mae comes back. Why don't you grab a seat in the living room?"

"Nah. Thanks, bro, but I'm happy to help out. Feather Anne, whatcha want me to do?"

Feather Anne had already gone back to slicing tomatoes and had either not heard the exchange or had decided to ignore it.

"Nick, you slice up the cantaloupe and honeydew melons. Brandon, cover those trays back up with the clear wrap so they don't get nasty looking."

Brandon and Nick attended their respective tasks dutifully, but not without several unfriendly stare downs and glares hurled behind Feather Anne's back. If she knew, she didn't acknowledge any of it.

Mae returned a short time after, looking pale and drawn. Brandon's heart lurched for her. Mae and William had been like an adoptive family to him over the years; they'd always been that in his mind: *Mae and William*. It seemed unimaginable there'd be no *and* after Mae's name from now on.

"I'm so sorry, Mae," said Brandon.

He gave her a brief, gentle hug, then drew away feeling awkward. Brandon had always thought Mae was one of the most beautiful women he'd ever seen but thinking this had also made him shy and tongue-tied around her. Feather Anne, of course, caught on and teased him mercilessly in the earlier years of their relationship.

"So," she'd say, "should I invite my sister to the movies with us? I bet she'd share her popcorn with you."

She'd use that sing-song, teasing tone and Brandon would get mad and flustered and tell her to shut up and stop being weird. He'd told Ricky about it once and he'd slapped his palm against his forehead and passed down some hard-learned lessons about girls.

"Listen, little brother." Ricky had clapped him on the shoulder and sat him down. "When a chick points out another pretty girl to you—doesn't matter who it is—you always, *always* say this: *she's all right, but she's no you.* Works every time."

Brandon had flushed and stammered, "I don't—don't like her. Geez. Not like *that*. She's, like, she—"

Ricky laughed, dipped his head down closer to Brandon's, and said, "Dude, there isn't a man in Chance that doesn't think Mae Huxley is hot." He straightened, shot a glance over his shoulder—probably checking if Brianna was in earshot—and added, "But that's beside the point. Feather Anne is fishing for a little reassurance from you. Give it to her, and all will be well. Trust your big brother-in-law Ricky."

Despite his misgivings and how dumb he felt saying it, it had worked. The next handful of times Feather Anne brought up her sister's good looks—or rather Brandon's awareness of her good looks—he told her that she was the only one he had eyes for. Or something like that, only not as smooth. He was thirteen at the time; he had no game. Still, Feather Anne had eventually stopped fishing.

This present-day Mae Huxley was no less beautiful than she ever was, despite the paleness and dark circles under her eyes. This Mae, in her grief and stoicism, her straight spine and sad smile, somehow managed to be even more breathtaking than before.

A wave of pity for William overcame Brandon. That poor guy, to miss out on a woman like Mae. He imagined he and Feather Anne living their life—the house, the kids, the whole works—and knew if he had to part with Feather Anne and not have a life with her… it didn't bear thinking.

His eyes welled—for the wrong reasons—and he turned on his heel and returned to the kitchen. He heard but tried to ignore Nick's almost too casual, "Hey, Mae," greeting but it got under his skin.

He was making it known to Brandon that *he'd* been a part of this ordeal from the beginning; had already given his condolences and been a help to the family. *Asshole.*

"How did—is everything all set?" Feather Anne sought her sister's gaze and held it.

Mae nodded. "The wake will be Tuesday from six to nine. The memorial is Wednesday morning at nine."

"Tuesday? I-I thought it would be on Monday," said Feather Anne. Her expression seemed puzzled.

"Yes. And I'm glad you're here, Nick. There's something I want to discuss as soon as Bruce gets here."

Brandon winced internally. *She was glad Nick was here.* She hadn't said that about him. He looked at Nick for his reaction and found it interesting. He didn't seem surprised or even curious, which meant he was in on whatever this discussion was.

He looked next to Feather Anne, who appeared confused and suspicious. She was trying to catch Nick's eye—this irritated Brandon beyond words—but Nick wouldn't make eye contact with her and instead busied himself with arranging the stupid cantaloupe on the platter.

"Okay," said Feather Anne, drawing the word out and narrowing her eyes at Nick and Mae. "Where's Tree and Gina?"

"They went to Gina's house to pick up the twins for me. I-I have to tell them still. I haven't been able to…" Mae trailed off and stared down at her hands in her lap.

Feather Anne set a plate and a teacup in front of her sister, gave her a quick, one-armed hug, and ordered her to eat. "You'll need your strength for that. I'll be with you when you tell them, if you want."

"Thank you," said Mae. "I think—I think I'd like to tell them alone. I-I'm not sure yet. But thank you."

They watched as she moved food around the plate. Perhaps sensing their eyes on her, Mae looked up. "You're a bunch of little mother hens, aren't you? It's very sweet." She looked to Nick, then to Brandon, and said, "Feather Anne is very lucky to have you. Both," she amended.

Brandon's chest swelled. It was petty, he realized, but Mae had singled him out and added Nick as an afterthought, *Take that, dickhead.* He tried to wipe the smirk off his face before anyone saw it. Naturally, Nick saw it and shook his head. Disapproval? From *him*? Please. Yet, somehow, he felt chastised.

"Make yourselves a plate, guys. We'll eat with you, Mae," said Feather Anne.

Brandon was starving, so he didn't need any further encouragement. He couldn't give two shits if Amendola was hungry, so he paid no attention to him. With the way the chairs were situated around the island—three along the long side, two on each end with Mae in one of the end seats and Feather Anne beside her—Brandon hurried around the trays loading food onto his dish. He had to get back around to the chair beside Feather Anne before Nick did.

"All this has made my appetite not what it usually is," said Nick.

He snagged a slice of melon and sat next to Feather Anne. Nick eyed Brandon's full plate caustically. Neither Feather Anne nor Mae looked up, but Brandon's face heated, nonetheless. Nick chanced a sly smirk at him before resting his hand on Feather Anne's back.

"How you holding up?" Nick asked Feather Anne.

Brandon watched this, mute and furious. Feather Anne shrugged one shoulder, then she looked at Nick, eyes slitted.

Ha, she's going to call him out for making a move in front of me.

She said, "You haven't eaten anything since yesterday, have you?"

Brandon's jaw dropped. *Are you fucking kidding me? How can you not see what he's doing?* He said none of this, of course. Instead, he leaned his back against the counter and shoved a slice of cinnamon raisin bread in his mouth.

Chew, glare. Chew, glare. Smile sympathetically when Feather Anne looks up. Yeah, he'd stand there and take it because of the situation. But bull*shit* if he'd go sit at the far end of the island like some outcast.

The doorbell rang. Feather Anne, Mae, and Brandon all yelled, "It's always open." The trio grinned at one another. It was something they'd picked up from that tv show, Fuller House that Mae and Feather Anne watched religiously.

See, Amendola? I'm an insider here, not you. Take that, fuckface.

Bruce came in looking harried and rushed. "Sorry it took me so long. Tenants at the—eh, never mind. Everything went okay?"

He gave nods around the room and kissed Feather Anne and Mae's cheeks. The last part he directed at Mae.

Mae set the still empty fork down and gazed up at Bruce, eyes red-rimmed and round. "As well as," she let the sentence fall off.

"Yeah," said Bruce. He squeezed her shoulder. "I'm sure. Did you…" he jerked his head in Feather Anne's direction.

"Not yet. I waited for you."

"You want me to…"

"No, I'll… then you…"

They volleyed back and forth like this, driving Brandon a little crazy. What the hell were they saying-not saying? Feather Anne had a similar expression on her face. As for Amendola, he looked down and seemed to be waiting. *He* obviously knew exactly what was going on.

"All right," said Bruce.

Immediately following, Mae said, "Feather Anne, you're going to New York tomorrow. Nick is bringing you, as planned, and I won't take no for an answer."

Feather Anne looked from Mae, to Bruce, to Nick. Not at Brandon. To Mae and Bruce, she said, "N-no. I'm not." To Nick, she hissed, "You couldn't leave it alone, could you?"

"Sorry, Feather Anne, but no," said Nick. He didn't look at all apologetic.

Feather Anne spun back to Mae, standing now. "No way. You need me here. *I* need to be here. There's no fucking way I can go and sing on some stupid show. It's not like I have a chance of winning, anyhow."

And, damn himself, but for as heartbreaking as it was to hear her lie to herself and them, Brandon wanted to shout his agreement. How was he the only one who thought it would be wrong of her to go? The other three—Mae, Bruce, and the asshole—sat there stoically, waiting for her to run out of protests.

"Feather Anne," said Nick. "It's a once in a lifetime shot. You can't give it up."

"Yeah, I can," spat Feather Anne. She crossed her arms over her chest and glared. Her chin quivered.

"No, sweetie. You can't because I won't let you. William would want you to do this; I'm certain of that. So, do it for him."

"That's not fair," said Feather Anne. The tears were streaming down her cheeks now.

Bruce spoke up. "We are so damn proud of you, Feather Anne. This is a really big deal, kid. You gotta do it."

"Feather Anne, you're pissed at me, but they needed to know. This is, like, a life-changing thing," said Nick.

He touched her arm, and she didn't jerk away like Brandon had hoped. Brandon had to say something.

"Can't she try out again next year?"

It was the wrong thing to say. The second it left his mouth, he knew it.

"Dude, *next* year? It's the last season. There is no next year."

Nick's look was full of scorn and disgust. And God damn it, he was right to look at him like that. He, better than anyone there, knew exactly how much this meant to Feather Anne. His selfishness had shone through and now there was no backpedaling.

"Yeah, no. I…" *Fuck*. Feather Anne stared at him now, her expression full of hurt and something else. She looked at him like she didn't know him.

Mae spoke, cutting across the awkward silence. "Bruce is right, Feather Anne. I could punch you for not telling me about this yourself." She sighed. "But I understand. You asked me before if there was anything you can do for me. Well, this is what. You can go tomorrow, kick ass, and get yourself into the finals."

"But what about—"

"Everything is taken care of. You won't be missing anything," said Mae.

Understanding lit Feather Anne's face. "You moved the wake and the memorial for me."

Mae was noncommittal. "It was the better day for everyone," was all she would say. She stood. "Listen, I'm exhausted. I'd like to take a nap before they come back with Evvie and TK. No one minds, right?"

"Go on," said Bruce. "I'll show myself out. Nick, maybe you, uh, can come help your old man out at the house for a while?"

Brandon never liked Bruce more than in that moment.

Nick hesitated, caught the look in his father's eye, and nodded. He slung his useless guitar over his shoulder, tugged Feather Anne's sleeve like a little kid, and said, "I'll call you later, okay?"

"Yeah," said Feather Anne, not looking at him. Brandon began to gloat internally at her coldness toward him. She grabbed his wrist as he passed her by. "Nick?"

He stopped and looked back at her. Brandon watched this unfold like a scene from a movie. A horror movie.

"Thank you."

Two words. That was all she said, and yet it sounded like so much more to Brandon's burning ears. He watched on as her grip on his wrist lingered and their gazes locked. He watched as the tension in Nick's face softened. Brandon wanted to puke.

Bruce's eyes were on him—he sensed it—and he looked down at his still full plate. He walked it to the trash and let the contents slide into the pail. Then he busied himself with washing it in the sink. He wanted to cry.

It may have been a minute later, or maybe five, but he and Feather Anne were alone in the kitchen. He dried his hands and faced her. She'd been watching him. Her expression unreadable. Was this where they were at? Two people who'd always known each other's thoughts before they were spoken, now staring as if they'd never met before.

"So," he ventured, "you're going to New York in the morning?"

She picked at a napkin in the island. "You obviously don't think I should."

"I didn't say that." His tone was defensive; not what he was going for. He tried again. "I'm just surprised."

"Way to make me feel like shit, Brandon."

She picked up Mae's plate and stacked it on top of her own with a hard clack. At the sink where Brandon stood, she motioned him away and ran the water full force over the plates. Her every move was packed with bottled anger.

"I'm not trying to make you feel like shit, Feather Anne. I don't want you to do something you might regret." Why couldn't he stop himself from saying stupid shit?

She wheeled on him. "Something I might regret, or something you don't want me to do because you're jealous?"

"I told you. I'm fine with the Nick thing." He lied. She saw through him. And because the hole had been dug, he dug in deeper. "I mean, it would've been nice to hear from you that he was the one driving you there."

"Oh, you're fine, huh? Sure didn't seem fine when you were shooting daggers at him earlier."

She ignored the driving part.

"Me? What about *him*? He had that smug look on his face every time you looked away, Feather Anne. He was goading me. Jesus, what do you want from me? The guy is blatantly making a move on my girl, and I'm supposed to, what? Sit back and trust him to act right?"

With ice in her voice, she said, "You're supposed to trust *me*, Brandon. You're supposed to support me and… and be *happy* for me."

He raked his hand through his hair. "I *do*. I *am*. I've been nothing but supportive and you know it. Maybe this is your way of—of deflecting or something. I think you do have feelings for this guy, and you can't admit it."

There, it was out. It made him want to throw up, but it was out. They were going to do this, right here, right now. Sink or swim, break up or stay together. Either way, he needed an answer from her. It was either him or the dickhead.

"Are you fucking kidding me? *This* is what's on your mind right now? I just lost the man who was like a father to me, and you are suggesting I have *feelings for another guy*? Who *are* you?"

The only thing worse than the contempt on her face was the sheer, naked hurt he saw in her eyes. What was he doing? How had he messed up so badly, so irreversibly?

Before he apologized yet again, she said, "I think you should leave now, Brandon."

"Feather Anne, I—"

"Please. Just go okay?"

His throat scratched like sandpaper and his chest hurt. "Okay, okay. Can I call you later?"

Her voice had lost all its venom and now came out a low monotone. "I'll, uh, I'll probably be pretty busy. So—"

"No, yeah. I get it." He hesitated, hoping she come in for a hug at least.

She folded her arms and looked away. "See you Tuesday?"

"Yeah, yeah. Of course. Uh, good luck tomorrow."

Her head jerked in a nod. He read it as a sarcastic, *yeah, thanks a lot*, way. There was nothing more to say. He left her standing there in the kitchen.

It wasn't until he stood outside that he remembered he didn't have his car. There was no way he'd hang around like a loser on her porch. Brandon swore under his breath and began walking home.

22 Brianna

Brianna drove around town for an hour after dropping off Brandon at Mae's house. If asked, she couldn't explain how or why the news of William Grant's unexpected passing shook her so deeply. They weren't friends, nor colleagues. They certainly didn't travel within the same social circles. Yet she *was* shaken.

In fact, the news made her physically ill. Her heart actually hurt… for *Mae Huxley*. Oh, and her poor, poor children. How unfair. How cruel.

She'd internally railed against the universe for giving her breast cancer, yes. But—truth be told—there was a part of her that believed she'd brought it on herself. Like some kind of karmic energy. She'd dismissed the notion as abruptly. To allow for that possibility would mean an acceptance of a higher power. *No, thank you.*

God was not a concept she'd ever embraced thanks to the lovely, sociopathic, abusive parenting of the oh-so-devout Gordon Beaurdreau. No. Things that happened were a matter of chance and human design, and that was all.

Yet, she couldn't stop the lament for a man even she found near perfect. *William Grant.* What woman in Chance didn't have a secret—or not-so-secret—crush on the man? He was, for wont of a better word, dashing. Charming. Handsome in that old movie star way. The man was a modern-day Cary Grant, for fuck's sake. *Eat your heart out, George Clooney.* And now he was… he was *gone*.

Something tickled Brianna's cheek, and she brushed at it. Dampness. Tears. She hated crying, yet there she was, crying over a man she barely knew. And then, she sobbed. So much so, she had to pull over to the side of the road.

After a minute or two, she composed herself. One glance in the visor mirror told her she needed her makeup bag and a tissue. There had to be some in her console; she was a mother. None. Glove box?

She leaned over and had popped open the compartment when a knock on her window made her jump. Charlotte Asheby.

"Jesus, Charlotte. You nearly gave me a heart—" she stopped and gulped. Poor choice of words, given the latest events. Her damned chin quivered, and she quickly turned her head away.

"Brianna? Are you… what's wrong?"

She couldn't stop herself. "What's wrong? What's *wrong*? William Grant—he's… that's—oh, damn it. Why am I reacting like this?"

She pressed the one scrap of tissue—a Dunkin napkin, really—to her nose and shook her head.

Charlotte reached through the window and touched her arm. "Because you're human and William was a wonderful man."

"Yes, but we weren't even friends," said Brianna.

She felt like such an idiot. Worse, like an imposter, like someone trying to hone in on other people's grief. Which was so stupid because who the hell would want someone else's grief? Wasn't there more than enough to go around? *She* had enough, for sure. Fucking breast cancer. And, damn it, she' started crying again.

"Brianna, you've had a rough year and you've stayed pretty stoic throughout. I think this is your mind's way of saying enough is enough."

"You can say that again." Brianna sniffed.

"Listen, I'm on my way to Mae's now. Would… you like to come by?"

"Don't you think that'd be weird? Hypocritical, even? I mean, Mae and I are not exactly friends."

Charlotte hedged. "Well, no. That's true. But your brother and her sister have been dating since forever. Geez, they'll probably get married one day.

That'd make your families connected for real. Think about it at least."

"Well," Brianna sniffled again and pondered, "I *did* drop Brandon off over there earlier. And he *will* need to be picked up. So, I suppose it's not totally bizarre for me to come by."

She was awarded with a smile from Charlotte, who she'd noticed to appear as teary-eyed as Brianna. "Good, I'll see you there."

Brianna let Charlotte pass her and followed her car back to Mae's house. She spent the short ride devising a way to help the Huxley's. A fundraiser? No, William would likely had made sure to provide well for his wife and children. A benefit in his name for a charity. Yes, that's what she'd do.

She felt better already; having a plan and something to offer instead of the same old sympathies and regrets. The banner appeared in her mind's eye. *The William Grant Gala for…* for what, exactly? Brianna shrugged. There would be time to figure that part out.

By the time she'd parked her car back in front of Mae's house, she had it all planned out—from invitations to attire and everything in between. Now she had a purpose and a reason for being there. Still, she paused at the steps, unsure.

"Come on. She knows you're coming, and she's glad for it."

Brianna's eyebrow rose. "Really?"

"Yes," said Charlotte, looping her hand through Brianna's arm. "Come *on*."

The sight of Mae—her face scrubbed free of makeup, hair in a loose bun, eyes over bright—made Brianna's breath catch. She looked like her teenaged self. So young and vulnerable. The sight— horrifyingly—forced fresh tears to her own eyes.

Mae stood and came around the kitchen island to Brianna. She tipped her head to the side and came in for a hug. The two women—the two non-friend women—embraced as if they'd gone through all of life's hardships side by side.

"I'm so very sorry, Mae," whispered Brianna in Mae's ear.

She slipped from Brianna's embrace, grasped her arms above her elbows and nodded her thanks. Mae inhaled deeply, and on the exhale, said, "Wine?"

"Please," said Brianna.

The others—Lotus, Marisol, and Rosabelle— greeted her somberly, but not coldly. She sat in the chair pulled out for her by Charlotte and draped her purse over the arm.

Mae slid a glass of red her way and said, "I was telling everyone the plans for... William." She filled Brianna in on the details. Then she asked, "Do you think Brandon would want to say a little something at the memorial?"

"Oh, I'm sure. He must be around here somewhere. Let's ask him."

"Oh," said Mae. "No, actually he left about an hour ago."

"He did?" Brianna was surprised and hoped he and Feather Anne hadn't had a fight.

Mae confirmed her fears. "I'm afraid they may have had a falling out."

Brianna suspected it had to do with Nick Amendola and Feather Anne's singing competition. She started. *The competition.* It was tomorrow. What was going on? Did Mae know about it? Should she tell her?

"Mae," began Brianna tentatively. She looked around the room at the others. They eyed her curiously. "N-never mind. It's nothing." She waved her hand and took a gulp of wine.

Even though it didn't reach her eyes, Mae smiled. "It's okay, Brianna. I heard about the show. She's going. I insisted. It's what both William and I would have wanted for her."

"Oh, Mae. That is, wow. That is amazing," said Brianna. She was thrilled for Feather Anne, and also sorry for Brandon. "I'm guessing she's going with that *Nick*."

She was unable to hide the disdain from her voice.

"*That Nick* is my son," said a voice from the kitchen doorway. Mia Amendola leaned against the frame and stared at Brianna with an iciness that rivaled her own. "and he's a good kid. Despite what you or anyone else in this town might think."

Brianna bristled. "I'm sure he is. *Now*. Didn't he—oh, well, I guess it doesn't matter." She left the sentence dangle on purpose.

Charlotte spoke up next, ever the diffuser of tension. "Uh, Mae. Before I forget. Katie sends her love. She wanted to be here, too, but they're stuck upstate for one more day. Billy's dad isn't well."

The others all began talking, too. Mia shot glances Brianna's way but kept her mouth shut. For the most part, Brianna stayed silent throughout the evening, too. Her position as the outsider never escaped her, although the other women behaved inclusively. Except Mia.

"I can't really wrap my brain around it yet, but I want to do something in William's honor," Mae was saying at the other end of the table.

Brianna's ears perked. Here was her opportunity. "Like a benefit? A-a charitable event? Maybe a—oh, I don't know—a gala?"

Mae hesitated and Mia jumped in. "Probably more like a scholarship. Right, Mae?"

Mae looked around. "Oh, I-I'm not sure. Both ideas sound great."

Brianna straightened and said, "Mae, both are completely doable. Complimentary, in fact. The proceeds from the *gala* can to a *scholarship* in William's name."

Mae's smile was wistful. "I'd like that. William would like that. Something for aspiring writers?"

"Perfect," said Brianna. "You have so much on your plate, though. I tell you what. Let me take care of the details."

Mae looked understandably taken aback. "Oh, Brianna. I couldn't ask you to do that. It's too much. You have your own—"

"Nonsense. I want to do it. Your husband was—" her voice wobbled, "he was such a lovely man, Mae."

The room fell into silent agreement. The other women nodded and wiped tears from their eyes. Brianna saw that it was settled. She stood, lifting her purse from the chair.

"I really have to leave now, but we'll be in touch, Mae."

Mae walked her to the front door, and the women held hands for a moment. "Thank you, Brianna. This is so kind of you." She looked down. When she looked back up again, she was smiling. "William always thought you were a hot ticket. His words, mind you."

Brianna laughed. "A hot ticket, huh? I'll take it, especially these days." She looked skeletal and pale. No one had to tell her; the mirror never lied. But she was getting healthier every day.

She drove home, finally, to her family. In her own driveway, she allowed herself a moment to soak it all in. How God damn lucky she'd been in her cancer scare. How grateful she was that her odds were better than good. That she had her beautiful children and damn near perfect husband waiting for her behind those walls. And that now, she had a way to help a woman she'd always secretly admired.

23 Feather Anne

Breathe. Just breathe.

It was five-forty-three in the morning. Nick would be there at six-fifteen. Her bag was packed with everything she might need. Change of clothes. Extra shoes. Makeup, hairbrush, perfume, phone charger, pen, paper, gum, throat spray. She even had Band-Aids for just in case.

"Here, I packed you a cooler." Mae walked in wheeling a blue thermal bag the size of a small refrigerator.

"When the hell did you have time to do that?"

Mae shrugged. "Couldn't sleep."

Feather Anne hugged her sister. Her talk with the twins had gone as well as expected. Which meant it was devastating, and gut-wrenching, and awful. She knew this not because Mae told her, but because she couldn't speak about it when asked.

"Mae, I don't have to go today. I can—"

"You're going and you're going to be amazing. I'm just sorry I'm not the one going with you."

"I would've been too nervous with you there, anyhow," said Feather Anne.

It was true. Her big sister sang like a pro and the only reason she wasn't on some singing competition show was because she wasn't interested. Having Mae there, watching her sing, would only get Feather Anne twisted up and anxious that she was doing her sister proud.

Mae elbowed her and said, "Come on. I made you some herbal tea. Sit with me for a minute before you go."

Feather Anne didn't think she was capable of sitting still, but there was no way she'd tell her sister no. Not now, not anytime soon. Perhaps the tea would calm her down. They walked quietly down the hall, careful to not wake the twins, who Mae had decided to keep home for the week.

On the couch, Gina snored softly. Feather Anne cocked her head and looked at Mae. Mae rolled her eyes and mouthed, "Wait till we're in the kitchen,"

They took their mugs to the breakfast nook and spoke in whispers. "What's she doing out there?"

Mae shrugged. "She wants to be available in case we need her."

"Oh," said Feather Anne. "Well, that's sweet. Don't tell her I said so, though."

"Too late, little shit, I heard you. Anyone ever tell you two you suck at whispering?"

Simultaneously, Gina's daughters said, "So do you."

Gina pulled a mug from the cabinet and set to making herself a cup of tea. They sipped in silence as the clock above the sink ticked. Feather Anne checked both it and her phone at about thirty-second intervals.

"So, you nervous?" Gina stared over her mug at Feather Anne.

She resisted the urge to say, "Yeah, duh," and instead nodded.

"Eh," said Gina, "You'll slay them. No doubt in my mind."

"Mine, either," said Mae with a smile.

She looks so small and frail. I can't leave her today. Mae must've read it in her eyes. She shook her head almost imperceptibly and sat up straighter.

"I have a lot to do today," said Mae. "I'll be too busy for... for anything. Don't worry about me, Feather Anne."

Feather Anne bit the inside of her cheek. She didn't want to cry. She wouldn't cry. She pulled out her phone and checked for messages. One came through as she blinked rapidly at the screen. It was Nick, telling her he'd be there in five. She stood, sloshing her tea.

"Easy there, killer," said Gina with a smirk.

Mae stood with her and grasped her shoulders. "Deep breaths, sis. Do your warmups, don't overthink it."

"Warmups. Overthink. I mean, don't overthink. Right." She licked her lips. "I shouldn't go. I'm going to stay."

Mae spun her toward the door and gave her a gentle but firm push. "Oh, you're going. Call when you get there and text us when you can." Nick knocked once and entered. "And you, keep an eye on my sister, got it?"

Nick tipped an imaginary cap and said, "Yes, ma'am. Will do."

Gina handed Nick an envelope and said, "For gas and incidentals along the way. Drive safe."

"Aw, you don't have to—"

"I want to. Now, do like Mae said, take care of our girl and keep her safe."

Feather Anne rolled her eyes at them and gave Nick an apologetic shrug. His expression was earnest and not mocking. It made Feather Anne blush.

He took the cooler handle from her and his hand lingered over hers. "You ready?" His tone was low, conspiratorial.

She swallowed hard. "Mhm," was all she squeaked out.

Nick grinned. "All right, let's do this."

He jerked his chin at Mae and Gina as a goodbye and wheeled out the cooler. Her sister and mother took turns hugging Feather Anne and for once, she didn't grumble about the PDA's.

In the truck, they were quiet. Feather Anne bit her nails and Nick thumped the steering wheel in time to the music. When they turned onto the highway on-ramp, only five words had been exchanged.

Him: "Rateliff or The Lone Bellow?"

Her: "Rateliff."

As they reached New Haven, her favorite song came on and she had to sing along. Nick joined in, quietly at first. By the second chorus they were belting it out and smiling wide.

When it ended, he turned down the volume and said, "There she is."

"Yeah, yeah. It's nerves. And…"

"I know."

They fell silent again, but only until Feather Anne saw a rest stop sign. "Bathroom break and coffees?"

"Roger that," said Nick.

They fueled up, grabbed coffees, and stretched their legs. Feather Anne cracked her neck and looked around. Highway, cars, half bare trees. She couldn't help but imagine what life on the road would look like. This? Probably. Sure, it was bleak on an overcast day. But something about the open road called her name.

She saw herself in a tour bus, guitar in her lap, a notepad and pen on the little tour bus table, and her head against the cool smooth glass as she watched the world whoosh by. Writing lyrics and humming tunes. Impromptu singalongs with the band. Creating music that moved people.

"Yo, daydreamer. Ready to roll?"

"Yeah, let's go."

Within fifteen minutes they were back on the road. Feather Anne dug out her battered notebook and a pen and started writing.

"Whatcha got there?" Nick glanced over.

"Song. Possibly. Came to me when you called me Daydreamer." She sang what she had so far.

It didn't surprise her anymore how unself-conscious she'd become around Nick. He spoke her language. He understood her.

"I like it. Sing that last line again."

She did, and this time he joined in, adding a layer and depth to the words that gave her chills. By the time they passed under signs for New Rochelle, they'd written the whole song, and sung it twice while he drove, and she strummed his guitar. She wasn't great, but she'd gotten much better under his instruction.

"Holy shit, we're almost there." Feather Anne's heart fluttered.

"Yep. Ready or not, it's go time," said Nick. His hands were tight on the wheel and his eyes scanned the road and cars around them.

"You've never driven into the city before, have you?"

"Nope," said Nick.

"You want me to be quiet so you can concentrate?"

"Yep."

She clamped her mouth shut and resisted the urge to ask another question. It lasted about ten seconds.

"So, do you really think I have a shot? Like a real shot?"

"Yes, Feather Anne. I do." At a stop light he chanced a glance at her. "I really do."

Someone honked their horn, and he returned his serious gaze to the road. She returned hers to the window where she people-watched. Young and old, every color, shape, and size. Groups and lone walkers and bike riders. Cigarettes dangling from parted lips, stocky dogs on short leashes, women in heels, men in heels. Laughing, shouting, minding their own business, panhandling for spare change.

Unlike Mae, Feather Anne loved every bit of the city. From the ugly to the beautiful. And the veritable melting pot of ethnicities, races, and cultures that made up this living, breathing, pulsating city? Don't get her started on the lure and appeal of its diversity.

Chance, Connecticut—great as it was—checked very few boxes in that department. Feather Anne's exposure to different ways of life seemed woefully inadequate in her mind and never as starkly obvious as when she visited the city.

"I've never been here without Mae and William." The realization startled her. Saying it aloud startled Nick.

He jumped. "Jesus, Feather Anne."

She laughed—couldn't help it—and said, "Settle down, nervous Nelly."

"Yeah, yeah. Pull up that app you downloaded. The one with all the parking garage locations."

"But we're, like, ten blocks away."

"Do you seriously think we'll find any parking close by?"

Feather Anne tapped her chin. "Ah, yeah. Good point." A minute later she ordered, "Turn right up there. Parking garage on the left."

They paid an obscene amount of money to the attendant who leered at Feather Anne from bloodshot eyes.

"Yous here for the competition?"

Feather Anne—a girl born for the city—said, "What gave it away?" She had Nick's guitar slung over her shoulder.

The attendant shrugged and waved her away with a chuckle. "Smartass," he said. "Good luck to ya."

They walked fast up the block, or rather, Feather Anne walked fast, and Nick struggled to keep up. He lugged the cooler, along with his backpack, a blanket, and two pillows.

"Slow down, will ya? We're two hours early."

"Yeah, but I want to get to Rockefeller Center and find a spot to chill. It's going to get packed there quick."

Even she'd underestimated how early they should've been there. The place swarmed with guitar wielding, singing, strumming wannabe superstars. The sign-in tables were unmanned but surrounded. Every so often security guards dispersed them, only for them to line back up again moments later.

"This… is… insane," said Nick, spinning in a slow circle with his mouth agape.

Feather Anne's head swam and the intoxication of it all made her dizzy. Skyscraper buildings loomed over them. Men, women, girls, and boys milled and sat about. A cacophony of mingled sounds flooded her ears.

She took Nick's hand and squeezed it hard. "We're here, Nick. We're actually here."

"No turning back now, kid." He gave her a lopsided grin and held her hand tighter, as if she might try to escape.

"Nope. No turning back."

And she meant it. Now that they were actually there, in the heart of it, with television cameras and banners and chaos—it was like the song she'd planned to sing for the judges—wild horses couldn't drag her away.

"Come on. I see a slice of real estate over there we can sit and rehearse."

He yanked her across the courtyard to a building-side spot. A young girl and what appeared to be her mother flanked them on one side, and a pony-tailed man with a banjo on the other.

They exchanged polite, nervous hellos, and gave one another the once over. Everyone there represented competition. Still, in less than an hour, they sang songs together and for each other, exchanged stories and backgrounds, and followed each other on social media.

It had been Nick's idea for Feather Anne to create a community page on Facebook, as well as a YouTube channel where they'd been quietly uploading covers and original songs they'd worked on together. They were both called simply, Feather Anne - Musician.

She'd asked Nick to put his name on the page and channel, too, but he said the spotlight was hers and hers alone. He'd content himself with going along for the ride, as he liked to say.

Feather Anne suspected it had more to do with his own insecurity and self-doubt. She'd suggested it to him once, and he'd shut her down for the rest of the day, so after that, she kept quiet. Now she bided her time, waiting for the right way and the right time to push him forward like he'd done for her.

"So, are you two here as, like, a duo?" The young girl had shoulder-length, peacock blue hair and large, black-framed glasses through which she ogled Nick with blatant adoration.

"I'm here for support," said Nick.

"Oh, cool," said the girl. Her tone and moon-eyes suggested she thought it was positively swoon-worthy of him.

Feather Anne resisted the urge to tell her they weren't boyfriend and girlfriend but figured Nick would make her walk home if she did.

"So, let's hear the song you're going to sing," said the girl to Feather Anne.

"I—well, maybe—"

Nick saved her. "How about we do an original for you instead?"

He knew she wanted to save Wild Horses for the show, and she was grateful. "Yeah, good idea. Let's do your song, Nick," said Feather Anne.

He unzipped his guitar case. Once sure the six-string was in tune, he began playing and let Feather Anne take the first verse. When it reached the chorus, they sang together…

You don't know my heart
You don't know how I protected it
from the very start.

You don't know my soul
The darkest places that it can
sometimes go
Stay out of my space
It will only keep you safe, if you don't
know my heart.

Feather Anne became aware of a video camera in her face and stopped abruptly. Nick, as lost in the moment as she'd been, looked up.

"Holy..." Feather Anne whispered.

A broadly grinning man with perfect, immovable hair stood beside the cameraman. He clamped a hand on Nick's shoulder and beamed at them with teeth so white they glowed.

"Hey guys, great stuff, really great stuff. Here's what we're going to do."

Feather Anne stammered, "Y-you're John St. James. Host of Greatest American Singer."

Another sharky smile. "That's right, sweetheart, I am. And I'd like to have a feature segment on you. How about that?"

"That would be—"

He held a palm out at her. "Now, I can't promise it'll make the cut, but you've got as good a chance any anyone. Heck, even more so with your pipes... and looks." He winked.

Feather Anne blushed. Nick scowled. She kicked him. "Thank you so much, Mr. St. James."

"Call me John. What's your name, doll?

"Feather Anne Byrd. I'm seventeen, and—"

"Hang on," said John St. James. "Is that your real name or a stage name?"

"Uh, real. It's on my birth certificate if you want to see."

He exchanged a look with his cameraman, and if Feather Anne was as good at reading people as she thought she was, that look translated as meaning "Jackpot."

John St. James said "No, no need." "Here's the plan. I ask you some questions, you answer them. We take a little stroll through the park, get some candids, and voila. Done. Sound good?"

Feather Anne blurted, "Hell, yeah, that sounds good."

The absurdly perfect looking man gave her a twinkling eyed smile. "Oh, I like you, little Miss Byrd. And I think the camera is going to love you. And you, too, boyfriend boy. Let's get your deal, too. Spill it."

24 The Brightsiders

Georgie watched Mae and her two children walk down the street from the living room window. One hand pressed against her cheek, the other, her heart.

"Should I go out there, Charles? They look so... bereft."

Charles joined her, nudging aside the curtain for a better peek. "No, sweet wife. Let them have their time alone."

She sighed heavily; a wordless, reluctant agreement. "It's not fair, is it?"

"No, I can't say that it is," assented Charles. "Nothing fair or right about it."

She dropped her hands to her hips and frowned up at her husband. "Did you hear that awful Jilly Jarvis in the grocery line this morning?"

Charles grimaced. "I'd hoped *you* hadn't heard her. Best to ignore idle gossip."

"Idle gossip? It was worse than that, I'd say. What was it she said?" Georgie tapped her chin. "I remember. *What did she think, marrying a man so much older?* Charles, I had half a mind to throw our loaf of French bread at her."

Charles pictured such a scene and laughed. "Would've served her right. But I'm glad you restrained yourself, dear. You mustn't let people like her get under your skin. Brainless twits with nothing better to do than judge others."

"Yes, well. Glass houses, is what I say to them." Georgie tutted and brushed imaginary crumbs off her blouse.

Charles kissed his wife's temple and said, "Precisely. Now come have tea with me. It's been a rough few days and you're bound to get sick after the travel and the shock of William's passing." His eyes became red-rimmed. "Can't quite believe it myself yet."

It was Georgie's turn to offer comfort. "Come. I'll put on the kettle."

Somehow, they shared a sense of guilt. They were nearing eighty-one and eighty-three, respectively. Their lives were as busy and full as when they were young—perhaps more now that they had all the extended family to share it with. Health-wise, they'd both had their scares, but were overall fit and strong. Fortune had remained on their side.

Then, there was poor William. Poor *Mae*. To have been so happy and in love to only lose it so abruptly. Such a profound loss for one so young. Now, she would raise her children without her beloved husband and their doting father.

This wasn't to say they wished it were one of them rather than William... just that they also wished it wasn't him at all. They wished the same as anyone else for their loved ones. A life with more joy than pain, more happiness than sorrow, and more of that liquid, fickle thing named time.

"How fortunate we've been, Charles. If only the same fortune could be Mae's."

Charles expression read surprise. "Oh, but it has been, my bride."

"Nonsense," said Georgie. *Her* expression exclaimed disbelief.

"Now, now. Before you bite my head off, try seeing it another way. Mae has experienced great love. She's been—and is—loved greatly."

"You're not going to give me your favorite, the price of great love is—"

"Yes, that. Grief. I'm surprised at you, Georgie. You're usually more practical than this." His tone was gentle despite the reproach.

She relented, deflating against the kitchen chair. "I'm not in the mood to be pragmatic. I'm in the mood to be obstinate and angry. Otherwise, I'll have to be sad."

Charles reached across the table and patted his wife's soft, warm hand. "All right. Shall we go outside and smash some dishes?"

She laughed despite herself. "Break dishes? Where on earth did that come from?"

Charles shrugged. "Oh, something Lotus said about anger therapy. Or something like that. It's all the rage, they say. Axe throwing, plate smashing, and whatnot."

Georgie pondered the idea. "Doesn't sound quite so absurd right now. Although, at our ages, we'd probably break a hip or throw something out of the socket."

"You're right. Best to leave it to the young and angry," said Charles.

The doorbell rang and Rufus and Mabel barked excitedly.

"Do you think it might be Mae and the twins?" Georgie's face lit up.

The fourth generation of Keith Huxley's progeny—TK and Evvie—brought no less joy to the Brightsiders than the previous. The affection ran both ways; the twins couldn't get enough of Charles and Georgie.

"Only one way to find out, dear," said Charles.

Georgie nudged him aside and opened the door.

"Hello, sweethearts. Come in, come in," said Georgie.

Mae flushed and gave a pained look. "I'm so sorry to stop by unannounced. The twins insisted on stopping on our way back from our walk."

"Don't be silly. Our door is always open to you. You come anytime you want."

"Evvie, TK, what do you say?"

Evvie said, "Do you have ice cream?"

And TK said, "Can I play piano?"

Mae tried to affect a scolding tone when she reprimanded them, but Charles and Georgie's laughter overrode it and they bound into the house as if they owned it. Even Rufus and Mabel—normally less sociable now in their older age—trotted and wagged at the arrival.

"Come," said Georgie to the mortified Mae, "let Charles wrangle them. You and I will go in the kitchen."

Mae followed Georgie, offering more apologies and calling warnings to the children to behave.

Once she'd sat down, Mae asked, "So, how *are* you? I'm afraid with... with all our..." She gulped and tried again. "I haven't asked about your cruise or how you're feeling, or anything."

Oh, how the girl broke Georgie's heart. So typical of her; in the worst days of her young life, and she was asking how others were doing. She stared at Mae a beat, then asked, "Tea or wine?"

When Mae hesitated, glancing out the toward the living room, Georgie added, "It's one glass, sweetheart. I think you've earned it, hmm?"

Mae's smile was self-deprecating. "Half a glass?"

Georgie nodded and poured for both of them and sat next to her. "It seems absurd to ask how you're doing. So, instead, I'll ask you what we can do to help you through this?"

Mae looked down, her brow furrowed, and she fiddled with her wine glass. "That's it, though. There's nothing. Nothing anyone can do to—no, that sounds so ungrateful. What I mean is--"

"I know what you mean, dear. No one can take away the pain. But I'm afraid they—we—are going to try. It's human nature. When someone we love is hurting, we want to make it better at fast as possible. Bear with us."

Mae's head bobbed almost imperceptibly. They sipped their wine and listened to Charles teach the twins their scales on the piano. TK seemed to have a natural affinity for it, whereas Evvie liked to sing. Just like her mother, sister, and grandmother.

Georgie waited and watched as Mae inhaled, held her breath, and released it through her mouth. There was something she wanted to say, and Georgie had to be patient.

Mae finished her glass and set it down with light plink. "William wrote letters for each of us. Me,

Feather Anne, the twins. James found them in William's office. He gave them to me on Saturday. I-I haven't opened them or told anyone yet."

"Oh, my sweet. How lovely *and* how heartbreaking."

"Do you think I'm a coward for not opening mine?"

"A coward?" Georgie was taken aback in earnest. "Not at all, Mae. Not at *all*. It's been three days since you lost your husband unexpectantly. It's been a whirlwind and you've barely caught your breath. Tomorrow and Wednesday are going to be very difficult. So, you read it when you're strong enough to, and not a second before."

Mae's breath came out ragged. "Thank you, Georgie. I'm not sure if I can handle it. I've been holding myself together, but it is by threads." Her voice trembled. "By *threads*, Georgie."

"And when those threads unravel, we'll be here, sweetheart."

"I know you will. Thank you."

"Has Feather Anne read hers?"

"No. I think I did something stupid. You know she left this morning for New York?"

"Yes." Georgie smiled. "She told us about it right after you insisted that she go. I think she wanted a second opinion from you-know-who out there." Georgie inclined her head toward Charles on the other side of the wall.

"I take it he backed me up, otherwise I'd have heard about it."

"It was a no-brainer. And so very gracious of you to send her, might I add."

Mae shrugged off the praise. "Yeah, well, I don't regret it, that's for sure. I do, however, regret slipping her letter into her backpack. She'll recognize William's handwriting—it was so perfect, and we often teased him for it—so she can decide whether to open it."

"Oh, my," said Georgie.

"Crap. It *was* a bad idea. What was I thinking? What if she reads it before she sings, and she cries so much she can't sing? It'll be all my fault." Mae covered her face.

"Okay, okay. Easy, now. I'm not saying it was a bad choice. Perhaps it will inspire her. Or, maybe she won't see it until after. Listen, what's done is done. Everything will be all right, you'll see."

Georgie wished she was as confident as she sounded. Feather Anne, with her tough exterior and devil may care attitude was, deep down, a sentimental girl who adored her surrogate father. Just as Mae locked her emotions in a box to protect Feather Anne and the twins, she'd been doing the same for Mae. Their quiet devotion to each other touched everyone who witnessed it those past several days.

"I should be there with her," said Mae.

"And if circumstances were different, you would have been. Let's not dwell on what's out of our control, but on what we *can* do."

"Yeah? What's that?" Mae sniffed and eyed her skeptically.

"Pray," said Georgie.

Mae blinked at Georgie, who stared back with unwavering conviction. It was hard to argue against. Charles had told Georgie so enough times in the past to make the older woman confident.

Mae searched Georgie's eyes and after a pause, she straightened and said, "Okay. That's what we'll do."

25  John St. James

"Bobby, are you seeing what I'm seeing?"

The cameraman tilted his head to see around the camera. "Yep. On it."

"Good. Count me down."

Bobby did as instructed, and on one, John St. James gave the camera his half-million-dollar insured smile. "All right, guys. We are here in the one and only Rockefeller Center with hundreds of musicians from all walks of life. Each of them waiting and hoping for their shot at the big time."

John St. James swept his arm out to illustrate his point and Bobby panned the crowd. He stopped and zoomed in on a gorgeous, leggy girl and her guitar strumming boyfriend. He zoomed back out and John St. James came back into view.

"Behind me is one such hopeful. What do you say we get to know her?"

"And cut," said Bobby.

"How was that?" John St. James rested his hands on his hips, tipped his head up, and let the makeup artist freshen up his face.

"Looks good; perfect intro for the taped segment."

"Should be a good one. If my gut is right, it'll be worth its weight in gold."

26 Miles

"I feel like… like everything I've been going through these pasts month is, like, trivial compared to what's happened to Mae."

Dr. Hannah gave Miles a brief smile and clasped her hands on her lap. "Mae is a friend, correct?"

Miles nodded. "Yeah. Salt of the earth. Good people. She owns the café in Chance."

"Oh," said Dr. Hannah with a frown. "I know the place. Best quiche I've ever had in my life." She caught herself. "I'm sorry. Something has happened to her, and it's causing some feelings of imposter syndrome?"

"Yeah, exactly. I feel like I'm a faker, or over-dramatic. Jesus, the woman lost her husband, and here I am whining about feeling sad. He was a lot older, by the way."

"Oh, my. Yes, that is tragic news. But, Miles, comparing these things is not beneficial. You can have reactions and emotions about your life, and about your friends' loss without invalidating one or the other."

"I guess. I think it makes everything else seem so small in comparison."

"Well, perspective is a wonderful thing to have. When we empathize with others and their experiences, we tend to have a better point of view on our own issues."

"Doc, I'm confused. Comparing is bad, but also good?"

Dr. Hannah smiled again. "Comparing is bad, having perspective is good."

Miles sighed and ran a hand through his hair. He understood. He didn't like it. Any of it. He said as much.

Dr. H. cocked her head at him. "I see you're feeling very distressed. Is it because of your friend, or something more?"

"It all makes me feel small. Like nothing we do *matters*. This guy—the husband—had everything going for him. *Everything*. Now it's gone. Poof. Just like that. Not a damn thing anyone can do about it."

"Interesting. You said *the husband had everything going for him*. I've heard you say this before... about yourself."

"Have I?" Miles glanced skyward. "Yeah, I suppose I have." He shrugged. "Well, it's true, isn't it?"

"By conventional standards, yes. But that's not where I'm going with this. Do you see yourself in a similar scenario? Dying *before your time*, so to speak?"

Miles looked down and nodded. "Yeah. I do. I've imagined a bunch of time. I, uh, pictured it so clearly it made me freaking cry. Pretty sure that's not one of the stages of grief, huh?"

The doctor set aside her notepad. "The stages of grief are, in a way, a fallacy. Not a deliberate one, mind you. But one who's original intent revolved around the terminally ill, and how they processed their emotions. There is no linear path and no *right* way to grieve."

Miles hands flew up, pushing away the direction of the conversation. "I-I don't even know why I used that word. Grief. I'm not *grieving*. I didn't even know William very well."

He tried to laugh, but it hitched in his throat and he forced a cough so he wouldn't cry. His reaction baffled and embarrassed him. The doctor watched and waited for Miles to say more; her owl eyes searching his face and taking stock of his body language. Miles sipped his water and stalled.

Doctor Hannah decided to cut him some slack, it seemed. "Miles, you *are* grieving. You're grieving several things, in my opinion, and yes, one of them is the death of a friend."

She raised a hand to ward off his rebuttal and continued. "You said he wasn't a close friend, but his death affects you. And that is okay, Miles. Give yourself permission to grieve."

Miles' head moved up and down. He sniffed. "It sucks."

"Yes, it does," said Dr. H. Their time was up and she walked Miles to the door. "Finding a way to help the bereaved often gives a sense of purpose," she offered.

"Yeah," said Miles, thoughtful. "Good idea. Thanks, Dr. H."

Miles left her office feeling—if not better—more focused and resolved. He would do something special for Mae, thereby making himself feel better, too. But what?

27 Feather Anne

Feather Anne's heart pounded violently against her chest long after John St. James moved on. Hundreds of people, and he'd singled *her* out of the crowd. It had to be a sign.

"Right?"

Nick looked up from his guitar. "Right, what?"

"I said, it has to be a sign," said Feather Anne. She gave him a shove with her boot.

"Uh, you didn't say that." Nick stared blankly at her.

"I did. Oh, I thought it. Whatever. It's a sign. I think." She started to doubt her conviction from seconds before.

"Okay, Feather Anne, chill. I can't say whether it's a sign, but I do know it was a good thing. He's coming back in, like, ten minutes to do the interview, so grab your notepad and jot down some things you want to say. It'll help you remember and not freeze up."

Feather Anne stuck her tongue out at Nick, but still rummaged around her backpack for her notebook. When she slipped it out, an envelope fell into her lap. She lifted it, frowning. She smirked. It would be from Mae, of course. A *go get em* note. She turned it over to see if anything was written on the front.

When she saw the handwriting, her nose and eyes prickled. *William.* William had written something to her before he died. But when?

"Whatcha got there?" Nick eyed her and tried to see the writing. "Let me guess. Brandon?"

She looked up at Nick, her eyes red-rimmed. "No. William."

Nick's neutral expression melted into one of sympathy. He set his guitar aside and slid next to her. She let him drape his arm around her shoulders and pull her to his side.

"Shit, wow. Are you…"

Feather Anne stared at her name in William's handwriting, blinking rapidly. "I-I don't know if I can. Shit. I don't know if I can't *not*."

If she couldn't hold back tears at the sight of his handwriting, how would she keep it together reading his letter? She'd been looking for signs non-stop that she'd made the right choice in going to the show; might this be the real one she'd been seeking?

"Well, whatever you—" Nick began.

"I'm going to read it," said Feather Anne already carefully lifting the seal.

Nick gave her space. He rubbed her back once and scootched back to his spot across from her. Feather Anne took several deep breaths and tried to steady her heart. But the first line did her in.

Hello, my girl.

If you're reading this… well, we know the rest of that sentence, don't we? Feather Anne, I remember it like yesterday, the first time I saw you outside the café. A feisty little waif; audacious and yet vulnerable. Even then, I saw great things in store for you.

Allow me to say that you have not disappointed. In fact, I could not be more proud of the brilliant, kind, gifted, and beautiful young woman you've become. Being a small part of raising you has been one of the greatest honors of my life.

My wish for you is that you realize your dreams and goals and never lose sight of who you are and who you are loved by. The big world is calling you, but know home is always there waiting for you. I wish also that you know great love, as your sister and I have. Without it, life is hollow. Let deserving people in, my dear. Regret is only in not taking chances.

And speaking of chances… I know all about the audition and the show. Silly girl, trying to keep such a marvelous thing to yourself! How, you're wondering? I may or may not have held the postcard with your acceptance up to the light. Sorry… or as you like to say, sorry, not sorry. I refuse to use the absurd 'hashtag,' though. It's a pound symbol for Christ's sake.

I digress. Know this. No matter what happens, I am so very proud of you. I always have been, and I always will be. If this competition is important to you, then give it your all. However, also know it does not define you or decide your chances at achieving your goals.

There is so much more I wish I could say. So many nuggets of hard-won wisdom to pass along. But these are things you must learn for yourself for them to matter. My advice to you, is this: enjoy the journey. Take it all in and live each moment as fully as you can. Try to not have regrets. Be authentic. Love with your whole heart.

These are things I've strived to do my whole adult life. My reward—deserved or not—has been my beautiful family. That I must leave you all is my one and only regret. Take care of each other and of yourself.

Finally, this little trinket was a gift from my mother when I was a lad. I leave it with you now and hope it serves as a reminder that you can always find your way home, no matter how far you roam.

Love always,
Your William x

With shaking hands, Feather Anne lifted the envelope again, and the object inside slid to the corner. She tipped the paper and a round, metal disk fell into her open palm. A small compass, pointing true north. She used the back of her hand to swipe away the free-falling tears and clasped the compass to her chest.

"Here," said Nick, passing a leather string to her.

Feather Anne slipped the end of the string through the hole at the top of the compass and tied it around her neck. She thanked him and folded the letter back up.

A shadow fell over them. John St. James and his crew. In a sappy-sweet voice—and with the camera trained on their faces—John St. James said, "Hey, sweetheart. Tell me about what's in that letter."

Feather Anne's natural impulse was to recoil from such an invasive question, but Nick caught her eye and conveyed his warning wordlessly. She took a breath and forced a smile.

"It, uh, it's a letter from my brother-in-law. He and my sister pretty much raised me." She waited until the quiver in her chin ceased. "He died on Friday. So, yeah…"

A long silence followed, then John. St. James said, "Let's cut here, huh? Give her a minute."

A pointy woman—pointy nose, chin, elbows, like an emaciated scarecrow—hissed, "Cut? Are you serious? This is—"

"Who's the executive producer, Gloria? Oh, wait, me," said John St. James, "and I say *cut here*. The girl will still be upset in five minutes, so calm down."

Feather Anne tried to smile at him to show she was grateful. He shook his head. "We're sharks, but we're not piranhas. Listen—wait, how old are you again?"

"Seventeen. I'll be eighteen in June."

John St. James rubbed his forehead with his fingertips. "Tell me you have a guardian with you."

"I do. Him." She pointed to Nick, who smiled crookedly and waved.

"Him? The boyfriend?"

Feather Anne blurted, "He's not my boyfriend. He's the legal adult I brought to supervise me. I have a letter from—"

"Okay, okay. As long as legal cleared it, we're good. So, here's the deal, Feather Anne. This—your personal drama—makes excellent television. Some might call it exploitive. In fact, some have. So, I want you to decide if you're okay with this airing. Once you sign the release, it's ours to use or not use."

Feather Anne looked to Nick for guidance. He shrugged and stammered, "I-I can't make that call for you, Feather Anne."

"Well, technically, you can," chimed in John St. James.

Nick gave him a sardonic stare before returning his attention to Feather Anne. "Whatever you want. I got your back."

She squeezed her eyes shut and pursed her lips. Then she left the first words that came to her mind burst from her lips. "All right. Let's do this."

For most of the morning, Bobby the camera man and his assistant followed Feather Anne around. There were other contestants she saw with a cameraman and assistants trailing them and she understood that at least some of them would be used in promo clips for the show and on the show itself. It would all depend on who made the cut.

Once Feather Anne signed in and took her number—she was contestant forty-seven, much higher on the list than expected—she and Nick found a place to sit inside the auditorium. They made friends with a few other contestants and formed a loose alliance in which they promised to cheer for one another, It was the first time Feather Anne had ever been comfortable with her peers. She fit in.

All too soon—and not soon enough—her number and name was called. "Number forty-seven. Feather Anne Byrd. Come on up."

Her legs wobbled like wet noodles and she wanted to throw up.

"You got this, Feather Anne," said Nick.

The others shouted their own well wishes and encouragement. She smiled a shaky smile, wiped her hands on her jeans, and climbed the stairs to the stage.

The lights were brighter and hotter than she'd anticipated. Everyone in the auditorium look like a sea of shadows. Except the four judges—R&B recording artist and five-time Grammy winner Aisha Grant, Country music star, Brett Handler, actress, model, and singer Viki, and producer and label owner of Next Records, Sebastian Bane—sat on a well-lit dais. They all started leaning into each other and whispering.

Finally, Sebastian Bane said, "Tell us about yourself, love."

She tucked her hair behind her ears and tried to smile. "Right. Sure. I, uh, I'm Feather Anne Byrd and I'm seventeen. I grew up in Chance, Connecticut, and, uh, yeah… that's it, I guess."

"Sorry," said Aisha Grant, "Did you say your name is Feather Anne *Bird*? Child, who thought that was a good idea?"

There was a ripple of laughter through the auditorium. Before she responded, Viki drawled, "Aw, stop, now. Come on. I love your name, Feather. Tres chic."

Brett Handler tried to get a word in, but Sebastian spoke over everyone. "All right, all right. Let's get on with it shall we? What are you going to sing for us, love?"

Feather Anne licked her lips. "Wild Horses? By The Rolling Stones?"

"Are ya asking us, or telling us, darlin'?" Brett Handler guffawed and winked at her. "Just teasin' ya. Go on and sing."

"Hold up," said Sebastian, "are you doing this acappella, love?"

"Well, I have my friend with me. He, uh, plays guitar. But the lady at the sign-in said I couldn't bring him up with me unless he's a contestant, so..."

"Aw," said Aisha, "that don't seem fair. Let's bring him up."

Sebastian argued, "He's not a contestant, Aisha."

Viki piped in, "Can he sing, sugar?"

Feather Anne exclaimed, "Yes, yes he sings great."

"Very well. Make him a contestant, too."

The foursome bickered back and forth loudly until, at last, Sebastian let out an ear-piercing whistle and shouted, "Enough." Everyone shushed. He paused theatrically, staring hard at Feather Anne, who'd begun twisting her ring around and around. "Let him play."

Feather Anne jumped and shouted, "Nick, get your ass up here," and everyone laughed.

Minutes later, she and Nick shared the stage; he on a stool slightly behind her, her standing behind a microphone stand. She looked back at him and nodded once.

When the song was over, no one moved, no one spoke. The silence made her ears throb. Feather Anne shifted her weight from one foot to the other. She stared at Sebastian, knowing he held all the power.

"Hang on a sec," said Sebastian. "Lou? Turn our mics off for a moment, will you?"

The foursome conferred. There was some head shaking, a fist thump on the table, then Aisha and Viki high-fived. Sebastian gave a faceless person in the sound booth a thumbs up signal.

"Ah, Nick is it?"

"Yes, sir," said Nick. His gaze was so calm, Feather Anne couldn't help but marvel. Neither could Sebastian Bane.

"You're pretty relaxed up there, son."

Nick shrugged one shoulder. "Yeah, well, I'm not really in the spotlight here, so…"

"And what if you *were* in the spotlight? How would you feel then?"

"Uh," said Nick, "Dunno."

A chorus of chuckles spread across the room. "Okay, let me try this another way. Would you like to try out for the show, right here and now?"

Nick started to say no, but Feather Anne spoke quicker. "Yes, he would. He's got an original song, too. Can we sing it for you?"

"Hell, yes," shouted Viki.

"Well, I've clearly lost control of this show already," declared Sebastian. He threw his pen in the air in what Feather Anne hoped to be mock frustration. "Go on, you two, sing your song."

Nick glared at Feather Anne, and she mouthed, "Play, damn it."

He hesitated so long that the crowd began to chant, "Sing, sing, sing," until he raised his hand and shouted, "Okay, I'll do it, geez."

Feather Anne grinned at him and said, "You take the lead, I'll jump in on the chorus."

"But that's not the way we—"

"Just do it, Nick."

He sighed and tuned his guitar. A hush fell over the room, as if they knew something special was coming their way. Then, they sang.

You broke into my soul
You covet what you stole
What was the reason?
I locked out what you seek
Afraid that love would peak
Then be out of season.
One glance into your eyes,
And I drop the thin disguise

You don't know my heart,
 You don't know how I protected it
 from the very start.
You don't know my soul,
The darkest place that it
can sometimes goes.
Stay out of my space
It will only keep you safe,
 if you don't know my heart.

I could blindly forge ahead
Pay no attention to the dread
 if I was to hurt you.
 It's better just to say,
that it was meant to be this way
and take God's cue
One glance in your eyes
And I dream about another try

But, You don't know my heart,
You don't know how I protected it
 from the very start.
You don't know my soul,
The darkest place that it
 can sometimes go.
Stay out of my space
It will only keep you safe,
if you don't know my heart.

Something tells me this might be forever
But I'm not sure
 you won't find something better...
Girl, stay out of my space
It will only keep you safe,
 if you don't know my heart.

After the last notes played, the hush remained. There was the scrape of a chair, and Brett Handler was standing and slow clapping at the duo. Viki joined him, and Aisha—though still sitting—clapped, too. The auditorium erupted with applause. Only Sebastian sat quiet.

Feather Anne and Nick's eyes were locked on him and him alone. They watched as he tapped his pen against his lower lip. They watched as he pivoted his chair around to see the rest of the room. They watched as he slowly stood up, clamped his pen between his teeth, and joined in on the applause.

"Very well done, you two," said Sebastian when the noise quieted. "Off you go, now. You've got some time before we announce who's moving on to the next round, so go amuse yourselves, or whatever."

They were dismissed. Together, Feather Anne and Nick walked off the stage and were shuttled into another room. Bobby the cameraman was back, and he followed them. Clearly, he'd be recording when they learned their fate.

28 Bruce

Bruce squinted at his reflection in the long mirror in the tailor's dressing room. Antonio—the tailor—squinted around his shoulder.

"You like, yes?" Antonio moved in front of him, tugging, brushing, and adjusting the suit. "It fit good, no?"

"Yeah, Antonio, it'll do." Seeing Antonio's expression, he added, "Sorry, you did a great job, especially on such short notice. I'm not a suit guy."

The tailor adopted a sympathetic frown. "Yes, yes, but times like these..."

Bruce needed no reminder of why he stood in front of a tailor's mirror in a suit he'd rather remand back to its prison in the back of his closet. William's wake that night, and memorial on the following morning dominated his thoughts all weekend and throughout Monday.

The chimes over the shop's door jangled and Antonio excused himself. Bruce changed out of the suit and back into his jeans, boots, and flannel shirt. As he walked down the narrow hall toward the front of the shop, he heard Antonio speaking with a familiar male voice. *No, anyone but...*

"Hannaford," said Bruce with a curt nod.

"Grady," returned Miles as coolly.

If this asshole make one snarky fucking comment that I'm must be glad Mae's on the market again, I swear to God...

"How's baby Mae holding up?"

Bruce took his wallet from his back pocket and slid his credit card out. He handed it to Antonio and said, "As well as can be expected."

Here it comes.

"Rosie's been crying on and off for days. To be honest, I'm off my game, too. William was a great guy."

Bruce cleared his throat and took his card back from the tailor. "Yeah, that he was." And because Miles had behaved so uncharacteristically normal, he added, "I'm, uh, having a hard time with it, too."

Miles shook his head. "It fucking sucks, man. One minute you're here, living your life. The next..."

Bruce heard the tremor come into Miles' voice and to his horror, his eyes began to sting, too. "You aren't fucking kidding, man."

Neither man looked at the other, but Antonio's eyes darted back and forth between them. "I get for you your suit, Mr. Hannaford. Is ready. Mr. Grady, I get yours, too."

When the older man left, an awkward silence filled the small storefront. Miles and Bruce spoke at the same time.

"You going to—"

"Mae said you're—"

They laughed and gestured for the other to speak. They both talked simultaneously again.

"Jesus," said Bruce with another laugh.

"Yeah, right?"

"Yep. Mae asked me to say something at the memorial. You?"

"I am indeed. You… ever do that before?" Miles looked at Bruce, then away.

"Speak at a memorial? Yes, once. Back when my uncle died. Shit, that was, like, twenty years ago."

"Did you—I mean, was it… shit, I don't know what I'm trying to say."

"Was it hard? Like, did you—"

"Okay, here is for you, Mr. Grady. And here is for you, Mr. Hannaford."

Saved by the tailor.

The two not-friends walked out onto Main Street together and stood there for another awkward moment. Miles car was parked behind Bruce's about six buildings up the street. They would have to either walk together or come up with a passable excuse—another errand, perhaps—to avoid furthering the awkwardness.

"Well, I gotta—" began Bruce.

"You wanna grab a beer?" Miles gestured to Lucky Lu's, then he must've registered what Bruce started to say. "Another time, I—"

"No, uh, yeah. Sure. A beer is good."

What? Wait, no. A beer? With Miles Hannaford? *Crap.*

Too late to back out. The pair checked traffic and crossed the street; suits slung over their shoulders for lack of anything better to do with them. Inside, they hung them on the coat rack and sidled up to the bar. Loo herself faced them from the other side; her eyebrows raised as she looked from one to the other.

"Fancy seeing you two here on a Tuesday afternoon. Together."

Miles and Bruce stammered the beginnings of an explanation, but Loo held her hands up to stop them. "Whatever, boys. People come in, do what they do, say what they say, and as far as I'm concerned, it stays here. I'm like a priest, or no, a therapist."

Loo flushed and at and away from Miles quickly. Bruce caught the look, and the tightening of Miles' expression.

"I'll take an Ultra, Loo," said Miles.

"Uh, make that two, will ya?" Bruce still puzzled between the two. When Loo moved down to the far side of the bar, he asked, "What was that all about?"

Miles swiveled on his seat and gave Bruce a sardonic stare. "Come on, really? Like you don't know." He scoffed and shook his head.

Bruce threw his hands out, palms up. "Dude, no idea. You gonna spill it, or what?"

Miles didn't let it go. "You mean to tell me Brianna Baker hasn't shared my business with the whole town?"

"Brianna Baker? I don't even talk to her. Not if I can avoid it, I mean. Hey, if there's gossip around about you, I'm not in the loop. What can I say?"

"Ricky Baker, then." Miles still wasn't ready to give up.

Loo set the beers in front of them and moved back to the far end of the bar. Bruce lifted his beer and gestured for Miles to raise his.

"To keeping our private lives out of Brianna Baker's gossip mill."

"A-fucking-men to that," said Miles.

They tapped bottles together and drank. After, they sat for several minutes in silence, neither knowing what to say next.

Bruce tried out a mutually appreciated topic. "The Pats are having a good start to the season. No surprise, though. Brady is—"

"I'm in therapy," said Miles. He kept his eyes trained on the television above the bar, even when Bruce's head jerked in his direction.

"Oh," said Bruce. His brow creased. *Had* he heard that? He couldn't recall.. But even if he had, why the hell would he care? Or judge, for that matter. "Well, good for you, man."

Miles snorted a laugh making it clear he thought Bruce didn't mean it.

"Seriously," said Bruce. "My folks got marriage counseling after they got back together. My dad was kind of against it at first, but after he said it was the best thing he'd ever done for himself and his marriage. So, if you ask me, I think it's a cool thing you're doing for you and your family. That's manning up, right there."

"Means a lot. Thank you, man," said Miles.

The two men had this exchange while looking up at the tv, and never once at each other. Because that's how men had conversations involving feelings and emotions; by not showing any of either.

Bruce finished his beer, ordered them another round, and finally looked at Miles, who appeared to be considering what he'd said. Man, he'd spent a long time despising the guy. But this was a different Miles Hannaford than the one he'd known since childhood.

This Miles held a conversation for longer than ten seconds. This Miles actually acted like he had a heart and half a brain. He was someone Bruce could, well, have a beer or two with. His wife was a doll, his kids, adorable. The fact that the guy was living the life Bruce wanted didn't escape him, either.

"I envy you, man," said Bruce unexpectedly. But he'd said it, so there it was.

"Me? No shit, huh? Why?" Miles looked at him as if he were crazy.

"Dude, you're living the dream. You got the whole package. Your own business, beautiful house, kids, dog, and the best girl in town besides…"

He swallowed and looked away. *Shit*. Well, there was the opening Miles had probably waited for. *Here comes the mockery*. He'll finish that sentence and lay on the taunts.

Miles did finish Bruce's sentence, but no mocking followed. All he said was, "Mae is a great girl. My freaking heart breaks for her, man. It's good that she's got you to lean on. She'll need people around who love her and know her best."

Bruce was speechless for a moment. Had Mile been secretly in love with Mae? Miles must've read his thoughts.

"And, no Grady. I'm not in love with Mae. I love her, but I've never been in love with her. Not like you have."

Bruce looked up sharply, but there was no teasing in his tone. He meant it purely and simply as a statement of fact. And understanding.

Miles yammered on. "Listen, me and you have never been tight, and that's my fault. I've been a real dick to you over the years. Truth is, I was always jealous." Miles shrugged at his confession. "I came in second after you all the damn time, man."

"Well, you're sure beating me now," said Bruce.

"All I'm saying is—this whole William thing, man—it's got me thinking about a lot of stuff. And mostly, I just want to, like, do better. *Be* better."

Bruce nodded slowly. He got it. His thoughts had been much the same, really. "It's that whole, *life is short*, thing. I get it. I'd be lying if I told you this hasn't shaken me up, too."

"I wish there was something I could do for her, man. I mean, something besides all the usual stuff."

"Well," said Bruce, squinching one eye, "someone is organizing a benefit at the end of October."

Miles' shoulders slumped. "Let me guess. Brianna Baker."

"Yeah. Guess even she's affected."

"How about that, huh? The Ice Queen thaws. Shit, I can't even say that without feeling like an ass."

"Oh, right," said Bruce, suddenly remembering Brianna's cancer scare. "Shit, man. This is what getting older is about."

"What," snorted Miles. "Getting sick, dying suddenly—"

"No, asshole. Being more sensitive to that stuff."

"Oh. Right," said Miles. He motioned for Loo. "Speaking of being more sensitive, I guess we should get our asses off these barstools and get ourselves ready for tonight."

"Yeah, you're right. It's on me," said Bruce, pulling out his wallet. "Well, I'm off to pick up a bunch of pictures Mae had printed up for tonight."

"You buy the next time," said Miles, dropping a twenty on the counter and waving to Loo.

Next time? Eh, that wouldn't be so bad, I guess.

Miles looked at Bruce and snapped his fingers. "I've got it. I know what I can do for Mae. You mind if I pick up those pictures instead?"

Bruce shrugged. "Uh, yeah, sure. They're under Mae's name."

They still had no choice but to walk to their cars together, but they kept to bro code and maintained a two-person space between them. At Miles' car, they stopped.

"All right, man," said Bruce, "see you in a couple hours."

"Yeah. See you there." Miles reached out his hand.

Bruce looked down at it, then shook it. Their first handshake since… ever. Hell, it only took them nearly twenty years, therapy, and a death to get them there, but, hey. It happened. Miles Hannaford and Bruce Grady were now—if not exactly friends—not enemies.

Bruce's first impulse was to call Mae and say, "You'll never guess what just happened," but that wouldn't be appropriate. It would be insensitive and selfish as fuck, was what it would be.

Feather Anne's words in the hospital came back to him. *He's not even in the grave yet, and you're making a move.* Every time he saw Mae after, that played in his head. When he anticipated Miles' snide remarks—remarks that never came—had it been because of his deep-seated guilt?

He tried in vain to tamp down the feeling with denial and busyness. What he'd admit to no one ever, was that Feather Anne's accusation wasn't wholly unfounded or undeserved. There was a small fire in his heart—one he'd thought he'd put out years ago— that reignited when William died. Now, he'd forever carry the guilt of it.

What Miles said in the bar came back to him as well. *She'll need people around who love her and know her best.* He embodied both of those things, He loved her and he knew her best. But was *he* the best thing for her right now? Could he be what she needed, selflessly and without hopes or motives of his own?

"Yes, damn it." He hit the steering wheel with the side of his fist. *No.* "I don't."

He ground his palms hard against his eyes, hoping to clear his figurative vision and only succeeded in blurring his actual vision. A text alert chimed on his phone. It was Mae.

So sorry to ask again, but will you check on the café? I can't bring myself to go yet. Sorry. Xo

Bruce stared for a long moment at the screen. What could he do? Lie, and say, "No can do, Mae. Busy." Or tell the truth. "Well, Mae. Fun fact. Your husband died a hot fucking minute ago, but, hey, I still love you and I'm kinda hoping there might be a chance for us in the appropriate length future."

What Bruce ended up texting included neither option, but a third one; the one he knew—deep down—he'd go with all along.

No problem. I'm across the street anyhow. Anything you need before tonight?

Seconds later, she replied.

Nothing I can think of. Thank you, Bruce. I don't know how I'd be getting through this without you. You're the best friend a girl could ever have. xo

His smile, ironic as it was earnest, stayed on his face as he climbed out of the truck again. He started and deleted several responses as he leaned against the truck door. At last he decided on the simplest, most honest reply…

xo

29 Mae

Mae's hand rested on William's pillow; her head turned to the window. Birds chirped. A light breeze carried dried leaves past her vision. The front door opened and closed. Then there was silence in the house.

Gina, Chris, and Feather Anne had taken the twins to Mystic Aquarium. It was, perhaps, a strange choice on the day of their father's wake. But they were five and needed fresh air and things that brought them joy. For Evvie, it was the belugas. For TK, the jellyfish and sharks.

They balked when Mae said she'd be staying behind; they wanted Mommy more than usual. But that was to be expected. She explained that there were things she needed to do, and she needed to be alone to do them. To Mae's surprise, they gave little argument after that. As if they knew Mommy hung on by a thread.

She didn't want for them to know that; she'd have to do better. She *would* do better. Right then, though, there was no pressure to pretend or hold herself together. Funny, now that she'd given herself permission to cry, the tears decided to not come.

Mae climbed out of bed and walked trance-like to William's closet. She ran her fingers along his shirts and sweaters, stopping on her favorite. The chocolate-colored V-neck that matched his eyes still smelled of his cologne and Mae pressed the fabric to her face.

On impulse, she pulled the sweater over her t-shirt, pulled on a pair of black leggings, and her hiking boots, and twisted her hair into a loose braid. From her nightstand, she slid out William's letter. For a while, she stood there, holding his words against her chest and staring at their empty bed, the space where his body should've been lying next to hers.

The compulsion to read the letter had woken her in the earliest morning hours, yet she'd resisted the urge. There was some place else she wanted to be when she opened it. Someone else's comforting presence she craved.

Fourteen minutes later, she sat cross-legged against the apple tree, across from the willow tree, and beside a small pond, facing her father's headstone.

"Hi, Dad," said Mae.

A breeze kicked up. She imagined it to be Keith Huxley, saying hello back to his daughter, and she smiled.

"I'm okay," she said, but her voice faltered. So, she corrected herself, "I will be okay. But no, I'm not okay right now. Is he with you, Dad? What am I saying? Of course, he is, and the two of you are charming everyone in sight, aren't you?"

Mae snagged a tissue from her bag and dabbed her nose. With a trembling hand, she extracted William's letter.

"This is going to be hard for me to read, guys. I suppose you figured that though, didn't you?"

Mae unfolded the two sheets of cream paper to reveal William's beautiful penmanship. The words swam, and she blinked rapidly. She read aloud.

My darling wife,

How I have loved calling you such. My wife. Yet, you have been so much more than that to me. My love, my friend, confidante… my voice of reason (and sometimes unreason). My joy, my absolution, my fulfillment. My everything, my Mae.

If I've never said so before, I say now: I have loved you from the moment our eyes met, and I will love you for infinity. Every moment I had with you and our family has been a blessing beyond my wildest dreams.

Mae stopped reading so she could slow her breathing. In through her nose, out through her mouth. Part of her brain screamed, "No. Stop reading it. Reading it makes him gone for real," The other side—the one that spoke to her in William's voice—said, "Go on, now. It will all be all right."

She read the rest to herself, keeping it for her eyes only. When she came to the end, she laughed through her tears.

"You'll like this part, Dad."

So, my darling. If fate has chosen for me to no longer be there with you, take comfort in knowing I'll be causing a ruckus alongside your father. I expect he'll have some jazz on the Victrola and a scotch waiting for me, based on what you've told me.

I am so very sorry for leaving you, Mae. But we knew reaching the golden years together wasn't in our cards. I am selfishly grateful you accepted such an unfair fact. For as much as you'll resist this now, know that love—a second chance at love—waits patiently for you. Don't resist for too long, sweetheart. Time is short, as we know all too well.

Yours Always xo

Mae folded the letter back into its envelope and leaned back against the tree. For a while, she watched the ducks in the pond and listened to the sounds of nature. She closed her eyes and drifted off into a twilight sleep in which she dreamed.

William and Keith appeared and sat beside Mae, one on either side. They smiled at her and took her hands in theirs. Together, without speaking, they watched a mother duck guide two little ducklings into the water. They watched as she bobbed her head under water and brought it back up again with a quick shake. The ducklings followed suit.

This went on for some time. Occasionally she would look at her father or William, and her heart would swell almost painfully at how beautiful both men were. They in turn smiled at her, speaking only with their eyes.

Everything is going to be all right. Everything is going to be all right. Everything...

"Is going to be all right." Mae startled awake.

She was alone, of course. At the pond, a mother duck led her two ducklings from the water. Mae experienced a moment of confusion, but then smiled. Dream, apparitions… it didn't matter. She felt lighter than she had in days.

Mae reread Williams letter. At his behest—and her resistance—they'd had those difficult discussions about the inevitabilities that plagued their relationship. William faced it pragmatically,

Mae, stubbornly. He'd prevailed though and made her aware of the provisions he'd made for her, their children, and even Feather Anne.

Even if she were to sell the café and choose to not work, they'd live comfortably if not extravagantly. Not that Mae would ever want to live that way or sell the café any time soon. She'd loved her life before William, loved it more with him, and now she would have to learn to love it again without him.

"Oh, William." She sighed.

A glance at her watch told her it was time to return home and prepare for the post-wake gathering in her home. It marked the second time in her life she'd had to do this. First, her father; now her husband.

Gina and Tree tried to convince her to have it catered, but she would have none of that. Besides, staying busy helped. There would time enough later, in the quiet *after,* for Mae to face her sorrow.

In the meantime, her focus would be on Evvie and TK. The twins, as young as they were, would adjust more easily than if they had been older. It made her both sad and relieved and determined to keep their father's memory alive for them.

Telling them of their father's passing had been the hardest thing she'd ever done. Evvie's outburst of tears and the slow, silent trickle from TK's big brown eyes were imprinted on her brain forever.

TK, ever the big brother by three minutes, put his arm around his sister and said, "It'll be okay, Evvie. Daddy is with Grampa now. Right, Mommy?"

Through her own tears, Mae had said, "That's right, buddy. Daddy and Grampa are hanging out in heaven together."

Mae had told the twins about the grandfather they'd never had the chance to meet for so long, they behaved as if they *had* known him.

Evvie, through gulping sobs, asked, "Are they watching Bringing Up Baby?"

Mae had fought hard against her own sobs and managed a smile. "Yeah, sweetie. I bet they are."

"I wanna watch with them, Mommy." Evvie's tears had slowed as a new idea took hold.

"Someday, Evvie. But not yet." TK had taken the words from Mae's mouth, reminding her again how much he was like William.

"That's not *fair*," said Evvie. Her chin quivered. "Bring Daddy back, Mommy. Bring him *back*."

TK, as much like his father as he was, looked hopefully at their mother. She read it in his eyes. *Is Mommy powerful enough to bring Daddy back from heaven?*

Mae shook her head once and wrapped her babies in a tight hug. They'd left the beach and walked home holding hands. She took turns looking down at the tops of their little heads—one fair, one dark—and a tidal wave of fierce love took her breath away.

She would be strong for them. There was no question of it in her mind. They would grow up knowing their father, not only from their own memories, but from talking about him, watching family videos, and looking at his pictures. Yes, it hurt now to do so, but in time it would get easier. Eventually, it would become natural.

But first, this temporary parting. This *until we meet again*. This *not goodbye, but farewell for now*. Mae wasn't ready; she would never be. But nonetheless, it was time.

She went home and changed quickly, not bothering with makeup or more than a perfunctory smoothing of her hair. Rather than black, she wore William's favorite dress. It was custom made for her in Italy to resemble a dress Audrey Hepburn wore in Charade with Cary Grant. Cream-colored, with a thin black belt, and cap sleeves. She'd adored it, but he'd loved it even more when he saw her in it.

When the children came home, they ate lunch together. Mae set their clothes on their beds, and they talked about the wake. Mae didn't hide her tears, nor did she tell Evvie or TK not to cry.

"It's our wake, we'll cry if we want to," said Mae with a smile. Being the son and daughter of Mae and William, they understood the reference and smiled along with her.

At three in the afternoon, she entered the funeral home to say a private goodbye to her husband. Gina, Chris, and Feather Anne would bring the children shortly before the wake began. She had a moment of heart-sinking panic when she realized she didn't have the pictures for the memory board and fumbled for her phone.

"Mrs. Grant? Do you need something?" The funeral director approached as if out of thin air.

"Oh, I, no. I mean yes, but… I forgot the pictures for the memory board. I'm going to call—"

"No need, Mrs. Grant. It's been taken care of."

Mae's shoulders sagged, and she sighed, "Bruce. Thank goodness."

The funeral director frowned slightly. "Ah, no. I believe he said his name was Miles?"

"Miles?" It was Mae's turn to be confused.

"Yes, Mrs. Grant. It's a DVD he brought, actually. It's all set up if you'd like to…"

"Yes, please." Mae wasn't entirely sure she was ready to watch it, but losing her composure alone seemed preferable to falling apart in front of everyone.

The director turned on the flat screen and handed her the remote. "It's all set. Just hit play. I'll give you some privacy."

Before leaving, he discreetly set a box of tissues on the chair beside Mae. When the doors clicked close, she took a deep breath and pressed 'play' on the remote.

The first image—William as a boy of about five years—made Mae smile. TK was the very image of his father. It gladdened her heart to see William's face and mannerisms in their son forever more.

As the image appeared and faded, piano music played. But when the images of William and Mae came up, the music changed to *I Can't Give You Anything But Love, Baby* and Mae had to press her knuckles to her chin to stop its tremor.

Miles had added short video clips, too. Mae and William at their wedding. Feather Anne and William chasing the chickens around the yard. William fishing with the twins. A family picnic on the beach. Zoomed in clips of William mugging for the camera, and more.

When the screen turned to black, and the music faded, Mae stood and looked to where her husband lie. The room was so silent. Not even the ticking of a clock disturbed the air. Soon the room would fill with hushed murmurs and low conversations. Sympathies and regrets spoken solemnly. Cheeks kissed, hands squeezed, wet eyes. Semi-discreet ogling of floral arrangements. Strangers—friends of William's from way back and all over the country—and friends.

She longed to have his sweater back on and to return home to her bed. To pull the covers to her chin and his pillow to her cheek. Instead, she stood straighter and tried to calm her charging heart. The funeral director opened the door and bent his head in apology.

"Sorry, Mrs. Grant. The first guests have arrived."

"Thank you, Richard."

She stood beside the casket and breathed slowly. TK and Evvie burst in, followed by the rest of her family. Moments after, her dearest friends walked in. One face remained missing.

"Where's Bruce?" Mae whispered to Feather Anne.

Feather Anne shrugged. "Said he was on his way."

The hours passed in a blur. She stayed beside William throughout; vexing and stressing Gina and Katrina who tried to insist she take a break and sit. Mae didn't *want* to sit, but she accepted the cups of water they took turns bringing to her and ignored the anxious glances they exchanged.

Halfway through, the twins showed signs of fading. Chris offered to bring them home and Mae let them go. They'd hung in long enough, and she'd been proud of them. *William* would have been so proud of them.

Ricky and Brianna Baker came in near the end, and Mae couldn't help but ask Ricky, "Have you seen Bruce?"

Ricky said, "Oh, yeah. He's in the lobby."

Miles, who'd sat with Rosabelle in the chairs closest to Mae chimed in. "He's been there the whole time."

Mae frowned. "Tell him—"

"Mae, I'm so sorry for your loss," said a woman Mae vaguely recognized.

Mae accepted condolences from another dozen or so guests before she attempted conversation again with those closest to her.

"Feather Anne, go out there and get him, will you?"

"Already tried. He said he'd be in in a minute." Feather Anne shrugged.

Mae bit the inside of her cheek. *What the hell was he doing?* There was only one way to find out.

"I'll be right back," said Mae.

She found Bruce sitting on one of the wingback chairs in the lobby.

"You look like a giant trying to fit in doll furniture." She laughed.

He looked up and grinned sheepishly. "Yeah, well, that's pretty much what I feel like."

"Why haven't you come in?" She had no energy for beating around the bush.

Bruce half shrugged and looked away. "I just… it's better if I stay out of the way."

"Better if you stay out of the way? What are you talking about? You haven't been in the way, Bruce.

You've been my lifeline. I couldn't have gotten through those first days without you."

Bruce had an empty paper cup in his hand, and he crushed it in his fist. "I'm afraid—I feel like—William…"

Mae understood. She could pretend she didn't like she'd done many times before, sure. But that wasn't fair to anyone. She sat in the chair beside him, took the crushed cup from him, and slipped her hand into his.

"William always knew… how you felt. He *knew*, Bruce. It never became an issue because he also saw what an honorable, good man you are. He trusted you and respected you immensely."

"Jesus, that almost makes it worse." Bruce tried to laugh, then sniffed.

Mae punched his arm lightly. She sighed. "We got history, you and I; what can we say?"

"Do we have a future?" Bruce covered his face, but not before Mae saw the color drain from it. "Fuck, shit. I'm sorry, that was a fucked up thing to say at—Jesus fucking Christ—your husband's wake. Fuck."

He rocked for a moment before he dropped his hands and looked at her. His eyes were red-rimmed and full of regret. A faint smell of alcohol wafted toward Mae.

She poked his forehead and smiled. "Go get some coffee and get your ass in there."

Mae leaned over and kissed his cheek, then returned to the viewing room. She would treat his accidental question as if it had never been spoken. It was forgiven even as it left his lips.

The service ended—a half hour after scheduled—and Mae mercifully went home. The twins were already asleep, but she kissed them both before meeting Feather Anne in the kitchen over tea.

"You got them to leave, huh?" Mae smiled gratefully at her sister.

"Yep, they headed over to the bakery to make pastries for tomorrow."

Mae's eyebrows rose. "Katrina, too?"

"Uh-huh." Feather Anne lifted her mug to Mae. "Cheers to making it through the worst day ever."

"We're not done yet, kiddo." Mae lifted her mug anyhow. "So, you gonna tell me what happened yesterday, or what?"

Feather Anne shook her head and made a zipping gesture across her lips. "No can do, sis. Thems the rules."

"Come on, it's *me*. I won't tell a soul."

"Let's just say… it's good. Like really, *really* good."

"So, that means you—"

"Uh-uh. That's all you get for now. Hey," she changed the subject, "that video was kind of awesome, huh?"

Mae nodded. "Yes. It was. I can't believe *Miles* came up with it."

"Yeah. I talked to Rosabelle to see where he had it done. She said he did it all on his own."

Mae pulled a face and said, "Who knew, huh? Anyhow, you're not off the hook here. How long do I have to wait to see this show?"

"Two weeks, and all will be revealed."

"Two *weeks*? Oh, come *on*." Mae gaped at her sister. "I'm a grieving widow. How about giving me a little joy here?"

"Ooh, that is low. Pulling out the widow card? Ouch. But still no."

Despite Mae's attempts, Feather Anne held true to her word and kept her secret. They talked for a while longer, then said their goodnights, knowing tomorrow held more sadness for them. Mae hugged her baby sister—who was suddenly so grown up—and thanked her.

At last, Mae climbed into her bed. William's sweater, his pillow cradled her. The tears she'd valiantly held at bay came unrestrained. They rolled and trickled from her closed eyes even as she drifted to sleep, where she'd see her husband again in her dreams.

30 Feather Anne

Twenty-seven people gathered in Mae's living room. The smell of popcorn and onion rings—two of Feather Anne's favorite snacks—permeated the air.

"It's starting," shouted someone.

Everyone clamored for a spot to sit and watch. Feather Anne sat front and center in the middle of the couch, a huge plate of untouched onion rings on her lap. Her mouth had watered at the thought of them all day, but now she couldn't eat a thing.

She had no idea how the show—her parts, specifically—had been edited together. Nor did she have a clue if they were even using hers at all. All she knew was that at the end, she'd have to tell her family she'd be leaving for L.A. in a week.

The show's theme song came on and everyone sang—off key—along. Mae squeezed in beside Feather Anne and clutched her arm.

"Oh, my God, it's finally on," she squealed.

Feather Anne smiled. It was awesome to see her sister with some color to her cheeks and life in her eyes.

"Yeah, so, shush. Everybody, shut up," Feather Anne yelled.

"Yeah, what she said," yelled Bruce from somewhere in the back of the room.

Nick, who sat on the floor in front of the coffee table, winked at her. Brandon, who sat on the other couch, gave her a thumbs up. They were okay. Not great, but okay. She'd see how *that* went after she told them the news.

"Welcome to the first night of…" began John St. James. The camera panned to a neon sign and everyone shouted, "America's Greatest Singer."

John St. James perfectly chiseled face filled the screen again. "This year our contestants are *electrifying.*"

Images of contestants flashed across a mock screen behind him. Everyone screamed and cheered when Feather Anne and Nick's faces flashed by. Feather Anne's palms were sweaty. Nick and Brandon's eyes were on her, but she kept her gaze on the tv.

John St. James was talking about a girl from Louisiana, then a boy from Texas. Then, in one of the most surreal moments of Feather Anne's life, she stared back at her own face on television.

"Folks," John St. James was saying to the camera, "you are not going to want to miss this one. I told you we were starting with a bang, and these two don't disappoint. One came as a solo act, the other, as support. But when they sang together… well, you'll see for yourselves. Ladies and gentlemen, your first look at Feather Anne Byrd and Nick Amendola."

The screen cut to a slow zoom-in on her and Nick in Rockefeller Center, but Feather Anne barely wrapped her brain around it. Right now, millions of people were watching this. *Her*. If it hadn't felt real before, it sure did now.

By the end of the segment—in which they'd shown Feather Anne reading William's letter, a clip of her walking through Central Park and feeding the ducks, and their interview—everyone in Mae's living room wiped away tears.

"That was beautiful, Feather Anne," said Mae softly.

"It's so embarrassing," said Feather Anne.

Her face burned like it was on fire. So many people watching her get emotional. It was mortifying, really. She'd rather sing and not do all the other stuff, but if she wanted to be on the show, this was part of the deal.

On the screen, John St. James was saying, "Now let's take a listen to these two, shall we?"

They showed almost the entire thing, cutting out the time it took to get Nick onstage and some other gaps. The room exploded in applause and congratulations for the pair, and she avoided Brandon's eye as she waved them all away.

A commercial break came, and everyone started chattering at her and Nick at once.

"So, tell us what happens next," begged Rosabelle.

"Nope, you'll have to wait and see," said Feather Anne.

Mia Amendola called out, "Good luck getting anything out of these two. I've been trying for two weeks."

"You mean with have to sit through a whole forty minutes before we find out? No fair, guys," groaned Chris.

When the show came back on, it was met with less excitement now that they realized Feather Anne and Nick were done for a while. When the group began milling about, Brandon made his way over to Feather Anne.

"So, you're both on the show now? Together? Is that what the big secret is?"

"Well, it's not a secret. I mean, it was a surprise, but, Brandon, no one knew until now."

Brandon nodded slowly. "Right. Yeah. Well, that's really, uh, cool. For you. You sounded amazing."

"Thanks," said Feather Anne.

Their awkward pause stretched out. TK saved Feather Anne by throwing himself at her legs.

"Feather Anne, you're famous," he exclaimed.

The Brightsiders and the Villeneuves followed behind him and asked about a million questions, during which Brandon wandered off and Nick joined her. Once, Nick casually rested his hand on her shoulder. Feather Anne imagined Brandon's eyes laser-beaming a hole in the back of her head. She stepped out from under his hand and excused herself to the kitchen.

There, a crowd of honorary aunties grilled her about John St. James. She escaped them under the guise of needing to 'check something.' The whole thing had gotten a little overwhelming, so she snuck out back.

"Hey, sport," said Bruce from the patio. "Making an escape?"

Feather Anne plopped into a chair across from him. "Just for a few minutes. It's crazy in there."

"I noticed. Proud of you, kid."

"Thanks," said Feather Anne. "You okay?"

"Me? Yeah, of course. Just grabbing some air. So, you two are heading off to the big time, huh?"

"I'm not—"

"Yeah, yeah. You're not tellin' but your buddy spilled it last night. Nick told me the plan. Don't be pissed at him."

Feather Anne rolled her eyes. "I knew he'd be the one to blow it. So, what do you think?"

Bruce picked at the label on his beer bottle. "Well," he began, "I think it's a pretty big deal. And a big commitment. *And* a big change. You ready for all that? Leaving school, your family?"

"I'll have a tutor. And it's only a few months," said Feather Anne.

"And if you win this thing? Then what?"

"I can't think about that yet. Besides, the odds are—"

"As good for you as any of them. Better, if you ask me. Shit, girl. You've got some serious talent. More than you ever let on to us, that's for sure."

"Thanks, Moosie."

"Moosie? Jesus, haven't heard that in ages. You're the only one I'd let get away with it these days, so you know."

She almost asked, "What about if Mae wanted to call you that?" But she stopped herself. After what she'd said in the hospital, she didn't think she could tease him like that ever again.

"Bruce?"

He looked at her.

"I am really sorry for what I said to you."

Bruce shook his head. "You don't need to apologize. You called it like you saw it. Besides, you weren't entirely wrong."

"Of course, I was. You would never—"

"Not intentionally, no. But I did want to be the hero for Mae. All I should've been doing was be her friend. William was her hero, not me."

"Um, it's 2020, Bruce. Us women? We're our own heroes, thank you."

She picked up his bottle cap and threw it at him. It hit him on his shoulder.

"Hey, ow," said Bruce.

"Didn't hurt, big baby."

"Did, too." Bruce grinned. He looked at her with a serious expression. "Don't stay gone too long, Feather Anne, okay? You go get those dreams, all of them. Just don't forget you've got a home right here, with us. And bring my boy back with you, you here?"

"Yes, sir." Feather Anne saluted.

"All right. Let's get back in there."

They stood and before Bruce took a step, Feather Anne tackled him in a tight hug.

"You were a Dad to me even before William. I love you, you big ape,"

She ran inside before he answered, swiping a tear as she did. They'd walked in in time for the last segment and Feather Anne took her seat back on the couch.

"All right, viewers. The moment you've been waiting for. Only two contestants—that can be duos or solo artists—will get an automatic Platinum Microphone Pass to the finale in Los Angeles,

California. The rest with have to duke it out next week. But first, let's take a break."

Groans erupted all around the room. Popcorn flew through the air and Mae yelled, "He who tosses it, cleans the whole house," and that stopped chaos quickly.

"It's back on," yelled Evvie.

"The first contestant—or contestants—to receive the Platinum Microphone is…. Ellie Jacobs. Congratulations, Ellie."

The room groaned as one again and the tension crackled.

"Remember, folks. There's only one more Platinum Microphone Pass. And it goes to… Feather Anne Byrd and Nick Amendola. Congratulations, kids. You're going to L.A."

The camera zoomed in on their faces, but no one paid attention. They were too busy whooping and hugging the two soon-to-be-famous singers in their midst. Feather Anne disengaged herself to seek out Brandon. Movement by the door caught her eye, and in a blink, the door close between them.

"Feather Anne, Feather Anne," several people called her name and she let them pull her back into the madness.

Nick looked at her, and he mouthed, "Here we go," and smirked.

She grinned back at him and mouthed back, "Here we go."

About the Author

Elsa Kurt is a multi-genre author, mentor, and speaker. She has written over a dozen novels, several short stories, and a book for aspiring and new authors called *You Wrote It, Now What?* When not writing or sharing her experiences in writing, publishing, and promoting, Elsa can be found gardening or spending quality time with her husband, daughters, and three dogs. Elsa loves to hear from her readers at authorelsakurt@gmail.com. If you've enjoyed this book, please review it at any of these places:

https://www.goodreads.com/author/show/151773 16.Elsa_Kurt

https://amazon.com/author/elsakurt

https://www.bookbub.com/authors/elsa-kurt

Visit Elsa on social media:

https://facebook.com/authorelsakurt/

https://instagram.com/authorelsakurt/

https://twitter.com/authorelsakurt

and her website, https://www.elsakurt.com